SCRAP

Mike Padgett

Grosvenor House
Publishing Limited

This book is published by
Grosvenor House Publishing Ltd
Link House
140 The Broadway, Tolworth, Surrey, KT6 7HT.
www.grosvenorhousepublishing.co.uk

A CIP record for this book
is available from the British Library

ISBN 978-1-80381-396-7
eBook ISBN 978-1-80381-397-4

For my family

Also by Mike Padgett:

As Far As We Can - a travel memoir

Thursday

1

I always suspected Jack Jagger was a bad payer. Nobody could be that well off and pay up on time. The other clue was the way he looked at you. It was like being weighed up by a bull. When I was building his pond, I told him my favourite joke, the one about the wasp in the shop window, and although he laughed out loud, his eyes never changed. Friend or enemy, you were only ten seconds away from a punch up.

I've said nothing to Deb, of course, or to our Gav. They've no idea what mess I've got myself into. They're used to seeing me walking around the house with a distant look on my face. Deb says all ex-miners look like that – miserable. I've tried to explain to her that for a start we're not ex-miners, we're former miners, and we're not miserable, we're angry. We just keep the resentment well hidden. Miners are good at keeping things under the surface. It must be all those years working underground.

I come down the stairs sideways, one step at a time, groaning and yawning and squeeze past Deb. She's standing in front of the mirror in the hallway, putting on her lipstick and I glance at her through the glass as I nudge past.

'If my breakfast's not ready,' I say, 'I want to know why. And if it is, I don't want it.'

Deb pouts and stares at her own reflection.

'You're not fast enough, lazybones. Goldilocks has eaten it all up.'

Somehow, despite the slow death of the village, most of us have managed to cling on to our sense of humour. It's like having a safety lamp shining deep inside.

I drop into my chair at the kitchen table the way I used to do after a tough shift at the pit. In those days the fatigue was a result of hard, honest graft. Now it's through scratching a living, arthritis and uncertainty.

'These lazybones are going as fast as they can,' I say.

'Well, if you'll not take any painkillers, I've no sympathy for you.'

Deb turns her shoulders and tries to see the back of her suede jacket in the mirror.

'Does this coat look okay?'

'Looks all right to me. I thought you were going up to the café to do a bit of decorating? I'm beginning to think you've got another bloke up there.'

Deb opens the cellar door and brings out two bulging carrier bags. There's a neatly folded red jumper with white stripes on top of one of the bags, and two pairs of blue shoes and a black patent leather handbag on top of the other. I move my creaking legs out of the way and watch her place the bags against the back door.

'What have you got in there?' I say. I don't know why I ask this question. I'm not really interested. Maybe it's the fear of being left out. Or maybe I'm looking for something to poke fun at to liven up the morning.

'Some of my old clothes and jewellery,' Deb says. 'I'm taking them up to the café before the big opening day. I'm going to give them all away.'

'Give 'em away? We've given enough stuff away. Good jobs. Security. A future.'

'Plenty of women in Brodworth will be able to make good use of them. I've had my wear out of them. Time for a change, and you never know, it might bring a few people into the café to nosey around and then they might decide to come back next week when it opens.'

I'll give Deb her due. She's only ever done waitressing and office cleaning and a few years as a home help but she's really got her teeth into this café business.

'Nice bit of marketing,' I say. It's all the praise I can find without digging too deep.

'Have you got anything you don't want that I could take up? Old clothes? Shoes?'

As I lift myself out of the chair to make my first coffee of the day, I hear a groan. I feel older this morning than I've ever done. I seem to have gone downhill these last few years since the pit shut. Deb seems to have got younger.

'You could tek my skeleton,' I say. 'See if you can swap it for a new 'un.'

'What about all that old gear you keep on the top of the cellar? It's been stuck in there for years.'

I spin round from the sink and stare at Deb as though she's accused me of killing somebody. I get upset at the least little thing these days and I don't know why.

'What old gear?' I say, angry at the aggression in my voice and even angrier that I'm incapable of doing anything about it.

'Them old pit boots and steel toe-capped wellies you got when the pit shut, and that fusty old helmet with the lamp on. They look like something out of a museum. It's like a shrine in there. It's time you got rid of them all.'

'I'm not giving them away to nobody. They mean a lot to me.'

3

'You never use them.'

I sit back down and hold onto my cup at a stiff arm's length. It looks as though I've dropped anchor for the day but I don't care. Deb lifts the carrier bags and tests the weight as if to demonstrate there's plenty of room inside for my old pit gear.

'Somebody might want them,' Deb says. 'A builder. Or a mechanic.'

'Or a plumber,' I say, and pull on the anchor even harder. 'I might need them wellies missen if I don't master this soldering technique. And I've only got another week to get it right. That's if they don't kick me off first.'

'What do you mean, if they don't kick you off first?'

I think about the money I owe the training centre and sigh at the low odds of getting the five hundred quid off Jagger before next Wednesday.

'Nothing. Just joking.'

'I hope so. We need you to be out earning money again.' Deb opens up the patent leather handbag as though she's having second thoughts about giving it away. 'And what about that old donkey jacket of your dad's? The one he gave you when he retired. It's been hanging in that cellar that long it's gone green.'

'You'd have a job on getting rid of that old NCB jacket. Not unless somebody called Norman Clive Barker or Neil Cuthbert Bothwell came in looking for one.'

Deb unfolds the red jumper with the white stripes and holds it up to her chin.

'My mother knitted this.'

'She did a good job,' I say. 'I've always liked you in that jumper.' I remember the first night Deb wore it down to the King George. She looked great. All the wives complimented her on the style and the quality of her mother's knitting and how much the pattern and the colour suited her. And I could tell some of the lads fancied her that night. 'It suits your skin.'

Deb has great skin. There's a few lines around her eyes now, but she still looks fresh even without make-up. Maybe it's because she's always smiling. I'm a lucky bugger.

She carefully folds the jumper and puts it back on top of the bag.

'I was thinking,' she says.

'Dangerous.'

'No, listen. I've got an idea and I'd like to know what you think.'

I can feel my stiff arm relax its grip on my cup and I keep quiet. Deb wants to know what I think. It always works, even when I know she's after something.

'If this women-only day I've got planned for Thursdays gets off the ground, and I'm convinced it will, then I thought it might be a good idea to ask the women if there was anything they wanted to learn or do on those days while they're at the cafe. You know, a craft or a hobby or a skill. Or anything they wanted to know more about, like, I don't know, rights and things. Then I could get a volunteer to come in to the café for an hour and do a little training session or give a talk.'

I grip my cup again. So that's it. She's trying to get me to do a training session on clearing a blocked toilet or fitting a tap washer or something. Not likely.

'We could do it over a cup of tea and cake,' Deb says. 'I've talked to Sheila about it and she likes the idea. It was something we talked about when we were working together in the kitchen at the miners' welfare during the strike. She thinks it would be great. A bit like a learning centre.'

'Sounds like a good idea,' I say, trying not to let Deb see I'm already getting worried at the thought of being asked to stand up in front of a room full of women and give a demonstration.

'Of course, I'd have to give it a few months before I could set it all up,' Deb says. 'I'd need to let the women get comfortable with the idea of the women-only day first.'

When I realise it's not going to happen for a while, the colour returns to my knuckles. Deb sees my shoulders relax and I know she's playing me like a fish.

As we look at each other, waiting for one of us to say something, our Gav's left hand appears on the balustrade, slowly working its way down the handrail. A yard from the bottom the hand stops moving for a second then there's a whoosh and a thud as Gav pivots the full length of the staircase from the landing to the hallway without his feet touching a step.

Deb shakes her head as Gav sits down next to me at the kitchen table and turns on the TV.

'You'll be breaking your neck one of these days doing daft things like that,' Deb says.

'I think that jump qualifies for the Guinness Book of Records. Take a photo of me next time, Mam. It could make me famous.'

There's a slice of cold toast on Deb's plate and I pick it up and butter it, laying it on thick, head to one side as though I'm creating a sculpture.

'I hold the record for vaulting down stairs, Gav,' I say. 'Back at your grandmother's I used to vault the full length every morning before I went to school, sometimes one-handed.'

'Aye, okay Dad.'

'I did. And your gran's stairs are twice as steep as these.'

'And I suppose if they'd had that stair lift in back then you'd still have been able to do it.'

'I would. With your gran on my back.'

Deb opens the back door and picks up the two carrier bags.

'Right. I'm off up to the cafe. Things to do. I'll leave you two to argue with yourselves in the school playground. Byee.'

'Hang on, Mam,' Gav says, and he jumps up and runs upstairs like a Thompsons Gazelle, then races back down just as fast, laptop in hand, lid open, eyes on the screen. 'Will this do for you?'

Gav puts his computer on the table and Deb peers at the screen and smiles as though she's looking at a bonny new baby in a pram.

'Oh, that's wonderful, Gavin. Exactly what I wanted. Don't they look superb. All of them. Which one do you like best?'

'I like the red and black version,' Gav says. 'If I wa' designing a training shoe or a car, they're the colours I'd use. But I don't mind the green one if you're going for a 'new age' look.'

They're as thick as thieves and I'm beginning to feel left out so I walk round the back of them to see what they're admiring. On the screen are eight tiny images of the front of Deb's café. It takes me a few seconds to work out that each picture shows a different shop front sign with the words DEB'S CAFÉ written in a style ranging from simple coloured lettering to fancy motifs and elaborate graphics.

'Which one do you like best, Phil?'

'The simplest one,' I say, and I sit back down again and turn off the TV seeing as nobody's watching it. 'It'll be cheaper to make.'

'Oh, come on, Dad. Don't be boring. They'll all cost about the same. It's the plastic board that's the expensive thing.'

'Plastic? What's wrong with a bit of half inch external ply and two coats of decent gloss paint? It'll last for years.'

'Here we go again,' Deb says. 'Putting the mockers on any new idea straightaway.'

My arm stiffens again and I can feel the reassuring strain of the anchor.

'Somebody has to be practical.'

Gav closes his laptop and laughs at me.

'Look at my dad's long face. Anybody'd think he was paying for it.'

'I'll finish up paying half,' I say. 'I can guarantee you that.'

'I'll ask Sheila what she thinks,' Deb says. 'She's got a good eye for these things.'

'There is one thing I wa' thinking about, Mam, while I wa' playing around with the design.'

'What's that?' Deb says, her eyes widening. 'Go on, I'm all ears.'

I'm all ears as well but I don't let Deb and Gav know. Instead, I take a slow drink of coffee and watch them over my cup.

'I know it's personal to you, calling it Deb's Café, but have you thought about something a bit more …I don't know, a bit more… eye-catching?'

'You must be a mind reader. I've been trying to think of a new name since I got the place. It's not easy.'

'You'd better make up your mind quick before you splash out on a new sign,' I say, looking out of the window, distancing myself without moving an inch.

Gav laughs again and says, 'You could have a revolving sign, Mam. When my dad calls in from work for his bacon sarnie, you could call it The Half Empty Café. Then when he's gone, you could swivel the sign round and call it The Half Full Café.'

I'm not quite sure what he means but I know he's taking the mick so I smile at Deb as if to say, 'Can you hear him.'

'Right. I will get off.' Deb says.

'Me too,' I say. 'The training centre calls.'

2

Garrett, the director of training, slips quietly into the classroom at a minute past nine with his clipboard pressed tight against his chest as though he's holding something top secret. He's already got me worried. He doesn't usually take the register on a morning so I know something's up. He slams the clipboard down on the trainer's desk so hard it makes the wiper board cleaner jump up and crash to the floor. The action startles a few of my classmates standing by the window with their backs to Garrett. They're looking at a central heating pump that somebody brought in this morning for us to strip down and play around with. When they see the director of training, they stop what they're doing and slink back to their desks the way my dad's greyhound used to do when it was caught kipping on the couch. That's Garrett all over – catch as many people off guard as you can then watch them react to your presence. The scraping of chairs and the scrunching of sandwich wrappings replaces the murmur of serious conversation and in less than a couple of minutes we're all settled and ready to hear what the director has to say.

Garrett looks over the top of his glasses and surveys the class. Anybody else would lift up their glasses, not keep them perched on the end of their conk, but it gives him an excuse to look down on us.

'Morning. Right. Bollocking time. Somebody's been taking all the milk again. I brought two five litre cartons in yesterday morning and now there's not a drop left.'

We all sit back with relief. It's only milk. Nobody's been caught cheating in their assessments or stealing copper pipe. I join the other students and point at likely culprits in mock judgement.

'Anyway, I'm warning the lot of you,' Garrett says. 'If it happens again, you'll be buying your own milk for the final week. Right. Second bollocking. Over to you, Peggs.'

Peggs Perkins, known as the Silicone Kid, has been standing by the door at the back of the classroom. He's got his scruffy green trainer's smock on as usual, the one with the greasy skid marks at the entrance to every pocket. Peggs is a walking miracle. The whole of his left arm is no thicker than his wrist and only his boney knuckles stop his watch from slipping off. His left leg is permanently bent and if you look closely there are no creases in his shoe.

'The workshop was left in a right state yesterday,' Peggs says. 'It was a tip. There were tools left everywhere and there was a ton of scrap copper and lead left on the benches. And nobody had swept up, neither. Me and Young Simon spent half an hour cleaning up after you'd all buggered off. Didn't we, Simon?'

Young Simon is sitting in front of me and he nods, licks his finger and scribes a figure one in the air. The students on either side prod him in the ribs and he pretends to be grievously wounded, twisting to soften the jabbing fingers.

Peggs is looking for an acknowledgement of bad behavior but our attention has shifted to Garrett who is now writing something in red on the whiteboard. When he moves out of the way I see two names.

Garrett points at the two of us. He must think we've forgotten who we are.

'I'll see you two downstairs when Peggs has finished in the classroom. The MD wants a word with you both.'

Young Simon follows my lead and removes an imaginary top hat and we bow to the rest of the class like a pair of Victorian gentlemen.

Young Simon is the baby of the class. Twenty years old, six foot tall with a pair of shoulders that puts the T in T shirts. On the first day of the course, he turned up in a flash red open top sports car and made a big thing of opening up his wallet in front of everybody and paying his first instalment in cash. He never came in the sports car again – he drives a little white van now – and most of us suspect he hired the convertible for the occasion. He's had a deep tan from day one despite the miserable weather we've had, and Hazel and Jean in reception go wobbly-legged when he talks to them.

Garrett picks up the board marker, tosses it onto the trainer's desk and goes out of the classroom whistling Fly Me to the Moon. Peggs waits until the director's footsteps reach the bottom of the staircase.

'Right. For you lot doing your assessments this morning, remember only one thing.'

Peggs picks up the red marker pen and writes 'CHEAT' in big letters under the two names on the whiteboard.

'It's never done me any harm,' he says. 'It's a skill for life when people treat you as though you're a bit slow just because you limp. You learn early on the only way to survive is to cheat.'

He wipes off the two names and his word of advice with his scruffy sleeve and leaves a good impression of a toxic red cloud on the board.

'Right. Come on. Into the workshop. Let's get cracking.'

It's more like creaking. I slot my pen down the spine of my portfolio and groan as I straighten up. Newspapers are reluctantly closed, chairs are pushed back under desks, students sling their overalls over their shoulders, and half eaten sandwiches and empty paper cups are shoved into the overflowing waste bin.

Garrett puts his ear to the MD's door and I put my hands in my pockets then some distant memory of school makes me take them out again. Young Simon pretends to bite his finger nails. Garrett knocks once and the MD's response is immediate.

'Come.'

I look round to see if there's a dog behind us.

'Ah. Good morning, gentlemen.'

We try to keep a distance from the MD's desk but Garrett nudges us forward. The MD is sitting in a high-backed imitation leather chair in front of a computer screen. He has a black earpiece behind his ear and although I know it's high tech and meant to show how important you are, I can't help but think of the big black slugs that hang around the window in my cellar when it's been raining.

'Well, only a few days left now before you set off into the lucrative world of plumbing,' the MD says. 'You're almost there. Now. Last week we agreed you would pay your final instalment by today. The girls in admin tell me they haven't received anything yet. Has there been a problem?'

The MD sits back in his chair and locks his hands behind his head. Every time he rocks the chair, the pivot mechanism squeaks like a mouse. I shift my feet and inspect the bare office walls and chrome steel furniture. Bundles of freshly printed company brochures are piled on top of the filing cabinet. The front cover shows Garrett in a pair of brand spanking new overalls with a spanner in one hand, a wad of cash in the other and a big smile on his face. Next to the pile of brochures is a photograph of the MD, Garrett and two other directors dressed in dark suits and black dicky bows outside a casino. The neon light above the revolving doorway says Las Vegas and the four directors are holding their thumbs up to the camera, faces full of glee.

I nod to Young Simon, encouraging him to respond, delaying my own interrogation for a few more minutes. Young Simon, cool as an alley cat, puts his hand in his pocket, pulls out a roll of fifty-pound notes and hands it over to the MD. The MD doesn't blink.

'Thank you, Simon.'

I'm mesmerized. The MD's fingers flick through the money with the expertise of a bank clerk and I'm still gawping long after the cash has been safely locked away in the desk drawer. I don't think I've ever seen a fifty-pound note before never mind ten of them together. Ten little pieces of paper. Five hundred quid. The office walls seem to close in on me.

Young Simon is almost out of the door when Garrett taps him twice on the shoulder.

'Hey, young man. Where are your safety boots?'

Young Simon looks down at his gold and white trainers.

'Up in the classroom.'

'Well-go-and-put-them-on-then before I stamp on your toes. You'll follow Health and Safety regulations when you're in this training centre like everybody else. Why you insist on wearing trainers in a working environment is beyond me.'

'Speed round the workshop.'

Garrett comes back in and shuts the door. I put my hands behind my back and breathe in, trying not to feel intimidated, and I keep telling myself that I'm the customer here.

'Now, what about you, Phil?' the MD says.

I inspect the green carpet tiles on the office floor. They're the same type as the ones Deb made me rip up when she took over the cafe.

'I still need a few more days. Somebody's let me down but I'm sorting it.'

Garrett's stare is like a blowtorch to the side of my head and he says, 'You've had seven weeks to find the money. I'm beginning to think you're pulling our plonkers.'

'Hang on,' the MD says. 'Let's keep calm. Go on, Phil.'

But Garrett won't let go. 'You've done nothing but complain from day one. I don't think you ever intended to pay up.'

I'd love to have it out with Garrett. Tell him to keep his opinions to himself. Ask him why he always thinks we're swinging it as soon as his back's turned. Tell him if he treated us like adults instead of trying to catch us out doing something wrong, we'd learn a lot faster and we wouldn't complain as much. But I need to stay calm.

Keep the MD on my side. He seems more understanding. I double check the carpet tiles. Maybe slightly greener but definitely the same type.

'Of course I'm going to pay up. I just need another day or two, that's all. You know where I live. It's not as though I'm going to do a runner.'

'We can't sign off your portfolio until we've received the final payment,' the MD says. 'The last thing we want to do is send you away without your qualification. You'll have difficulty finding work if you're not qualified.'

'I should have the money next week.'

I suspect this might upset Garrett and I'm right.

'It's to be hoped so,' Garrett says. 'You finish on Wednesday.'

The MD drums his fingers on the desk. Through the window I see two students carrying a ladder across the car park and I have to pull a face to stop myself laughing when the ladder and the students get stuck in the workshop doorway.

'Okay,' the MD says. 'Wednesday. But that's it,' and he presses his ear piece and stands up. 'Yes. Put him through.'

I worked out early on how the MD always seems to receive a call when he's had enough of talking to students. Coincidence or not, it's an effective way of ending the conversation. I put my head down and leave the office determined not to look at Garrett.

3

For the rest of the morning my head's all over the place and I can't concentrate on any of my practical tasks because I'm thinking about my qualification and what Deb and our Gav will say when I tell them that all that money I've spent on the course so far has been wasted. When it gets to lunch time, I've made up my mind to call round on Jack Jagger one more time in an effort to get my money.

The drive along the rough track leading to our house at the foot of the muckstack bounces me up and down in my seat, rattles the ladders on the roof rack and throws my tools around in the back. I used to laugh at the crazy jolting and noisy commotion. That was before years of graft underground followed by years of labouring above ground wrecked my body.

A pair of my old pit knee pads hang from the overhead telephone cable where it crosses the track close to our house. The day the pit closed, I tied them together and flung them over the cable as a futile, but satisfying last act of defiance. Now the knee pads are locked together through years of spinning and twisting in the wind. Whenever I come home from work after a back-breaking day mixing concrete or carrying bricks, passing under the knee pads is like crossing a finishing line, or a starting line, depending on whether I've earned a wage or not.

I ease myself out of the van and lean on the garden gate for a few minutes until I can stand upright. It's a solid gate, like the rest of the fence, made up of blue pallets that a mate of mine half-inched from a warehouse. I haven't bothered staining them green yet to match my shed because if things don't improve on the financial side, I might end up burning them to keep us warm.

Mining subsidence has affected all the houses round here and the whole of our terrace leans to the right. Our house, being the end property, looks as though it's straining to hold up the entire row. Maybe I should ask the council for a rebate. Upstairs, the curtains in Gav's bedroom are closed. Downstairs the kitchen window is partly open and I can hear the boos and laughter of daytime TV escaping over the gardens and garages.

It takes the usual three shoulder charges to open the door and the draught strip sweeps the morning post into a straight line. It's mostly junk mail and a few official looking envelopes. The flyers go straight into the bin and I drop the letters onto the kitchen table where Deb is sorting through her paperwork.

'All yours, Deb. Looks like more bills for your cafe.'

One half of the table is covered with forms and invoices, the other with coloured photographs torn out of home interior magazines. The glass fruit bowl, a wedding present from Deb's mother, has been pushed to the edge of the table and is empty apart from the withered remains of three green grapes. I lob my van keys into the bowl, the concave shape amplifying the sound of metal hitting glass. Deb doesn't move. She never looks up when she's wearing her reading glasses. Maybe it's because I once said I didn't think the red plastic rims suited her blonde hair.

'What are you doing home?' Deb says, still not looking up.

'I've just won the award for the best bit of soldering in the class so they've let me off early for the day.'

'A-ha.'

I rub my shoulder and try to rotate my tight neck.

'That door's getting worse. If we get any more subsidence, we'll end up wi' a busload of tourists gawping at us. Welcome to the Leaning Terrace of Brodworth.'

'You should have let me know you were coming home. I could have got something in for your dinner. I've just put the last of that steak pie I made yesterday in the oven for our Gavin.'

'I thought you'd be up at the café.'

I take a painkiller out of the cupboard above the fridge and swallow it dry while Deb has her head down. As I pull open the fridge door, Colin, the next door DIY neighbour starts drilling the party wall, tentatively at first before switching to thc full hammer mode. The plates above the microwave jingle and the pan supports on the gas cooker rattle.

'How many more shelves can Colin put up in that kitchen of his? It must be like a warehouse in there. He'll be putting them up for all the drills and hammers he needs for putting his shelves up. It's perpetual motion.'

'I might ask him to put some shelves up for me in the café,' Deb says.

I can almost see a little mischievous grin on Deb's face and I ignore her attempt to goad me. Deb would never let Colin do any work in the café. He thinks he's a perfectionist but he's as rough as a bear's arse. I think it's because he can hardly see. His glasses are like jam jar bottoms and I feel sorry for him sometimes especially when he's had a stab at being a builder. Like the other week when he built a little wall around his veg patch and he's standing there with a proud look on his face and all I see is the mortar thrown all over the brick faces as though he's used a spade to point the joints. But he thinks it looks good so who am I to criticize.

The fridge is full but the only quick snack in there is a todgy pork pie sitting on its own in the egg compartment. It'll fill a corner. I clamp the pie between my teeth and bang on the party wall. Colin stops drilling and I down the pie in two bites.

'We're doing tiling this afternoon. It's optional. I've done enough tiling in my life so I thought I'd nip out for an hour. See if I can catch a bloke in who owes me some money. But it'll be a complete waste of time, I know it will.'

'Will it?' Deb says, still not looking up.

'I think he must have a camera on his gates because every time I go round there, nobody's ever in. I once spotted him on his drive but as soon as he clocked me, he buggered off round the back of his big double garage.'

'Wear a disguise, then.'

'I owt to. Have you got a clown's outfit in your wardrobe?'

I imagine myself pressing the buzzer on Jagger's steel gates, looking pathetic in a ruffled collar and pointed white hat, a painted smile on my face and a custard pie in my hand. The way I'm feeling right now it would be a fitting disguise.

'And if he's looking out for your van, why don't you go on your motorbike?'

'Hey, that's not a bad idea, Deb. I hadn't thought about that.'

Deb scans the newly arrived letters, putting them into an order that baffles me. Somebody comes on the TV playing the bagpipes and I reach over the table for the remote.

'Can I turn this down a bit? You can hear the thing in the garden.'

'Turn it off if you want. It's only on to keep me company.'

The kitchen goes quiet and a blackbird starts singing from the top of the garage and I put my hand on Deb's shoulder.

'Do you know. When I hear that blackbird singing, all my troubles disappear.'

Deb puts her pen down and takes off her glasses.

'How much does this man owe you?'

As I've already said, I've no intention of telling Deb how much I'm owed and I'm definitely not about to tell her who my debtor is. She would only drill me, keep on asking why, why, why, and if I wasn't careful, I would end up telling her how I'd been that desperate for work to pay for my training course that I'd done a job for Jack Jagger. Yes, that Jack Jagger. The man who made money out of the sale of the house we lost six months into the miners' strike. And I would end up telling her how I now owe money to the training centre, all because of Jagger's debt. She would look at me and shake her head and tell me what I already know – that I'm a fool.

'It's only a few quid,' I say. 'Not much. I'll manage.'

'Good. Don't forget the rent's due for the cafe. You said you'd go half with me for the first two months.'

'I know I did and I will. No need to keep reminding me.'

Deb knows how to stick the knife in. Nobody else gets under my skin the way she does. It must be love. I take the change out of my pocket and shuffle the coins as though I'm panning for gold.

'Is our Gav still in bed?'

'I don't know if he's in bed but he's up in his room. He's working on a design for the café menu board, and he's doing a spreadsheet for me.'

I've no idea what a spreadsheet is. Something to do with bedding? I lean over Deb to get to the jar we keep at the side of the TV. She doesn't move even though her work is now in the shade. I shake the contents of the jar to separate the dead batteries, buttons, fuses, paper clips and whatever else is in there, from the small change but no pound coins come to the surface. Not even a fifty pence piece. Deb tries to move out of my shadow.

'Phil, watch what you're doing. Can't you see I'm working? Just because you're in a bad mood doesn't mean to say you have to make me feel bad as well.'

I want to say at least it would make me feel better. Jump in this hole with me for ten minutes. It's grim down here.

Deb scoops up her paperwork and files it in a box in the sideboard. I know I've upset her and when she closes the kitchen window and puts on her coat, I try to help straighten her collar.

'I'm sorry, love,' I say. 'All this training and chasing about for my money is beginning to get to me.'

Deb twists away from my clumsy attention and straightens the collar herself.

'I'm going up to the café. I've a lot to do before next Thursday.' Deb closes her eyes and lifts up her chin in mock martyrdom. 'Somebody's got to go out and earn a living round here.'

'Yes. Go on. You can laugh. Get your crowing in while you can. There'll be two of us earning a living next week,' and then to myself I add, 'With any luck.'

Deb drags a heavy cardboard box from under the table and with the load balanced on one knee tries to open the front door.

'Look out,' I say. 'I'll get it. No need to be stubborn.'

As Deb steps outside, I make a show of peering into the open box. There are rolls of expensive-looking wallpaper packed tight, and on top is a bag of adhesive and a brand-new burgundy paste brush still in its plastic wrapper.

'I don't believe it,' I say. 'Harris? And Laura Ashley? How much has that lot cost us? We've a dozen rolls of woodchip on top of our Gav's wardrobe. Never been touched.'

'Woodchip?' Deb says, shaking her head. 'You've no idea have you.'

'And we've a boatload of brushes like that in the cellar.'

'I know we have. I've been down there to have a look. Have you seen the state of them? They're that stiff I could sweep the path with them, front and back.'

Deb's wit makes me feel happy. It takes my mind off the money I'm owed and the fix I'm in. It sharpens me up and warms me through. But even so, I have to have the last word.

'They just want cleaning, that's all. A bit of turps and they'll be like new.'

Deb pauses on the path and adjusts her grip, her small frame leaning back to counterbalance the load. She still looks good. Not bad for fifty.

'Hang on,' I say, stepping outside. 'Give us it here. I'll take it up in the van. I've just about got enough time.'

'It's okay, I'll manage. You'd better get off and see if you can get that money you're owed.'

4

I lean my trail bike against a silver birch tree half way up the muckstack. The young tree, like all the trees covering the tip, is no thicker than a pit deputy's stick and it bends with the weight of the motorbike as though the wind has caught it. The sun still hasn't got out and when I take off my helmet and gloves, I have to rub my numb fingers which are as white as the bark on the silver birch. As I'm waiting for some colour and feeling to return, I count the number of daffodils still in flower among the dying clumps at the side of the tree.

'Nice,' I say aloud. 'Ten. One for each fifty quid owed.' I shake my fist then slyly look around. If anybody's watching me from behind the trees, I'll be getting a visit from the men in green jackets. The surviving daffodils look a bit weak close up but they'll have to do. I talk to them in confidence and snap off their stems one at a time.

'You might just be the key to my future.' Snap. Snap. 'All I want you to do is hold your pretty heads high.' Snap. Snap. 'Let me do all the yapping.' Snap. Snap. 'And if that doesn't work.' Snap. Snap. 'Well. Looks like I've been shafted and I'll have to take back what's mine.' Snap. Snap.

I take my lead sheet knife out of my top pocket and cut the stems to an equal length. The sap is as sticky as phlegm and I curl a dock leaf around the knife blade and wipe it clean. The bike seat makes a good workbench and I set to work fastening the stems together using the pink ribbon I found in one of Deb's drawers. On my first attempt, the bow falls apart when I try to tighten the tails. On my second effort, my finger gets trapped in the knot. Third time, I'm lucky.

As I thread the bunch of daffodils down the front of my jacket, I laugh at my lack of knot tying skill, wondering how I've managed to tie my shoe laces for the last fifty years. I pull on my helmet and start up the bike, still smiling to myself. Then I remember where I'm going and I snap down my visor.

'Right Mister Jagger,' I say aloud. 'Time for a different approach. The Debt Man cometh.'

I zig-zag around the silver birches back towards the gap in the fence at the bottom of the muckstack. The ground is soft and the young trees are evenly spaced and I soon find a rhythm, building up speed, the thin twigs and fresh leaves brushing against my shoulders, left, right, left, right. I'm just beginning to enjoy myself, imagining I'm in the final of the slalom on Ski Sunday when I hear a shout above the noise of the bike's engine. A man and his dog stand motionless in front of me less than ten yards away. I grab the front brake and stomp on the back and the forks dive and the rear wheel locks, sending the bike sideways. In panic I dig my boot into the ground and the bike straightens up and comes to a halt six inches off the man's leg. He never moves. He's either very brave or he's in shock. Even the terrier freezes, not barking until I put both feet down and kill the engine. The man lets the terrier yap and strain on the lead for a few seconds then he gently pulls it back to his side.

'Tha wants to slow darn a bit, lad. It's not a race track, tha knows.'

I put my hand out to quieten the dog and let it sniff my leather glove. My heart is still bumping and when I lift up my visor, I recognize the owner.

'I wa' just enjoyin' that, Frank.'

'Bloody 'ell. Is that thee Phil? Thar a bit old to be scramblin' up an' darn t'muckstack, aren't tha? Shut up Bess. That's enough. I thought it wa' wun a' them young tearaways off yond estate.'

'It's a good job tha sharted,' I say. 'I nivver saw thi.'

'It's a good job tha not deaf, then.'

Frank, as usual, is wearing the grey anorak he wore when we were on the picket line together. There's never been much meat on Frank. At the pit we used to call him the King of Skiffle because the ribs on his back stuck out like a washboard. After the pit shut, he gradually lost what little fat he had on him and now his anorak is baggy at the shoulders and the sleeves come down to his knuckles.

Frank is looking at the daffodils poking out of the top of my jacket like ten little yellow joeys.

'Has tha got thissen a new job then, Phil? Flower arrangin'?'

I gently tuck my jacket lapels around the daffodils as though I'm trying to keep them warm.

'I might finish up doin' that if things carry on as they are.'

'I've got used to doin' nowt,' Frank says, and he strokes Bess's head. The terrier looks up at him as though she understands everything he's saying and everything he's not saying. 'She keeps me company. Don't you, lass. I'd be lost bart her.'

I look around the muckstack. It's softer and greener than it was when we were working here. It might not be increasing in size any more but it still dominates the skyline and overshadows the houses. It's private land now and the whole tip has been fenced off. The British Coal Corporation sold it off a few years ago. Nobody in Brodworth knows for sure who bought it. Some say it was sold off at a giveaway price, thank you very much, to the former pit manager, lucky bastard, and he was going to put his sheep on it. Others thought a developer had got his hands on it and had plans to turn it into a ski resort. The joke going round Brodworth is that all the miners who lost their jobs when the pit closed will be gainfully employed building a hundred ski lodges using left-over pit props.

'It don't seem two minutes since we were diggin' a mile under here for a livin', Frank.'

'It seems a long time to me.'

'And it don't seem two minutes since we were scramblin' up and darn here in t'freezin' cold,' I say. 'Scratchin' abart like animals for any slack we could find to tek back home to keep our families warm.'

'I've bin cold ever sin.'

Frank is a good guy, a good worker, never missed a shift, and always with something dry and witty to say. But when the pit closed, he turned into one of those men who could talk all day without altering his sad tone and he would bring you down if you let him. Frank's missis isn't a bundle of laughs, either, and I often wonder what the atmosphere must be like in their house. No wonder she lives in the front and he lives in the back.

'Anyway, I can't stop, Frank. I've an urgent job on.'

'Lucky thee.'

I hope Frank doesn't tell anybody down at the working men's club about the near miss with the bike and I hope even more that he doesn't mention the daffodils. Word would soon get round that I'd picked them for Deb and I would never live it down.

My eyes are wide open from the near miss and I ride like a learner through the gap in the fence and back onto the lane that leads to the town centre. The gap appeared within days of the fence going up and I'll guarantee the missing rails are now on the side of somebody's pigeon hut or on a shed on the allotments.

The thin clouds that had been shading the sun all morning and cooling the air on the muckstack are slowly disappearing. As I turn into the high street the sun breaks through above the working men's club, distorting the light coming through my scratched visor, sending coloured needles across my vision and fracturing the shops and vehicles in front of me. By the time I flip up the visor I'm only ten yards from hitting the front end of a wheelchair. It's a good job I'm only going steady. Two near misses in ten minutes. Jagger must be getting to me.

It's Julie and her lad, Carl. Julie lives a few doors down from my mother-in-law on the council estate. She's in her late twenties. She used to be a nurse before she needed a wheelchair and Carl is her carer. He's nine. Wherever she goes, he goes, riding on the back like Ben-Hur. I once gave him a couple of quid and told him he was a hero and to go and treat himself. He went straight into the co-op and came out with a bunch of red roses for his mother and I nearly choked.

When I nod to them, Carl recognizes the trail bike and he puts his thumb up.

'All right, Phil,' he shouts, unsmiling, like an old miner.

'Champion, Carl,' I shout back, and they ride their wheelchair up onto the kerb opposite the chemist and the automatic door slides open for them.

I leave the high street and after a mile turn down the country lane leading to Jack Jagger's house. The sun is bright now and it flickers through the trees in the woodland to my left. The shadows on the road look like patches of new tarmac. I have the lane to myself and the feeling of being alone and protected at the same time warms me up and my smile returns. After a mile the trees begin to lose their height as the wood thins out and the competition for light is reduced. The view opens out on to a hilly landscape of pasture and drystone wall. There's a flat line of trees running across the hill, parallel to the lane. It's all that's left of the branch line that once connected Brodworth colliery to the rest of Yorkshire and beyond.

A lone biker appears round a sharp bend ahead of me and we nod in respect as we pass within a few feet of each other. There's still hardly any traffic and my little trail bike is running well. With the trees gone, my only company is the power line running alongside the lane, dipping between its wooden poles. The shadow it throws onto the tarmac undulates like the flight path of a bird and I follow it all the way to Jagger's house.

5

There's a high brick wall around the property and an even higher hedge behind. All you can see of the house from the road is the chimney stack. I stop outside the locked gates and pike through the bars. My luck is in. Jagger hasn't emigrated after all. He's on his drive washing a 4x4 pick-up. There are two men with him, doing nothing other than watching him rinse off the soap suds with his hosepipe. I could have done without the company. I switch off my engine and put the bike on its side stand. A lorry thunders by, its slipstream almost blowing the little machine over.

Doubts about confronting Jagger begin to creep into my head. Maybe all this is a stupid idea. Maybe I should just get back on my bike and ride away into the sun, back to the training centre and face the music. Why put myself through all this conflict? But I know I can't leave it any longer. Time is running out.

I pull the daffodils out of my jacket, straighten the pink bow, and press the intercom button on the wall. There's a faint buzz from somewhere near the garage and Jagger lifts up his head. I wave the flowers at him, trying not to stare at him, hoping to appear nonchalant, looking away, down the road, up at his trees. The two stone lions reclining on top of the gate pillars seem to look down on me and sneer as I lift up my visor and lean into the intercom.

'Flowers for a Missis Jagger.'

The two men, one heavy, feet planted on the drive, the other, wiry and fidgety, point and laugh at Jagger. He sprays them with his hosepipe, making them cower and curse, then he comes steadily down the drive. Doesn't even turn round to see if Heavy and Wiry are plotting their revenge. Top dog.

Jagger approaches the gates, moving his head from side to side, trying to see around the bars and fix both eyes on the motorcyclist delivering flowers for his wife.

'Who's sent these?'

I deepen my voice.

'No idea, mate. I'm just the messenger.'

Jagger's eyes switch from me to the bunch of flowers to the bike and back again. It looks like he's going to turn round and saunter back up the drive. Tell his two mates it's some nutcase flogging flowers nicked from the roadside. My hand begins to shake and sweat from my forehead trickles into my eyes. I think about pushing the flowers through the bars, jumping back on my bike and riding away. But I don't get the time to think about where that escape might lead because Jagger presses his key ring and the gates whir open, slow and weighty.

'Give us them here, then.'

I take off my helmet, glad of the cooling air, trying not to smile and look weak, trying not to stare and look hard.

'I thought that'd fool you, Jack. Can we talk about my money?'

Now it's Jagger who doesn't know whether to smile or stare.

'There's no need for all this bollocks,' he says. 'All you had to do was ring me.'

'I've been cut off.'

Jagger sets off up the drive, back to his laughing mates, and I keep right behind him. There's a white van parked on the drive and the big grey mongrel standing on the driver's seat is snarling at me through the windscreen. Jagger picks up his hosepipe and carries on spraying his vehicle. He won't look at me.

'That's never that Golden Flash thing you were bragging to me about, is it?' he says.

'No is it hell. This is just for running around on.'

'I've got a bigger engine in my lawn mower.'

Wiry and Heavy laugh at Jagger's wit. But it's forced laughter, too loud to be genuine.

Well-manicured lawns and borders form the front garden and there is a sickly-sweet smell of oil seed rape in the air from the field next to Jagger's house. The only sound on the drive is the jet of water drumming into the hollow wing of the 4x4. Jagger doesn't seem in much of a hurry to speak. He must think I'm just going to stand there for five minutes then slope off. I try to start up a friendly conversation and if he takes it the wrong way, tough.

'New motor, Jack?'

The vehicle has the same personal registration plate he had on his previous pick-up. This beast looks more powerful, three litre maybe, bright red with JAGGER PROPERTY ENTERPRISES in gold letters down the side.

'I'm still struggling to get you your money, Phil. Like I said last time, somebody owes me for a big job and until I get paid for that, I can't pay you or anybody else. I should have it by next week and you're top of the list.'

'That's what you said last time. It's been eight weeks, Jack. Eight weeks. If I don't get my money this week,

I won't have a next week.' I'm on the verge of saying, 'You're just taking the piss,' but I stop myself.

The first stage of panic begins to tighten my chest. I try to convince myself that Jagger could be telling the truth. That there's still a chance of getting my money this week as long as I control myself. The one thing I don't want to do is upset Jagger, especially in front of his two buddies. I take a deep breath and try to sound businesslike.

'I was beginning to think you were avoiding me.'

'Who me?' Jagger says, looking offended.

Wiry and Heavy laugh again and Jagger smirks. I know how ridiculous I look – a bunch of daffodils in one hand, crash helmet in the other, one against three. I try to block out the two men and concentrate on Jagger.

'You never answer your phone when I ring you and you never answer that buzzer on your gate when I call round, neither. Every time you see my van pull up you disappear round the back of your garage. I know you've seen me.'

Jagger appears to be fascinated by the appearance of a rainbow in the spray from his hosepipe.

'I'm not trying to avoid you,' he says, not looking at me. 'I've told you. You'll have your money in another week or two. Three at the latest. Guaranteed.'

One week. Two weeks. Now three weeks. With each extension of time, another breath of air is squeezed out of my lungs.

The bike ride to Jagger's house has stiffened my back and neck but I manage to turn my shoulders and look across the big front garden through the trees and shrubs towards the ornamental pond at the side of the monkey puzzle tree. The pond is half hidden among the greenery and I can just make out Jagger's son and daughter – they're about four or five years old – splashing each other and jumping around in the water in their little coloured wellies.

'I put my heart and soul into building that pond for you.'

'I know you did and I'm very happy with it. The kids love it. Look at them. They think it's a paddling pool. I can't keep them away from it.'

Each time Jagger pulls on the hosepipe it tightens around his bucket of soapy water. I think about telling him he'll be pulling the thing over if he isn't careful. Have the upper hand for once, even if it's only for a second, instead of begging for my money.

A tractor pulling a trailer packed with straw bales rumbles by on the main road, its noise rising as it passes my bike, falling again as it disappears behind Jagger's high wall and hedge. For a few moments the stench of diesel overpowers the scent of oil seed rape.

'Haven't you got anything? Not even a hundred? At least that'd cover me for that liner I ended up paying for out of my own pocket.'

'I've nothing, Phil. How many more times can I tell you? Anyway, loosen up. It's only five hundred quid.'

I scan Jagger's face for a hint of understanding but there's more empathy in the stone eyes of the two supercilious lions on top of his gate pillars.

'It might only be five hundred quid to you. It's a fortune to me and I need it bad.'

'We've all got problems,' Jagger says, turning the nozzle to full force. 'Come back in a couple of weeks. But make sure you give me a ring first.'

Water ricochets off the bonnet into my face blinding me for a second. But I don't move. Don't want Jagger to think he's come out on top. I wait for Wiry and Heavy to start laughing again but they stay silent. The mood has changed. The door has been slammed shut and I no longer feel like begging for my money. The clown's outfit has gone. Now, the flowers and helmet feel like a sword and shield. I want what's mine and I'm going to do everything I can to get it.

The big grey mongrel in the white van must have sensed the change in atmosphere. Smart dog. The thing is going crazy now, trying to break out of the side window, its jaws snapping into the glass, smearing it with saliva, the van shaking with the ferocity of the attack.

I'm being ignored by all three men and I know if I stand there any longer things could turn nasty. I set off back to my bike and only wipe the water off my face when I know they can't see. Half way down the drive I stop and turn round.

'I'm not writing it off, Jack. I'll get what's owed to me one road or another. Every penny of it.'

Jagger and the two men look at each other in bewilderment as though I'm trying to explain Newton's law of gravitation to them. I take a few more steps then turn again, this time pointing the daffodils at Jagger.

'I was banking on that money this week. My future depends on it. My family's future depends on it.'

One more step. One more turn round.

'You made a killing out of me once before. You're not going to make a killing out of me again.'

'You were daft enough to go on strike,' Jagger says. 'I was smart enough to make money.'

Jagger says something to Heavy and Wiry. It sounds like, 'These ex-miners never fucking learn.'

Then Wiry rolls a coin down the drive. The ten pence piece comes towards me like a little guided missile. I'm back on the picket line. The coppers and their overtime. The miners and their struggle. After all these years, the sight of a rolling coin still has the power to deaden my stomach. I stamp on the money and stuff it deep into my pocket as if to say, 'Thank you very much. I'll have that. It's a penny from heaven.'

6

The curtains in Gav's bedroom are still drawn when I get back home. I half-fill a pint pot with water from the kitchen sink tap, wash a painkiller down, and drop the flowers into the glass with little attempt to arrange them. The stairs in this old terrace house are getting a bit steep for me these days and I pull hard on the handrail and listen to the treads creak in sympathy with my sore joints. Gav's bedroom door is half closed and out of the gloom comes the zip-zap-pow piercing sound of space age gunfire.

'Gav.'

'What?'

I push the door open slowly so as not to surprise him or let in too much light. The curtains are closed and it takes me a second or two to work out that he's sitting up in bed with his computer resting against his bent knees. His face, eerily lit by the glare from the computer screen, looks like an advertisement for the ghost train in the amusement arcade at Scarborough. At eighteen, he's as long-limbed as me now. Spitting image, everyone says. Luckily, they joke, he's inherited Deb's brains, which I have to admit is true. Gav never had to work hard at exams. He could have gained a few GCSE's, his teachers said, if he'd stayed on and applied himself. But all his mates were leaving, and nothing we said made any difference.

'I thought you were helping your mam? Doing her a design and a spreadsheet or something, whatever one of them is.'

'I've done 'em. Want to have a look?'

The screaming space battle stops and Gav turns his computer round for me to view the screen.

'So that's what a spreadsheet looks like,' I say, still having no idea what it's supposed to be.

'And what do you think to my design for my mam's menu board? Good eh.'

'That's neat. How do you draw stuff like that on a computer? And all in colour,' I say, totally baffled by the process. It's all too weird for me, and frightening. All this technical magic.

'It's easy. You just have to keep playin' with it and don't be frightened of doing any damage. You'll not blow owt up.'

Gav turns his computer round, hits a button, and the space battle resumes.

There's a narrow gap between the wardrobe and the end of the bed and I have to turn sideways to squeeze through to get to the window, almost tripping over a pile of trainers.

'Don't open the curtains, Dad.'

'Wouldn't you rather be outside on a day like this? The sun's shining.'

'Is it comin' up or goin' down?' Gav says, without taking his eyes off the screen.

I'm beginning to think there's something wrong with me. First Deb won't look at me. Then Jagger. And now our Gav.

I run my fingers along the pack of woodchip wallpaper on top of the wardrobe, feeling my way over the hard curves beneath the thin plastic film until I find a loose roll.

'Well. Only another few days to go now, Gav. Just think, if you'd come on the course with me like

I suggested, we'd have been ready to start work together next week. You and me, side by side.'

I aim the roll of wallpaper at the blank wall above Gav's head, using it like a pointer to highlight imaginary words on an imaginary screen.

'I can just see it. Steele and Son Plumbing'.

When Gav starts laughing, I can't tell whether he's laughing at the battle taking place on his computer screen or at my proposal for our future together as plumbers.

'Steele and Son Plumbing?' Gav says. 'What a joke.'

OK. It's not the space game.

'You only want me to join you because you need somebody to do all the heavy liftin' for you.'

My heart sinks when Gav knocks me back like this. I'm serious about us working together. Dead serious. It would have been the happiest day of my life if he'd joined me on the course. I'd have found the money for it somehow. But sometimes it sounds like it's the last thing he wants to do. When I slide the wallpaper back into the pack on top of the wardrobe, it feels like I'm pushing a bolt across a door.

'At least it'd be a proper job,' I say. 'Better than getting up to whatever it is you're getting up to with those mates of yours. Cars coming and going. Whispering to each other on your mobile phones.'

'Dad. I've applied for loads of proper jobs, as you call them. On line, and by letter, and what have I got? Zilch.'

'We've no idea what you're doing half the time. Your mother's always worrying about you. Wondering what you're getting up to.'

'Not even a reply from most of them.'

Gav stretches over and clicks on the bedside table and grabs a bundle of newspaper cuttings from the shelf underneath. He peels them off one by one and points to dozens of advertisements circled in red ink.

'I bet I haven't had ten replies in total and all of 'em said the same thing. Sorry, you haven't got the experience. Course I haven't got the experience. How can I get the experience if nobody'll give me a job?'

'Exactly. So why not come in with me? What have you got to lose?'

Gav slams the pile of cuttings down on the table, hitting the lamp base and knocking the shade off its holder. He turns out the light and the smell of hot dust drifts past me.

'It was all right for you,' he says, staring into his computer. 'You left school on Friday and then went straight down the pit on Monday.'

I can feel the anger and frustration catching fire inside him. He's turning in on himself and I can't blame him. I know how important work is for me, for my own self-esteem, never mind for a youngster just setting out in life. But I don't have the words or the skill to push too hard, and I must admit, I don't have the guts either. Don't have the guts to tell him about my own hopes and fears of finding work for us both. I tell myself that's the last thing Gav needs to hear. But I'm not sure. I don't know how to handle this frustration. It's a weakness on my part. I've never been good at opening up to Gav. And he' just as bad. My only strategy is to try and be funny, try and lift both our spirits, and hope neither of us gets in deeper than we want to.

'How do you mean I left school on Friday then went straight down the pit on Monday? Get your facts straight, Gav. I never went to school on Fridays.'

'We'd be lucky to find enough work for one of us nivver mind two. No thanks. I can earn more in a day with my mates than you can in a month.'

'You forget, Gav. I sacrificed my job for you an' your mam.'

'Oh, here we go,' Gav says, slamming the lid down on his computer. 'Miners' strike, repossession, startin' all over again. That wa' years ago.'

I hold on to the door jamb for support. When I see the dark, stooping figure looking back at me in the wardrobe mirror, I feel sad and I push my shoulders back and stand as tall as my sore bones will allow. My eyes have got used to the dim light now and I can see the strange mix of anger and lack of interest on Gav's ghoulish face.

'I went on strike to save my job and I went on strike to save a job for the future for you. Me an' your mam wouldn't be struggling now if we'd won. We've been running uphill ever since. I can't even get hold of enough money to finish paying for my training. I could end up getting kicked off the course with no qualification and then it's back to square one.'

I let that last sentence dangle, hoping Gav will show some sympathy which might then allow me to open up a little about my own, urgent predicament. But it doesn't work.

'Dad, I'm not lendin' you any money, if that's what you're after. You still owe me for that can of diesel I bought you last week when you ran out. If you're that hard up, why don't you sell that Golden Flash that's been stuck in the garage forever?'

7

Light rain speckles my visor as I turn off the high street and ride down the alley between the charity shop and the betting shop into the car park behind Deb's café. There's no need to count the cars. There are only two, parked close together as though keeping each other company, and a dry rectangle of tarmac, evidence of another just gone.

I paddle the bike through a pile of empty bottles and cans, polystyrene food trays and black bags of rubbish ripped open by dogs, and park the two-stroke behind a big grey wheelie bin. Rain clings to the sides of the bin like blisters and when I swing my leg off the bike, I end up with a damp patch all down the front of my jeans.

It would be a lot easier to park where the cars park but it's best to keep the bike out of sight of the hooded youths that hang around the car park. The shopkeepers are always complaining about the threatening behaviour of these yobs, as they call them. I've told them not to worry. They're friends of Gav. Soft as a wellyfull of taddies, the lot of them. But I'm not daft. Being soft wouldn't stop them nicking my bike. It might not be worth much, but it would give them hours of free entertainment racing up and down the old muckstack, ripping tracks between the silver birches, only stopping when the bike ran out of petrol.

All the windows and doors at the back of the shops are boarded up or secured with steel bars. Even the toilets, with their tiny opening lights, hardly big enough for a kid to squeeze through, have heavy grills fitted over the glass. Most of the gutters and soil pipes are covered with anti-burglar paint and all potential footholds are wrapped in razor wire. The arse end of shopping as I call it.

The smell of fish and chips blowing out of the fish shop's extractor fan a few doors down from the café intensifies as I lift up my visor. At the side of the greasy grille, a woman in a white smock and mesh hat inhales deeply on a cigarette and studies me as I pull off my helmet. It's Deb's mate Sheila. She works at the chippy. She's had her hair done short and spikey and dyed jet black. I don't think the harsh colour suits her pale complexion but I wouldn't say anything to her, even if she asked me outright what I thought of it. I'm not that insensitive despite what Deb thinks. I've noticed the other women working at the fish and chip shop and the women in the charity shop have had their hair done the same so it must be the fashion.

Sheila's face is lined through hard times and smoking, and she has a bitter look that melts away as soon as she smiles.

'Pissed yourself again, Phil,' she says.

I look down at the rain patch on my jeans and try to rub it dry.

'It's age, Sheila. I'll be dribbling like an old man afore long. You all right, love?'

'I'm fine,' Sheila says, and she takes another drag on her cigarette. 'I'm getting some fresh air. I've been in there since half ten this morning. I'm knackered. Ready for home.'

'Telly on? Feet up time?'

'Ooo no. I look after my grandkids on a night now. My daughter's managed to get a cleaning job in an office block in town. It's from six till ten and then she does another two hours early morning so I'm looking after them for her. It tires me out but it helps her and I love it. Ah, here they are now, the little darlings.'

Sheila throws her cigarette down among the litter of tab ends and almost before the car stops, her two grandchildren jump out and run up to her screaming their heads off. She lifts them up, one under each arm, their legs kicking the air with pure joy, her face transformed and the long hard shift forgotten.

I go into the café through the back door. Deb is behind the counter, diligently polishing the inside of a glass, her head and the glass held at the same angle as she twists the cloth. When I look over the counter through the stacked chairs, the step ladders and the tins of paint, I see two men tucking into a meal at the table against the big front window. It takes me a second or two to work out that it's my mates, Barry and Dave.

'Hey up. What are you two doing in here? We don't open till Thursday.'

'They thought it was still Madge's Snack Bar,' Deb says. 'They didn't know I'd bought it.'

'We didn't know it had shut down.' Barry says. 'But your good lady kindly rustled up a hearty meal for us both.'

'And very tasty it is too,' Dave says, and he sticks his fork into a fat sausage.

'It's a good job I had plenty of food in the fridge,' Deb says.

A lorry goes by on the main road and the glass in the front window rattles. Deb has asked me a dozen times to repaint the frame. She thinks it's a ten-minute job but it needs rubbing down to the bare wood to make a decent job of it, which will take days. I told her I'd do it when I'd finished my training but as usual, we ended up arguing about priorities and she told me to leave it. She would do it.

'I hope you're charging them the full rate, Deb,' I say as I put the kettle on and offer to make Barry and Dave a drink on the house. Deb picks up a carving knife and sloshes it around in the sink.

'You've just missed a young couple,' she says, wiping the blade clean. 'They popped in to see when we were opening. The lad said he does a bit of joinery and he said if I wanted, he'd make me a menu board for outside, a proper one with hinges and legs. It'd look really professional especially with our Gavin's artwork on it.'

'What was he after?'

'How do you mean what was he after? Nothing. He was just being friendly.' Deb pauses and I know what's coming. 'Well, he did say they were wanting a patio building at their new house.'

'See what I mean.'

'I said you'd have a look at it for them. I think it's a really good offer.'

Deb's eyes dazzle me. They're as bright as a child's eyes on Christmas morning. I drop two tea bags into the tea pot and scald them. I don't feel like playing Santa today.

'I'm not doing any more jobs for favours. You know it's cash I need. And anyway, I'm too busy.'

'Too busy?' Deb laughs but the knife in her hand looks dangerous. 'You've been on holiday for two months.'

'On holiday for two months?' I stir the pot then point the steaming spoon at the brown stain covering half the ceiling. 'Who's been up on the roof then and fixed them leaking tiles?'

The stain was nothing to worry about, the letting agent had apparently told Deb before she took on the lease. Just a little leak but it's fixed now, he said. When Deb passed this information on to me the next day as we were having our tea, I asked her why she hadn't told me the agent was coming round.

'He's taken you for a ride,' I said, 'because you're a woman. It's obvious to anybody the ceiling's still leaking. There's no way I would have let the agent get away with that. No way.'

Deb had calmly sipped her tea and said, 'I did tell you about the appointment but as usual you don't listen.'

I can't remember anything about an appointment. But I'm not going to argue. I flip the tea pot lid down and steam belches out of the spout. Barry makes room on the table for the three teas.

'I haven't seen you two knockin' about for ages,' I say. 'I thought you'd emigrated.'

'Dave's been abroad,' Barry says. 'He's been workin' in Sheffield.'

'I was doin' a bit of delivery drivin' but the firm's gone bust,' Dave says. 'They all seem to shut down as soon as I get there. Our lass's started callin' me Mister Receiver.'

'That's because she knows you're always nickin' stuff,' Barry says, pointing his fork at Dave and laughing.

Dave takes a drink of free tea.

'Ah, lovely,' he says. 'Deb makes a grand pot of tea.'

'Never mind Deb. I made that.'

Deb looks up from behind the counter.

'The first one this year.'

'How's tricks, Phil?' Dave says, pouring three heaped spoons of sugar into his tea.

'Bad in bed and worse up.'

Dave pours a fourth spoonful in.

'I say, Dave. Go steady with that sugar. You're eatin' into our lass's profits.'

'It's okay,' Barry says. 'He doesn't stir it.'

I rub my eyes, making little circles with my fingertips.

'I'll be a lot better next week when I've finished my training. Eight weeks is a long time not to be earnin' a wage. It's tough tryin' to make do on weekend jobs.' I watch Deb open the back door and take a black bag of rubbish out to the bins. The inflow of fresh air reaches the table, diluting the smell of bacon. 'Especially when Deb's spendin' like she is on this place.' I point at the shiny laminate wood floor. 'She made me rip up all the old carpet tiles the previous owner left and had me put this lot down. I got them second-hand but they still cost us nearly fifty quid. There was nothin' wrong with the old tiles, just a bit worn out that's all, like me.' I notice a scuff on the new floor and I spit on my finger and rub at it. 'And she's gone and bought a load of lamps and light fittings and paintings and drawings of the sun and the moon and God knows what.'

'The stars?' Barry says.

'Probably. There's boxes of stuff all over the place. And there's a load more in my garage. I can hardly get to my bike for 'em and I've had to put my sidecar outside. Chandeliers, apparently. Can you believe it?'

Dave's knife and fork hover above his black pudding. 'You're joking?' he says. 'Chandeliers for the garage?'

Dave looks like a pirate with his long straggly hair and the gap in his front teeth. He lost the tooth early in his twenties when a cricket ball hit him in the face. It was the first and last time he played any sport.

'Not *for* the garage, Dave. *In* the garage. They're for in here. Don't be giving Deb any more ideas.' I lift my cup up to the light from the big window. 'And look at this. I can't even get my finger through the handle.'

Dave and Barry try to push their fat fingers through the delicate handles on their cups. When Dave succeeds in threading the tip of his little finger through, Barry accuses him of cheating and we all laugh. I'm feeling better now. I'm on form and loving it. Acting around with my mates, my preoccupation with my qualification and the worry about Gav's future temporarily forgotten. I check to make sure Deb hasn't returned from emptying the rubbish.

'I know she's graftin' her backside off,' I say. 'I've never known anybody work as hard, but I've told her, she's tryin' to make this place too posh. She's plannin' to open up one day a week for women only, can you believe. I think that's why she's spendin' all this money on all these fancy things. All these things to do with light.'

Dave pulls a face as though he's just found something in his black pudding that he doesn't like the look of.

'Women only? Why?'

'It's the modern way, Dave,' Barry says, and he quietly continues to cut the rind off his bacon.

'Don't ask me why she's doing it,' I say. 'But between you two and me, I think she'd make more money forgettin' that idea and keepin' it open every day for everybody. A no-nonsense café where anybody can walk in any day of the week. All folk want is a strong pot of tea, a decent helpin' of pie an' chips and some good banter. They'd be happy for ever. Blokes round here don't want all this hoity-toity stuff.'

Dave and Barry nod and I take this as proof of our superior business acumen. I'm kidding myself, of course, and I know Dave and Barry are agreeing out of politeness and that's okay.

'But it's her café and you know what she's like. She'll do what she wants with it.'

A young woman with a little lad balanced on her hip comes up to the window and stops to read the notice about the big opening day. Images of Spider-Man, Superman and Batman pose aggressively on the kid's T-shirt, and when he taps on the window and pulls a face at us, Dave slowly lifts himself up out of his chair, expands his chest and growls at the lad like a wild man. The youngster laughs and wriggles into his mother's chest and although the woman smiles at Dave's antics, she sets the kid down on the pavement and they walk away.

'Nice one, Dave,' I say. 'We're looking for a marketing manager. You could rescue this place.'

'I haven't got the time.'

'I thought you said you'd just been made redundant?'

'I have. I've decided I'm goin' to make a livin' on the internet now.'

Barry looks at me and we raise our eyebrows.

'They reckon you can make a fortune buyin' and sellin' stuff on there with these new-fangled auction site things,' Dave says. 'Look at all them billionaires in America. A lot of 'em started up their businesses in their garage.'

'You haven't even got a garage,' Barry says.

'I've got a hut. It's all right laughin'. Somebody I know's just sold half a dozen old hessian sacks on there. He found 'em in his coal house and they still had the original coal merchant's name on. He got a fiver apiece for 'em.'

'Watch out Bill Gates,' I say, and we all take a swig of tea.

'And how's it going with you, Barry?' I say. 'Busy I hope.'

'As busy as I want to be. Did you say eight weeks training to be a plumber?'

'I did. I've spent a fortune on it and I still can't bend pipe and solder joints. None of us can.'

'God help us. They're basic skills. I did a five-year apprenticeship to qualify as a plumber when I left school. Five years at college plus on-the-job training.'

Barry has the cleanest hands I've ever come across in the building trade. No matter what job he's done that day, no matter how much lead or grease he's handled, by tea-time his hands are as scrubbed and weathered as driftwood.

'You're going back a long way there, Barry,' Dave says. 'I didn't think they had copper in the Stone Age.'

'Hey,' Barry says. 'It was good training in them days. That was when a trade meant something. When firms talked about quality and safety, not shareholders and bonuses.'

'I could have done it at the building college,' I say, 'but I've heard they've never any money. You end up reusing old bits of copper fittings and fighting over battered old radiators. And it's a right palaver to get on one of their courses. You need a certificate just to fathom out who to ring up. Open days, testing, enrolment forms, work placements, NVQ's.'

'My last supervisor had an NVQ,' Dave says. 'Not Very Quick.'

'Honestly. It's like being back at school.'

I remember the wasted time at school. All that algebra rammed down our throats and never used since. All that time devoted to kings and queens from centuries ago and nothing about ordinary families from round our way. Being forced to listen to A Lark Ascending when we could have been outside in the fields learning about the real thing. I could never see the sense of it. All I wanted to do was play football and count down the days before I started work. The main motivation had been to have fun and avoid being caught which was a skill in itself. I reckon I deserved a certificate in perseverance. But deep down I know I wasted an opportunity and sometimes I do regret missing out on an education. But I would never say that to anybody. That would be admitting failure and I could never do that.

'I've been saving up for the last two years to pay for it,' I say. 'Me an' Deb's not been away for God knows how long. But at least the training centre's only a few miles away so I've not had to fork out on accommodation like some of the others have had to do. It must have cost 'em a fortune.

'I've taken every job I could get my hands on to pay for the thing. All the crap that nobody else wanted. Jobs paying next to nowt. I was that desperate I even did a job for Jack Jagger and I hate the guy. I hate him even more now. He still owes me five hundred quid for a job I did for him two chuffing months ago.'

'I know one or two who's still waitin' to get paid for jobs they've done for him,' Dave says. 'They've all bar written it off. Somebody was sayin' they think his business is struggling.'

'You're jokin', Dave?' I say.

'I'm not. He's had to lay off a few men.'

'Chuffin' great,' I say, folding my arms tight and looking out of the window for something or somebody to glare at. 'Goodbye five hundred quid.'

'Jack Jagger,' Barry says, looking over his shoulder and lowering his voice. 'What a character. I've heard some stories about him. He started up his business during the miners' strike. Buying up repossessed houses for next to nothing then selling them on. Look at him now.'

'Tell me about it,' I say, and my jaw tightens. I'm back on Jagger's drive watching the little coin missile roll towards me. Barry can see something is bothering me and like a true mate, he changes the subject.

'You're brave taking on a new job at your age, Phil.'

'I had to do, Barry. I couldn't have gone on much longer doing heavy building work. It was killin' me. It's alright for all these salesmen and office workers and bankers. Hardest thing they ever do is push a pen.'

'Or hit a keypad,' Dave says.

'When you have to work, and I mean real physical work for a living, it takes it out on you.' I push my chair back and stand up. 'Neck – pit. Knees – roofin'. Back – concretin.' I touch each named part of my body as I go along. Dave and Barry look at me as though I've invented a new dance. 'I was six foot when I left school. I've all on to straighten up to five foot nine now. God knows what I'll end up doin' if this plumbin' doesn't work out. Taxi driving? Decorating? Window cleaning?' As I sit down, I remember my close encounter with Frank. 'Flower arranging? Not a prayer.' I shake my head at my own suggestions. 'Everybody's at it. But I aint goin' on the dole or the sick for nobody.'

Barry in a serious voice says, 'Have you ever considered working in a Call Centre, Mister Steele? The work isn't physically demanding and you're entitled to a toilet break three times a day, whether you want one or not.'

Even though I know Barry is joking, just the thought of working indoors forces me to react.

'Me? A battery hen? No thanks.' If we'd been outside, I would have spat on the floor. 'No. I'll be done for, lads. Finito.'

My anger is tempered when I catch Dave trying to push his index finger through his cup handle again. I nudge Barry and we secretly watch Dave struggle. When he looks up like a guilty little boy, we laugh out loud and Barry bangs his fist on the table and I wipe a tear from my eye.

Deb comes back from emptying the rubbish and as she washes her hands in the bowl, I see her head tilt towards us.

'Hey, be quiet, lads. Deb's listenin'. She might think I'm happy.'

'That'll be the day,' Deb says without looking up. 'He's only happy when he's working on his Golden Flash.'

'Haven't you finished that Golden Flash yet?' Barry says. 'It's years since I last saw it. I think you were in the middle of rebuilding the forks.'

'Come round and have a look. I'll be in my garage on Sunday morning. Unless I drop on some work from somewhere.'

'I might do that. About eleven?'

'Perfect.'

'I'll bring some copper pipe with me and show you the basics of pipe bending if you want. And soldering if we have time.'

Now it's my eyes that dazzle like a child's on Christmas day.

'That'd be brilliant.'

I take a big sup of tea and the cup handle doesn't seem so tiny after all.

Deb calls out as she rinses her hands under the tap.

'Phil. Can you keep an eye on the café for me for half an hour just in case we get anybody coming in wanting to know when we're opening up? I want to write up the new menu for the big day and I don't want disturbing.'

Dave is quicker than Barry.

'How long does it take to write pie an' peas?'

Deb dries her hands down the front of her apron.

'Cheeky sod. I'm going to open up with an Italian theme. Pizza, pasta, risotto, tiramisu. A bit of continental flavour to spice up the taste buds.'

Now Barry has a nibble.

'That should bring the locals in. Most of 'em hate foreigners round here.'

I'm enjoying the ribbing and I'm waiting for Deb's response. She's smart and I know she'll not back off.

'Anyway, you two aren't invited,' Deb says, and she points her finger at Dave and Barry, switching between the two of them for emphasis. 'It's women-only that day. Old women, young women, working women, women at home, unemployed women, energetic women, disabled women, lonely women, shy women, struggling women. You'll have to find somewhere else on Thursdays to get your fried bread and black pudding.'

Barry winks at Dave as they stand up to leave.

'Oooh. Hear that, Dave. A full house. Sex, class, *and* racial discrimination.'

They shut the door behind them and the front window rattles as though it's about to fall out. Deb appears to be talking to the suds in the bowl as I pour the cold dregs of tea from the three cups down the sink.

'That window wants fixing,' she says. 'It'll put people off coming in.'

The laughter has gone out of the door with Barry and Dave.

'It'll not be the window that puts people off coming in, Deb. It'll be because nobody's got any money. Everybody's skint. The only way you'll fill this place up is if you start giving the food away.'

'If you think I'm going to spend the rest of my life cleaning other people's houses and then come back home and be at your beck and call, you can forget it.'

'I'm not saying that.'

'What are you saying, then? You've got your plumbing job and your Golden Flash. Well, I've got my little project, now.'

Friday

1

The mornings are getting lighter now. It's not eight o'clock and Deb's already gone up to the café, scrubbing walls and floors and things. It's still fairly dark in the garage and the fluorescent tube takes forever to kick in. It's the same ritual every time. Ear cocked at the hesitant clicks and ticks as though I'm listening for something to hatch. Wait three seconds until I hear the bump from above. Then watch the light bring life to the Golden Flash.

I lift the blanket off the bike and check the machine over. There's no visible dust but I wipe the seat and petrol tank with a clean rag in a sort of reflex action. The bike looks great in this light and I can't resist swinging my leg over the seat, settling into the riding position, twisting the throttle and pulling in the levers like a big kid. The unmade track at the back of our house is transformed into a long sweeping desert highway and the muckstack becomes a high mountain range.

When the low sunlight enters the garage and overpowers the artificial light, the fun ends and I put the blanket back over the Flash. As I'm locking up, Gav comes out of the kitchen door zipping up his bomber jacket. I can't believe what I'm seeing. He's never up this early and I rub my eyes and look at my watch pretending to be in shock.

'Bloody hell. We're up early, aren't we?'

'I might have finally got myself a job.'

My face lights up and I rush to snap the awkward padlock shut and shake his hand.

'Hey, that's fantastic, lad. Well done. What is it? Where abouts is it?'

'It's at a garage. They want somebody to set up a computer system for them.'

'Just up your street.'

'They said if I did a good job, they'd look after me and put plenty of work my way. They've got loads of contacts in the motor trade, all over the north.'

'That's brilliant. Aren't you going to put a tie on? First impressions count, you know. You can borrow mine if you want. It's my funeral tie but it should be okay.'

'I'm not wearin' a tie. They'd laugh their heads off if I went dressed up. I know the owners. Me and my mates do odd jobs for 'em now and then.'

Of course, I'm dead chuffed at the news that my lad might have found employment at last, and yet I can't help feeling a bit sad that he's not talking about joining me as a partner in Steele and Son Plumbing. Deb would say I'm being selfish again and maybe I am. But it doesn't feel like that. I'm trying to help the lad get a job with a future. A skilled job that involves working with his hands so that he'll never ever be without work. I stop arguing with myself and push my thoughts to the back of my mind.

'Do everything they ask you to do and don't give them any backchat,' I say, almost adding, 'like I did at the pit,' but I don't because I'd be lying, 'and you never know, this might be the start of a great career.'

Gav drops into his car seat and lowers the window. He checks his hair in the mirror and winks at me.

'I might have finally got a job.'

He races out of the track, tyres throwing up dust and gravel, and I smile as the car merges into the traffic on the main road.

'I hope it goes well, lad,' I say aloud to myself. 'I really do.'

Gav's noisy exit from the area brings Colin, the DIY next door neighbour out of his little wooden shed at the bottom of his garden. The man stands at the entrance with a four-foot length of dowelling against his shoulder like a sentry with a rifle. When he sees the joy on my face he stands at ease, takes the dowelling off his shoulder, and pretends to play a snooker shot.

'Have we won the lottery or something, Phil?'

'No. Better than that, Colin. Our Gav might have found himself a job.'

'Good for him. I hope it's not as a driving instructor.'

I have to nod in acknowledgement of Colin's wit. On any other day I would have answered back. Probably asked him if he came out of his little cuckoo clock hut on the hour every hour, but I'm feeling good so there's no need to repay the sarcasm.

It's early and I decide to take a detour to Jack Jagger's house before going to the training centre. The radio is on full belt and I sing along to every song, making up job-themed words where I don't know the lyrics. I only stop singing as I approach Jagger's house with its locked gates and the two supercilious stone lions looking down on me. The defensive barrier of steel gate and high wall and hedge looks more solid and a lot higher than I remember and I spend the rest of the journey trying to work out if there is any way to break into the grounds without being seen.

My desk is at the back of the classroom next to the wall of windows which face south. At the start of the course, in a sunless March, the solar gains were welcome but now as May approaches, whenever the sun comes out, we all wilt. A couple of weeks ago on a really sunny day, I half-jokingly complained about the heat to one of the directors. 'You could grow tomatoes in here somedays,' I said. 'Plumb tomatoes.' But the director didn't seem to get the pun. He told me the room used to be the canteen in a small engineering firm before the company went bust. When Plumbdeep moved in, it had only taken the training centre team six weeks, the director said with pride, to turn the gutted engineering workshop into an approved plumbing training centre.

I knew the engineering firm well and was sad when they shut down. The engineers there had been good to me over the years, re-boring the barrels of the Golden Flash, skimming the cylinder head, and fabricating all sorts of bits for the bike no matter how small and intricate. The company was always busy and had a waiting list a mile long. But when the pits closed, unemployment went up and their business went down. Not long ago, I saw one of the engineers who used to work there. He said he was filling in his time as a tyre fitter at Remolds and Retreds.

Now, in the classroom, the trainer delivering the Water Regulations session hangs his white company jacket over the back of his chair and closes the blinds. I keep a record of the number of slides he's using and when it reaches ten five-bar gates, I abandon the count and idly sketch myself on my Golden Flash soaring over a drystone wall in an open field. I'm usually rubbish at drawing but this effort doesn't seem too bad and I slide it left across my desk to Kath the Gardener. Kath must be in her late twenties or early thirties and as I keep reminding myself, she's a lot younger than me. She's a former landscape gardener from Scotland and the only woman on the course. You wouldn't know she was the only woman because she always wears baggy clothes when she's out of her overalls and she keeps her long red hair tucked up under a black baseball cap. I've only ever seen her hair once and that was for the few seconds it took her to beat the dust and cobwebs off her cap after she'd been working under the floorboards all day. Kath is good at soldering and she always comes top in theory and that's why, whenever I can, I make sure I'm always by her side. Well, that's what I keep telling myself.

Kath shades in the drystone wall and turns the field into a colourful wild flower meadow. She slides the enhanced sketch back to me and I nod my approval before sliding it to my right to Robert the Farmer. Robert looks bewildered but I don't laugh or say anything, especially not in front of Kath. I know it would embarrass the man. Poor Robert. Strong and tanned on the outside and as green as his fields on the inside. I remember how it had taken three weeks of gentle ribbing, nibbling away at his thin skin, watching how he reacted to others, before he was able to look me in the eye during a conversation. Even now, when he's talking, his sentences occasionally trail off into a mumble as though he doubts the value of his own words.

After looking at the sketch for a minute and scratching his head, Robert draws a cow riding a Suzuki trail bike leaping over the wall and flowery meadow alongside my BSA Golden Flash.

The slides are appearing and disappearing at a blurring pace and the fan on the computer projector is humming like a bee trapped in a jar. I rest my chin in my hands and look around the classroom. Even in the dimness I can tell that many of the students, young and old, have succumbed to the heat and monotony and given up the fight to keep their eyes open. The atmosphere takes me back to the Friday afternoons at junior school when the teachers used to gather everyone into the assembly hall to watch a boring film about tribes and wild animals in Africa or life in the army, just so they could take an hour off from teaching. One Friday they showed us a newsreel about the Queen and the Royal Family. I was convinced nobody had taken any notice, but a week later, and it could have been a coincidence, somebody a few doors down from our council house painted God Save the Queen on their outside toilet in white gloss paint.

The hypnotic hum of the projector in the darkened, airless room, begins to overpower me. My eyes close and I imagine the day my Golden Flash is finally on the road . . .

. . . *the blanket comes off and the 1954 BSA 650 cc Golden Flash sparkles as though it's lit from within. The paintwork is in the original gold colour. The alloy rocker covers above the black cast iron cylinder head and barrels are highly polished, and the twin chrome exhaust pipes curving out of the head, flow backwards and terminate in parallel tapered chrome silencers.*

I ride out of the garage into the sunlight like a bird set free from a cage. With a salute and a grin to the wide-eyed hooded youths circling on their pushbikes on the street corner, I wind my way through the labyrinth of narrow streets, junctions and roundabouts until I get to the quiet, sweeping lanes of the open countryside.

When I ride past a gap in the hedgerow the throaty roar of the big engine vanishes and everything goes quiet. It's as though the noise has jumped off the bike, raced around the perimeter of the field, then jumped back on again, breathless, as the line of hedges resumed.

The quiet lane follows the gentle rise and fall of the landscape. The dense hedgerows are set well back and the grass verges are wide enough to race horses. A pheasant with its head held high trots into the lane from the vegetation on the left. It sees the Golden Flash and stops two strides from the safety of the other side. Unsure of what to do, it turns round, head still held high and sprints back to where it came from. A blackbird fires out of the undergrowth on the other side, skimming low over the surface of the lane, almost passing under the bike before disappearing into the hedgerow opposite.

The lane becomes narrower and the bends tighten and the hedges lean into my shoulder like a row of spectators. We take to the air and I lift up my visor. The gentle breeze warms my face and I stand tall on the footrests and soar over the woods and fields towards the horizon . . .

. . . The projector goes quiet and I open my eyes. In the kitchen at the side of the classroom somebody is filling a kettle, the jumper washer banging as the tap turns off. Noises from outside drift up into the classroom. Somebody hammering at a bench inside the workshop across the yard. A hole being drilled in a brick wall in the car park.

The trainer opens the blinds and we all shield our eyes from the harsh light reflecting off the whiteboard. In the car park below, my trail bike looks lost among the cars and vans. The student with the drill is shrouded in a cloud of brick dust. A hosepipe drains into a puddle at the side of a skip. Next door in the supermarket car park, customers wheel trollies in and out of the store. As soon as a car moves out of a parking space another takes its place.

I'm still only half awake and I can't help reading, for the hundredth time, the poster underneath the clock on the wall. 'Become a Plumber with PLUMBDEEP: Earn a Good Living. Develop an Exciting Career. Learn Skills for Life.' It's short and snappy and whoever dreamed it up did a good job. Let's see.

All around the classroom, students uncurl slowly as though a stone has been lifted from on top of them.

'Everything we've discussed is covered in your copy of the Water Regulations,' the trainer says as he turns off his computer and unplugs the projector. 'Make sure you know it from front to back. Finally. Now that you're coming to the end of your training, let me offer you a word of advice about setting up your own plumbing business. Whatever you do, don't try and copy every other plumbing business out there. The key to success is to be different. Find a niche and give it everything you've got. Okay. Any questions?'

Silence. I push myself off the desk and straighten up to let the blood flow back into my arms and neck. I feel sorry for the trainer. He's not what you would call dynamic. I can't relate to nine tenths of the regulations he's talking about and I've never heard of, never mind seen, most of the plumbing fittings popping up and down on his never-ending slide show. I don't think I'm alone in thinking this judging by all the blank faces around me. Somebody ought to tell him but nobody wants to risk having their portfolio rejected. The most I dare offer is a bit of well-meaning sarcasm.

'Can we just go back to slide number two?'

There are groans, arm stretching and yawns as though it's time to get up for work after a good night out but no one has the energy to respond. Standing up is hard enough.

I join Kath and Robert in the slow procession of students leaving the classroom.

'What did you think to that, then?' I say. 'He lost me when he introduced himself.'

'Don't worry, boys,' Kath says. 'All we have to do is remember the details on every slide he showed, otherwise we could be found guilty of spreading Legionnaires' disease and spend the next ten years in jail for manslaughter.'

Robert stops dead, causing the queue behind to falter and split in two to get past.

'Thanks, Kath. That's really cheered me up. It was bad enough having to worry about foot and mouth breaking out on my farm without having to worry about ten years behind bars.'

The back of Kath's baseball cap draws me on as she leads the three of us down the crowded staircase. The industrial stair carpet is cheap and thin and there is more noise from our footsteps than from our mouths.

'I bet you wish you were still a gardener, Kath,' I say. 'Just tetanus to worry about.'

Kath half-turns, smiling.

'Tetanus and poverty.'

There's a pause opposite the reception office at the bottom of the stairs as we queue to get into the car park.

'That trainer was as boring as hell,' I say, 'but he's given me an idea. You know when he said don't be like everybody else – be different? Well, I was thinking. When I get my Golden Flash finished, I could use it to market my plumbing business. That'd make me and our Gav stand out from the crowd. Two plumbers on a classic British motorbike.'

'It would,' Robert says. 'But what about all your tools and materials? How would you carry all of those around on a motorbike? I wouldn't be able to carry anything on my Suzuki.'

'I wouldn't use it for doing any plumbing. It's much too precious for that.'

I can just see all the plumbing tools and materials Robert would take to a job. They'd probably be the same big spanners, hammers and wrecking bars that he uses to fix his farm machinery. He would need a tractor and trailer to carry them all. Imagine parking that combination outside a customer's house and walking into the bathroom with a two-foot wrench to change a fragile ceramic tap disc.

'Much too precious,' I say. 'I'd just use it for advertising, like when I'm measuring up a job. Leave it on the drive with a big sign on the back with Steele and Son Plumbing plastered all over it. And I could get some business cards printed with me and our Gav sat on it.'

I'm thinking and talking at the same time, surprising myself at my sudden creativity.

'Hey, and I've just had another brainwave. I could call it, Golden Flush Plumbing. Do you get it? Golden Flush, as in toilet flush?'

Kath and Robert glance at each other and make no comment. I know they think I'm joking but it doesn't stop me feeling pleased with myself for the first time in weeks.

When we finally get out into the car park, the students ahead have formed a group near the workshop entrance and are listening to a bloke I haven't seen before. The stranger is wearing grey overalls, so heavily streaked with white jointing paste and silicone sealant you could mistake him for a soldier in camouflaged combat clothing. The guy is holding court, enjoying talking in between drinking his free training centre tea.

'Yeah, twelve months ago,' the stranger says. 'Peggs took us. Is he still here?'

We all nod.

'Bloody hell. God, he was a rough sod when we had him. We used to call him the Silicone Kid. Whenever you'd got a problem job, he used to say, "Put silicone sealant on it. That'll fix it." But he was a good trainer and he was a right laugh and he'd never see you struggle.'

At the back of the group, Jim Watts, the oldest student in our class and a former IT contractor before being made redundant, asks the question most of us want to ask.

'What's it like out there? Have you found much work?'

'Plenty,' the stranger says. 'There's stacks. I was doing odd jobs to start with, not making much money, but now I'm fitting central heating with a plumber I met a few weeks ago. He's red-hot. It's a piece of piss.'

Another serious question, this time from Kath.

'How did you meet up with this other plumber? Has he been through here as well?'

I'm keen to hear the stranger and so is everyone else, even those who are confident of finding work at the end of the course. There's no fooling around now.

'No,' the stranger says. 'I got chatting to him at the plumbers' merchant about a month ago. He overheard me asking about a shower I was having problems with and he told me what to do and he said if ever I got stuck to give him a ring and he said if ever he needed a hand, he'd ring me. Anyway, I rang him this particular day, before I started working with him, to ask him about some drains I was working on. It was about eleven o'clock and I said to him, "Where are you?" and he said, "I'm at home. I've just first fixed a central heating installation this morning, all plastic." I said, "This morning! It's only eleven o'clock." and he said, "Yes, it's easy. Just bash a hole in the outside wall and feed the plastic pipes through, one length after another. It's a piece of cake. Fish it out where you want it to come up for the rads. Job done." So I said to him, "What about clipping?" and he just laughed and said, "What's that?" He's a right laugh. We've been working together ever since.'

Nobody says anything. They're probably feeling like me – relieved there's nothing to be afraid of out there, and also a bit shocked that we've paid all this money to be no more than a glorified labourer. The stranger knocks his tea back and goes off to chat to Hazel and Jean in reception, and we all pull our overalls on and drift towards the bays and benches to work on our assessments and complete our portfolios.

2

At precisely half past ten the Fat Pie Man enters the training centre car park and honks its horn. Peggs limps out to the van to get the training staff order in first. Then Garrett steps out of his office, cups his hands like a market trader and yells, 'Down tools. Tea break. Fat pies. Get-your-fat-pies-here. Biggest-pies-in-all-the-world.'

I finish cutting the last few threads on a steel pipe as the hungriest students clamber out of their trap doors or drop their tools where they stand and jog out to the van. I'm not drawn to the smell of sizzling hot fat drifting over the steaming counter, where the chubby vendor in his smart blue and white striped apron has set up shop. And I'm not drawn to the sound of sausages and eggs being fried or the sight of salt and pepper pots, mustard and sauce bottles neatly lined up on the shiny, warm stainless steel counter like trophies. I'm not drawn because I've no money.

Instead, I join other students in no hurry, pushing my way into the tiny workshop toilet, jostling for position, a lattice of arms over the soap dispenser and the inadequate, single point electric water heater.

When I emerge into the sunlight, Robert and Kath are leaning against my van eating their sandwiches. I slide open the side door and sit on the step, eyes on the ground.

'Not eating again, Philip?' Kath says.

'I had a pie yesterday.'

'You look as though you could do with a square meal. Do you want to share my sandwiches? Freshly made this morning by my lovely landlady.'

'No thanks. I'll survive.'

'You can have one of mine,' Robert says. 'Free range bacon from my own livestock. Or should that be deadstock?'

'No, you're right.'

Kath opens her sandwich and rearranges the generous slices of cheese and red onion rings. My stomach rumbles and I swallow my saliva.

There's a discarded sink plug and chain on the car park floor close to my back wheel, and to take my mind off eating, I stretch out and nudge the plug with my foot until the chain is straight.

Robert says, 'Did you manage to pay your final instalment this morning, then, Phil?'

'No. I've got until Wednesday. Don't say anything to anybody, but I'm struggling to find the money.'

'That's tough,' Kath says, and she takes another bite of her sandwich and the smell of onion fills the air. 'How are things back home?'

'Getting better,' I say. 'Our Gav might have got himself a job.'

'That's tremendous.'

'He's fitting a computer at a garage for somebody today. He thinks it might lead to more work.' I check my mobile phone then put it back in my pocket. 'I thought he would have sent me a text to let me know how he was getting on, the little bugger. He never tells me anything.'

I smile as I remember the look on Gav's face earlier this morning as he smoothed his hair in his car's mirror.

'He's dead chuffed. You ought to have seen his face.'

'You look chuffed, as well,' Kath says.

'Do you know, it's heart-breaking to see him. I feel really sorry for the poor lad. This is the first bit of success he's had in over a year. He's tried everything, and I have as well for him, but there's nothing. Can you believe it. No job at his age. Nothing to get up for on a morning. No regular wage. No workmates.'

'No regular wage and no workmates?' Robert says. 'Sounds like farming.'

'It was another world when I was his age. Everybody had a job. If you weren't cut out for a suit and tie you could always find a job at the pit or if you didn't mind travelling a few miles you could always get a job at the steelworks in Sheffield.'

Kath nods. Somehow, I know she's listening even though she keeps rearranging her sandwich and doesn't look up at me. I pass the plug from one foot to the other.

'I know we all moaned about the pit, about the muck and the wet and the heat and the danger and all that, but it was like being in a big club. We looked after each other, and I don't just mean us that worked there. Everybody had something to do with the pit. All the shops. The buses. The doctors. Everybody. We were all connected up somehow.' I nod at Robert. 'Apart from the farmers. They were always a funny lot.'

'We had two coal fires,' Robert says, and he smiles into his bacon sandwich.

'I can well believe it,' Kath says. 'My dad tells me it was just the same in Glasgow with the shipyards.'

'I can imagine. I'm not saying they should have kept the pits open for ever. That'd be daft. But there should have been something else there for us before they shut the lot down. Nobody ever asked us for any ideas. You're talking about the lives of whole families.' I pick up the chain and pull at the plug to see how firmly it's attached. 'I don't know what else I could have done for the lad. He doesn't listen to me any more. Whatever I say to him, he thinks I'm talking crap. He's probably right. What do I know?'

'It sounds as though you think you've let him down,' Kath says.

I screw up my face. She's hit the spot again.

'I think I have let him down. All these years working my socks off and nothing to show for it. Nothing to give him a lift up with. Maybe he'll forgive me one day.'

'He'll not need to forgive you, Philip. He'll understand.'

I think about my dad and about all the years we never got on. How I despised him sometimes. How I blamed the old man for everything. Not wanting to go anywhere or do anything other than fly his pigeons at the back of the pub and go for pint in between shifts at the pit. Not standing up to some of the sharks down at the working men's club even though he could have hammered them in his prime. And then one day something flipped and everything made sense. Maybe I see myself in my dad. Maybe Kath is right. Maybe it is about understanding.

'I hope so,' I say. 'I've got him to worry about on one shoulder and our lass to worry about on the other. She wants me to take her to Leeds now to look for some second-hand chairs for the café. As if we haven't spent enough on the place. I sometimes wonder if I'd have been better off on my own.'

Kath makes me say things, things I didn't even know I'd been thinking. I try to imagine what it would be like sitting in a cold flat, in front of the telly all night long with a pizza and a can of lager, only seeing our Gav when he wants to see him. No. Not good. I shake my head.

'Then again, if ever Deb kicked me out, I'd just be another statistic. No thanks.'

'We're all just a statistic,' Robert says. 'Just dust and ashes.'

Peggs comes out of the workshop into the car park and informs everybody that it's a quarter to eleven and would we please mind coming back in to continue our assessments. What he actually says is, 'Get your lazy backsides in here – if they did a certificate in tea drinking, you'd all pass with distinction.'

I swing the plug in the air by the chain like a missile and when I let go, it loops all the way across the carpark into the skip. Kath stands up and knocks the crumbs off her overalls.

'I don't know what you think, Robert,' she says as the three of us amble across the car park. 'But being single is not as bad as people make out.'

'It's not,' Robert says. 'It's worse.'

'At least you never lose an argument,' I say.

'I've been on my own for four years now', Kath says. 'My husband was a bastard – a bullying bastard, and I'm glad I had the guts to leave him. It was a rough time but my parents were there for me until I got back on my feet. I survived.'

'Lucky you,' I say. 'My mam and dad wouldn't be able to help me. I don't just mean because they've no money. They're too old. My dad just sits there at the kitchen table all day long doing his horses and my mother works round him and gets his dinner ready.

They're just waiting for the big clock of heaven to strike midnight. They're going nowhere.'

'I know the feeling,' Robert says.

Kath empties her water bottle down the drain outside the workshop door.

'What about you, Philip? Where are you going?'

I laugh out loud at Kath's question. I hadn't thought about that one. Ever. None of the blokes I know talk about where they're going. Maybe the women do. Deb is always talking about wanting to move on. Where that might be is a mystery to me. But, no, the blokes say nothing. We just shut the future off, skirt round it, talk about cars, get drunk, look for scapegoats, buy lottery tickets, curse politicians and foreigners, resent anybody who's done well and only trust those who haven't. None of us go beyond what's happening around us that week. What's the point? We'd all end up depressed.

'Where am I going, Kath? Leeds by the looks of it for some second-hand chairs.'

3

The most obvious sign that the training centre was once an engineering workshop is the floor-to-ceiling roller shutter door operated by long, rattling chains at one end of the building. I remember it being used to load and unload light goods. Now the door is the main entrance into the training centre workshop and every time I hear the thing go up or down it reminds me of the cage at my old pit.

There are metal benches as big as table tennis tables in a line down the centre of the workshop. Along one side is a row of identical wooden training bays built with open doorways facing the benches. Each bay is the size of a tiny bathroom with a raised floor for the installation of underfloor pipework. To allow for drainage from the toilets and the baths and basins, the bays stand a foot away from the external wall of the building, creating a narrow unlit gap behind the row. A kind of no man's land.

One day during week two of the course, out of curiosity I shone my torch into the gap to see if there was anything interesting behind the bays. In among the cobwebs and dust left behind from the original engineering shop floor were fresh items of waste – sawn off bits of three by two timber smelling of pine, short coiled cast-off lengths of electrical cable, cut-offs of scrap pipe and fittings, and empty screw boxes and cigarette packets – all damp and stranded in puddles of waste water on the concrete floor as though the tide had just gone out. The following day I squeezed unnoticed along the gap, torch in hand, and found a handful of unused shiny copper elbows and tees abandoned in the puddles. I filled my pockets and later that afternoon when nobody was watching, the fittings went into my van stock. Fruits of the forest, I told Kath and Robert.

Now drills drill, blowtorches blow, and the smell of hot, smoking flux fills the air. The thud of lead sheets being beaten into chimney flashings on the metal benches acts as bass to the tinny music coming out of the workshop radio. It's noisy, warm and cosy. There is a job to do. I'm happy.

As I'm drilling a hole in the bay wall to fit a basin bracket, Peggs appears at the doorway of my bay. I'm behind with my assessment but I never view Peggs as an interruption. I always learn something from him. Not always about plumbing.

'At last. A trainer,' I say. 'I've been looking all over the place for somebody to show me how to level my bath.'

'I can't be everywhere. Anyway, come on, have you paid your final instalment yet?'

The work area is so small, when I sit down and straighten my legs to rest my knees and back, my feet stick out of the bay and Peggs has to stand to one side.

'No. I've got a few days' grace,' I say. 'I used my negotiating skills. The MD wanted me to pay it off in interest-free instalments over the next five years but I said I wasn't having any of that and so we agreed I'd pay him in full on Wednesday.' I rub my knee caps as though they're carrying the weight of the debt. 'All this chuffing hassle because of your mate, Jack Jagger.'

'Hey, he's not my mate. He gives me plenty of jobs, so I make sure I stay in his good books. In fact, I got a little job off him only last week. It's at one of his flats. You can have it if you want. I'm a bit busy. It's twenty quid standard rate for repairing a leak on a toilet. A bit of easy money for you.'

'Off Jagger? No thanks. I'm not doing any more work for that bloke ever again. He's done me once. Never again.'

'He'll not do you. Here. I'll pay you upfront out of my own money.'

Peggs pulls two ten-pound notes out of his wallet and I see half a tank of diesel.

'Take plenty of silicone sealant with you and don't use any parts. Jagger doesn't like paying for parts.'

I take the cash without looking at it, and thrust it deep into my pocket, out of sight.

'It's a good job I'm desperate.'

'Come on,' Peggs says, picking up my spirit level. 'I'll show you how to level up your bath.'

With my knees and neck creaking, I roll over onto my back and slide under the bath. As I put my adjustable spanner on one of the bath legs, Peggs shouts a warning.

'Make sure you keep well away from that electric cable under there. It's live.'

I know he's having me on. I'm about to scream and pretend I've been electrocuted when there's a loud crack on the bath side making me jerk and bang my forehead. When I ease myself from under the bath, Peggs is holding a length of plastic overflow tube behind his back.

'Thanks,' I say. 'That's all I needed.'

We're laughing at each other's disabilities when we hear Garrett's voice a few yards away. Peggs puts the plastic tube and spirit level down as though they're red hot and I slide back under the bath just as Garrett's brown brogues and blue socks appear at the entrance to my bay.

'I hope you don't think that's going to pass, Mister General Builder.'

I roll over onto my hands and knees and slowly get to my feet.

'Peggs has already checked it,' I say.

'It looks fine to me,' Peggs says. 'There are one or two tweaks to make but other than that it's finished.'

Garrett turns his back on Peggs.

'I don't care what anybody else says. I'm the director of training and I'm telling you that assessment is not up to the required national standard and there's no way I'm going to pass it.'

I stick my chin up and mirror Garrett's stance. I'm ready for a confrontation if that's what he's after.

'What's wrong with it?'

'Step outside and I'll show you.'

Students stop what they're doing and curious heads appear out of bay doorways. Garrett stands to one side to let me out then enters my bay and inspects my work, pointing and criticizing.

'Basin not secure. Bath not level. Radiator not level and not in the correct place. No toilet seat. Not enough fall on the basin waste pipe. Copper pipework to the toilet too far away from the wall and not clipped the correct distances. Do you want me to go on?'

My classmates are nudging each other and laughing, willing me to respond, putting me under pressure. I'm embarrassed and I'm angry. Garrett is calm. I try to act calm. Try to ignore the coiling up inside my stomach. If it was just him and me in the workshop, I'd tell him to back off or else. But there's an audience.

'But apart from that do you like it?'

'I think that's a bit over the top,' Peggs says. 'He's redone a few things that weren't right and we couldn't find a toilet seat and we've run out of plastic bolts. I told him not to worry, it'd be fine. It's as good as any of the others. If you're going to knock this one back, you might as well knock everybody's back.'

Garrett takes no notice of Peggs' plea for understanding. He just stands there with a supercilious look on his face like the stone lions on Jagger's gate and says, 'Has this been tested?'

The coiling inside my stomach tightens. I'm losing it. Garrett's slow-timing is getting to me. I'm close to cashing in my stamps.

'Of course I've tested it,' I say, somehow stopping myself from calling him a jumped up little tosser.

'Really?'

'It's been under pressure for two days and there's not been a single leak. The toilet flushes and all the waste pipes work. You checked it all with me, didn't you, Peggs?'

'Yes. No problems.'

Garrett turns on the bath tap. Nothing comes out. I'm baffled. Same with the basin. Not a drop of water.

'That water's been on all morning,' I say. 'Somebody must have been in here and turned it off.'

I look around the audience expecting one of my classmates to hold their hand up and say, 'It was me,' and we'd all laugh, but nobody does. Garrett steps out of my bay.

'Well go on then,' he says. 'Turn the isolation valve on.'

Students move in closer, trying to gauge the temperature of the conflict. The valve is under the basin and I have to get on my knees and turn the slot with a screwdriver. Immediately water spurts from a loose connection and hits me full in the face. It feels like ice cold fingers tearing at my lips and cheeks and trying to poke my eyes out. There are cheers from my so-called classmates. Half-blinded, I grope for the valve and eventually get the screwdriver into the slot and turn it off. My hair is heavy with water and the cold liquid runs into my ears and down the back of my neck. I get to my feet and lean over and squeeze out the excess onto the bay floor.

'That was sound before I went for my tea break. Somebody's been in here and loosened that connection.'

The anger in my voice and the wild look on my face silences the laughter. Garrett has won.

'Let me see this attempt before you assess it again, Peggs,' the director says. Then he turns his back on me, picks up a used steel fitting discarded on the floor and lobs it across the workshop. It lands in the scrap bin and he punches the air as though he's scored an injury time winner. He crosses the yard to the main office singing, 'Fly Me to the Moon,' each word deliberately off key.

4

When Peggs turns off the workshop radio to signal lunchtime, I take off my wet overalls and drape them over a warm radiator to dry out. My T-shirt clings to my chest and my jeans grip my thighs and within seconds it's like standing naked in a cold draft.

'Look at this, Robert. I look as though I've pissed myself. I think I'll nip home and get changed. Want to come? We can be there and back in under an hour and I can show you the Flash while we're at it.'

'Go on then. There's nothing to do here.'

Robert tries to hold on to the dashboard and at the same time catch the somersaulting copper fittings and screw boxes coming to life in front of him as the van passes under the hanging knee pads and bounces along the track behind our terrace.

The terrace was built over a hundred years ago to house colliers. It must have looked handsome when it was first built with its solid red brick and uniform slate roof. When we first moved in after losing our semi in the strike, we knew all the families because everyone was linked directly or indirectly to the pit. Everyone used the same shops, the same doctors, the same pubs, the same clubs, the same buses, and the same schools. Gradually, following the pit closure, most of the families moved away and now the terrace is full of strangers with high fences. I only know them by the cars they drive.

Robert clambers out of the van and surveys the terrace. He has a strange smile on his face and I can tell he's not impressed. It's not a pretty sight any more. Some of the owners have replaced their section of slate roof with concrete tiles which wouldn't look so bad if the new tiles were the same style and material. Now the terrace roof looks as though it's been patched up using whatever materials the various roofers could get their hands on. And then when you look at the mishmash of garages and fences...

I drag my trail bike out of the garage to create a bit of room and Robert settles himself against the door as though a film is about to begin. Like a magician waiting for the drum roll to end, I pause then slip the blanket off the Golden Flash.

'V-e-r-y nice,' Robert says. 'Very nice. It looks brand-new. Have you done all this yourself?'

'Just about. I had a bit of help from a bloke I know who owns a bike scrap yard. What he doesn't know about bikes. He helped me rebuild the engine and gearbox but I rebuilt the forks and the rear suspension myself. The clutch, the brakes. Everything else.'

'It's immaculate. It's a bit tidier than my Suzuki. There's no cow muck on it for a start.'

'I'm hoping to get some muck on this before long,' I say as I take hold of the handlebars.

'I can't wait to get the last few bits finished and give it its first ride. I'm thinking of going up to Scotland on it. That's where I got it from.'

'Kath's country, eh. I wish I had some spare time to take a break. I'd have a ride up there with you on mine. But I've that many things to do to get ready for that wonderful day when the removal men ...'

'If you fancy a break, why don't we have a ride out on the trail bikes? We could go up to the Biker's Café, that one just off the A1.'

Robert shrugs.

'Monday nights are the best,' I say. 'Loads of bikes get there, and the weather forecast is looking good.'

'I could do. I'd have to warn my mother and dad first. They'll have to look after themselves for an hour or two.'

'When do you and your mam and dad have to leave your farm?'

'It won't be long now by the sound of things. The council are putting it up for auction. Apparently, they need the money. Liquidate their assets, I think is the technical term.'

'Line their pockets, more like.'

'I was talking to Lord Havem last week, he owns Wenthem Hall and most of the land next to where I farm, and he said there's been plenty of interest.'

'Somebody'll have their eyes on it,' I say. 'It could be a famous TV star.'

'We were hoping Lord Havem would buy it, or maybe another farmer. Then they might have let us stay on for a few months, maybe even longer. I could do a bit of labouring if necessary and we could always move into one of the outbuildings – there's plenty of them. We'd even live in a caravan on site if we had to.'

Robert keeps scratching the palms of his hands and the skin is red and flaking.

'I don't know how my mother and dad will cope. They've lived on that farm almost all their lives.'

'That's bad. We lost our first house so I know how bad it is having to start out all over again. It was a tough time.

I had a good job at the pit and Deb was in her element looking after our Gav – he was only a nipper. Brand-new house. Brand-new furniture. We had everything we ever wanted. And I'd dropped on this Golden Flash up for sale in Scotland. It was in bits in a box but it was all there, and the bloke had a battered old sidecar to go with it so I bought that as well. I paid cash there and then. I'd always dreamed of owning a Golden Flash.'

I clean a spot off the handlebar mirror with my sleeve. I'm back in the garage at our new semi, checking through all the bike bits in the box, Deb nursing our Gav at my side, excited as me.

'We thought we were set up for life. We had a twenty-five-year mortgage like everybody had, and we'd taken on a bit of debt to buy all the furniture and things we needed to set up a home like everybody did. Then we went on strike and we couldn't pay the mortgage. Even when Deb found a part-time job down at the sewing factory, and my mother and her mother helped us out looking after our Gav, we still couldn't pay it. Six months into the strike, the building society took the house off us, and the bailiffs took everything else.'

'Your family had it tough,' Robert says. 'I don't know what to say.'

'At least my marriage survived. Not like some miners' marriages. And I managed to hang on to the Flash,' I say, my smile returning. 'Every time I come in here, I'm straight back to those good times.'

Robert crouches down and inspects the finish on the engine casings and the unblemished chrome on the exhausts.

'I can see why the bike means so much to you,' he says. 'What does it sound like?'

'I don't know. It's not been kicked up since I rebuilt the engine and gear box. The kick-start's knackered, but I've got my feelers out for a new one.'

I fetch the kick-start from the bench at the back of the garage. Deb's cardboard boxes take up so much room I have to hold my arms in the air like somebody wading through waist high water. Robert inspects the lever and I point out the damage to the splines.

'It's cracked right through,' I say. 'See? I daren't risk it. One kick and it could snap. I'm hoping my mate at the scrapyard'll be able to find me a new one. If he can't, I'll probably end up buying a full gearbox. But I can't afford that at the moment.'

'Why don't you get it welded? I could do it for you.'

'I didn't think it could be welded. And I didn't know you were a welder.'

'I'm a farmer. You have to be able to weld. I'll put it on my to do list. Barring a stampede or a case of mad cow disease this weekend I should have it done for you before we finish our training.'

'That's twice in two days you've come home at dinner time.'

We both look round and see Deb standing outside the garage door.

'Are you trying to catch me sitting around watching the telly or something?'

Robert looks the other way.

'I thought you'd be up at the café, decorating,' I say.

'I will be in a minute. I'm just finishing off some paperwork and my ironing.'

Deb re-ties her hair, holding the clip in her mouth before pushing it back into the knot.

'Hello. Have you come to buy Phil's bike?'

Robert's face turns red.

'No. I've already got one.'

There's a late April breeze in the air and the cold bites into my damp underwear.

'Have a good look round it, Robert. I'll just nip in and get changed. I'll not be long.'

In the bedroom, I peel off my wet jeans, underpants and T-shirt and wrap a towel around my waist. Thankfully, the two ten-pound notes that Peggs gave me are damp but not damaged. I bundle my clothes under my arm and half way down the stairs the cold hits me again. Years ago, I removed the door and casings between the kitchen and the stairs as well as the door opposite leading into the front room because Deb said she wanted a modern open-plan design. I have to admit she was right. The new set-up definitely lets in more light. But the house is a lot colder now and the gas bill has gone up.

The TV in the kitchen is on and a live audience is alternately clapping and jeering at some sharp-suited interviewer baiting somebody's wicked partner. The ironing board is set up and there's a pile of clothes stacked in a basket ready to be ironed. On the worktop above the washing machine, there's a bunch of invoices clamped to a notepad with a bulldog clip. It only takes me a second to see the price Deb has paid for some of the stuff for the cafe. She must have spent hundreds. Half of it mine. All the money we'd saved up for a few days away. No wonder she's kept these invoices well hidden.

As I put the notepad back on the worktop a photograph falls out and lands face up on the lino. It's a shot of Betty's Tea Rooms of Harrogate, all clean and shiny, and there's a line of people queuing all the way round the corner. On the back Deb has drawn a neat sketch of the interior of her own café with details of a new design and colour scheme, plus a key showing where the materials can be purchased. It's like discovering a secret plan to set fire to money and I shake my head in bewilderment. I slip the photograph back inside the notepad and as I'm packing my wet clothes into the washing machine the back door opens and our Gav comes in, pizza in one hand, mobile in the other. He doesn't say a thing, not even commenting on why I'm in the kitchen with a towel wrapped round my waist at half past twelve on a day when I'm supposed to be at the training centre. Gav ends his phone conversation, sits down in front of the TV and flicks through the channels until he finds a noisy cartoon. He appears to be in no hurry. There is no sign of pleasure in eating the pizza and his eyes never shift from the cartoon.

'How did you get on then?' I say.

'How did I get on with what?'

'With that computer job.'

'It only took a couple of hours. There were three of us in the end doing it. I thought they only wanted me.'

Gav repeatedly presses the remote control and a confusion of pictures and sounds appear and vanish.

'Did they say anything about any more work for you?'

'They said there could be.'

'Cheer up then. It's a start. Things might be brightening up for you at last. I've had a good morning, as well, seeing as you ask. I've won the lottery. I've had two new knees fitted. And the training centre's just told me you can come and do the same course as me for free.'

A little smile softens Gav's face. The kitchen smells of herbs and burnt cheese.

'That looks a tasty bit of pizza. What's on it?'

Gav rips a small piece off and offers it up without looking. I try to eat it in one go but a slice of salami falls onto the lino. My knee joints crack loudly when I bend down to pick it up and while I'm on one knee Gav leans over and taps me on both shoulders with the remote control.

'Arise, Sir Plumber.'

'Very funny.'

It takes me a few seconds to get up and I have to hold onto the sink and heave myself up in painful stages.

'Hey, Gav. I've got a little plumbing job to do tomorrow if you fancy giving me a hand.'

Gav flicks through more channels and increases the volume and I have to shout.

'It'll be good experience for you.'

Gav mutes the TV, says, 'I doubt it,' then turns up the volume again.

There's a pair of clean jeans and a jumper in the ironing basket and I get dressed and return to the garage. Deb is still at the entrance and Robert is half hidden behind the Golden Flash. He looks relieved to see me.

'Robert's got a farm not far from here, Phil. It's near Delton. Him and his mother and dad are going to be thrown out soon.'

'I know.'

I try to enter the garage to reassert my ownership but Deb is in the way so I make myself comfortable by leaning on one of her cardboard boxes.

'Don't lean on that, Phil. You'll damage it. I was just telling Robert, I nearly married a man from Delton before I met you. When I was a teenager. His name was Robert, as well, funnily enough.'

'You're always telling people that. Everybody in Brodworth knows you nearly married a man from Delton before you met me.'

'He was in his thirties,' Deb says. 'He was a bit of a well-to-do. He always wore an immaculate suit and always looked dead smart. He was an area sales manager for a vacuum cleaning company. Travelled all over the country.'

I mimic Deb, taking over her story in a gossipy voice. 'And he had a beautiful bright red Jag with real leather seats, and he had this gorgeous flat in Whitby overlooking the lighthouse.'

Deb ignores my teasing. 'We used to go there every weekend in summer. Fish and chips on the quayside watching the little fishing boats heading for the lighthouse, chugging into the harbour with all the gulls following them.'

'Like the gulls following my tractor when I'm working the land,' Robert says. 'Ploughing my lonely furrow.'

'It was magical. He said he had an apartment in Spain, as well, but I never got to see that.'

'Surprise. Surprise,' I say, staring at the garage roof, pretending to yawn.

Robert comes out into the daylight and I slyly check the Golden Flash for any sign of fingerprints.

'That was in the days when I thought men with money were worth chasing,' Deb says. 'I would have done anything as a teenager to escape my dad. Anything for a better life. I keep telling Phil, he was lucky I grew out of it and married him instead.'

'I've always been lucky, Robert.'

'I still think I could have done better, though,' Deb says, and she laughs at her own dreams. 'Mind you, Phil's always telling me he could have done a lot better, as well, aren't you? I think we've both got a point.'

It foxes me why Deb is so willing to talk this openly to strangers. I can't understand it. No hanging around. Straight in there. Yet she never seems to upset anybody. If I tried that I'd finish up being laughed at and probably end up in a fight. And look at Robert, now. Listening to every word.

'Has Phil told you about my café?'

Like a matador working a cape, I swing the blanket over the Golden Flash in an exaggerated flourish. Nice one, Deb, I say to myself. I've brought Robert here to look at my Flash. We haven't got time to listen to you going on about your café.

'No, not really,' Robert says. 'We only talk about work and plumbing. Where is your café?'

'It's on Brodworth high street. I've only just taken it on. It was just a snack bar when I got it but I'm determined to make it into a successful café. Something I can be proud of. We didn't have much to be proud of when we were growing up. My dad was a womanizer and when he wasn't spending his money on his ladyfriends he was spending it on drink. It got so bad he used to lay into my mum whenever she asked him for anything for us or for the house. He used to hit her regularly. Poor old mum. She did everything, absolutely everything all on her own, and she hardly had the strength to pick up a duster because her heart was that weak. She can hardly get out of bed, now. I don't know if you're religious, Robert, but as far as I'm concerned there's no justice in this world.'

Robert moves his head. It's neither a shake nor a nod.

'I'm opening the café up next Thursday. I'm trialling a women-only day the first day and if it goes well, I'm going to make every Thursday a women-only day.' Deb stares at me for a second. 'That's if I get a bit of help with all the decorating that needs doing.' She turns back to Robert. 'It's an idea I've had ever since I worked in the soup kitchen during the miners' strike.'

'Don't talk about the miners' strike to Robert,' I say, ducking an imaginary flying brick. 'He's a farmer. Farmers hate miners.'

I know I'm exaggerating and I know Robert is a tenant farmer not a landowner. He's a decent guy and I've no idea which way he votes and no desire to draw him into an argument so I smile and try to sound as though I'm only joking.

'All you rich landowners. You thought Maggie was a saint.'

Robert answers without a hint of his usual trailing off.

'Governments. Unions. What's the difference? Neither of them ever helped me and my family.'

That shuts me up and Deb continues her story.

'I want to build on the good things that came out of working in the soup kitchen. It was a great time. We had a regular routine. Everybody worked together and we were all occupied in a good way, a very good way. Women of all ages helping and supporting each other, sharing everything, reassuring each other. It was that same feeling of shared experience and support you got as a new mother in the clinic.'

I find myself listening to Deb as I lock the padlock on the garage door. She's never said anything as detailed as that to me before about her upbringing. And never said anything at all about why the idea of a women-only day at the café means so much to her. Not that I can remember. I scratch my head and think hard. No. Nothing.

'Well, it's been nice talking to you, Robert,' Deb says. 'Best of luck with your plumbing and I hope you and your parents manage to survive the move out of your farm. No family should be forced to move home. If ever you're in Brodworth at any time, please call round at the café. You'll be most welcome.'

'Thanks. I might do that. I could do with a break.'

'And of course, your mother can come round any Thursday she likes and enjoy the company of other women.'

'I'll let her know. She doesn't get out much but I'm sure she'd welcome a change from talking to boring old me and my dad all the time.'

'Come on Robert,' I say. 'It's time we were getting back. I don't want Garrett jumping on me again.'

'I hope you make a success of your café,' Robert says. 'It sounds exciting.'

We climb into the van and as we bounce back up the rough track, under the hanging knee pads, I glance sideways and notice Robert has a little smile on his face.

'You know more about my wife's life than I do,' I say.

'She told me all about your life, as well.'

'That wouldn't have taken long.'

5

When we get back to the training centre, we go straight into the workshop to work on our practical skills. It's quiet. Most of the other students have finished the last of their assessments and are upstairs in the classroom, killing time, waiting around for Garrett to sign off their completed portfolios.

Half an hour later Kath comes into the workshop and offers to coach me and Robert on our soldering technique. I'm still rubbish and even Robert, despite being able to gas weld and MIG weld, is finding it difficult to master the skill. I don't seem to be putting on enough solder and Robert's problem is the opposite. Neither of us is confident of making a watertight joint which is pretty scary considering we're on our own as from next week.

Kath makes it look easy. She's like a surgeon performing an operation, and I'm fascinated with the delicate and controlled way she uses her fingers. She's relaxed and unhurried and is just about to let us have a go when old Arthur, the part-time workshop painter, appears at the side of our bench.

'Now then, Arthur,' I say, pasting flux onto the copper pipe and fitting. 'How's it going?'

Kath turns off her blowtorch and the workshop goes quiet. Arthur takes off his beret, gently stretches the headband, and settles it back on his head in the same groove. He has a gentle face and although he hardly ever smiles, I can tell from the old man's soft, watery eyes that he's neither shifty nor gullible.

'Are they taking it all in, Kath?'

'They're trying their best, Arthur, bless them. But it's not easy for them. They're only wee boys.'

'You can learn anything with time and good tuition,' Arthur says. 'I went to night class for years when I wanted to learn new ways of painting. I've learned how to do all sorts of techniques from marble effect to gold leaf application. Anything that interested me, really. I'm seventy-five and I'm still learning.'

'Is there much money in painting and decorating, Arthur?' Robert says.

'Not at this place, there isn't.'

I watch for a cynical smile or a raised heavy eyebrow but there is no hint of judgement.

'We're all classed as self-employed. No holiday pay, no sick pay, no pension. But it suits me. I've never been interested in making lots of money. I just love what I do. I know I'll have to stop one day but I hope that day is a long way off. Me and the wife are comfortable enough. We've got a nice little bungalow, we go dancing every Monday night, I do a bit of weight training during the week to keep fit, and the grandkids come up every Friday. And when she wants to watch something on the television I get out of her way and go upstairs to do a spot of painting.'

'Do you mean painting?' I say, pretending to emulsion a wall, brushing up and down with big strokes. 'Or painting?' and I swap the broad brush for an artist's fine brush held between my thumb and finger. I've suddenly become aware of my fingers after watching Kath.

'I paint things like plant pots and old watering cans, that kind of thing. Anything I can get hold of really.

Every month I take them to a little market place near Wakefield. It's members only but it's free to join. It's unique in that no money is allowed to change hands. Everything is done by exchange of goods. It's like a little self-contained community and I always pick up enough bits to start all over again. It's very satisfying.'

'It must be great if you can manage like that,' Robert says. 'I think I ought to have retrained as a painter and decorator instead of a plumber. At least you don't have to be able to spell.'

Robert points to the roped off area between the benches where the floor has recently been painted green, and where Arthur has chalked WHET PAYNT on the floor.

'Even I know you don't spell wet paint like that,' Robert says.

'You do if you want people to take notice of it,' Arthur says, and he scratches at a speck of green paint on his thumb nail. 'Did I hear you've got a classic motorcycle, Phil?'

'Yeah. I've got a BSA Golden Flash. First registered in nineteen fifty-four. I got it in nineteen eighty-three, just before the miners' strike.'

'A lovely motorcycle. I used to have a BSA Road Rocket when I was a lot younger.'

'Nice. That's the sports model whereas mine's more of a grand tourer.'

'That's right. They were both excellent British bikes in their prime. Classics now and worth a few pounds today, I should think.'

'I hope so.'

'I used to love working on my Road Rocket. I'm not a fan of modern motorbikes. They're marvellous pieces of engineering but I wouldn't dare touch them. They're not meant to be maintained by the owner. Manufacturers these days must think we all want somebody to wipe our backsides. It's the equivalent of being in a nursing home.'

'Thanks, Arthur' Robert says. 'I've got a modern bike.'

I laugh but Arthur's expression remains the same. Kath rubs Robert's back and his face turns red.

'I never thought about it like that,' I say. 'But you're right. There's nothing like taking something like an old bike engine to bits. Touching the parts, feeling what they're made of, holding things up to the light to see if anything's worn, talking to your mates to see what they think, then putting it all back together. Otherwise, you might as well be a robot.'

'Hey, steady on,' Robert says. 'Now you're saying I'm a robot in a nursing home.'

Arthur fastens the top button of his white overalls and turns up the collar.

'Well, I have a wall to paint. Good luck with your plumbing.'

It's only three o'clock in the afternoon and despite needing more time to practise my soldering and pipe bending, I take off my overalls, put my plumbing manual and portfolio in my van, and along with all the other students, leave the training centre for home. We're encouraged by Garrett to leave early on Fridays to avoid the rush hour traffic. But I know from talking to Peggs that the real reason for the short day is to enable the training staff to prepare for the free 'taster' course which they run every Saturday.

The one-day course is aimed, according to the Plumbdeep brochure, at those considering taking up plumbing as a career but are not yet committed to attending the full in-depth, eight-week course. I attended one of their weekend courses – I even persuaded our Gav to join me.

I remember it well. No more than nine participants were allowed on the course. We were split into three groups with one trainer per group and we were treated like royalty. Every question we asked was answered with respect and every attempt at a practical task was applauded, literally applauded by the trainers. The course even included complimentary chicken legs, sausage rolls and pork pies. And there was plenty of milk for your tea.

6

On my way home, I turn onto the high street ready to shoot down the back lane leading to our terrace when I see a small gathering of people outside the Miners' Welfare Institute, or Stute as it's known. They're staring up at the extended arm of a crane as it swings over the building. There's been talk of something happening with the Stute for a while. Two years ago, the windows and doors were boarded up and last month a developer put up a six-foot high hoarding around the whole site.

My neck is craning, which I suppose it would be looking up at the jib fifty foot in the air. The Stute is being demolished. The grey slates of the red brick building have been removed, exposing the structural roof timbers, and the triangles of bare, dusty rafters frame a patch of sky that nobody has seen from this pavement for over a hundred years. The ground judders under my feet and there is a heavy scraping sound of what I assume is a bulldozer at work behind the hoarding. Only the tip of the exhaust pipe sticks up above the boards, moving backwards and forwards, sending up snorts of black smoke every time the vehicle changes direction.

Among the gathering are a few pensioners, their shopping bags too heavy to put down and pick up again. They're standing well away from the figure sitting on cardboard in the locked doorway of what used to be the village cobblers. Nobody seems to be taking any notice of the cap he's holding then an old woman walks up and drops some coins into it. The man nods and when he stretches out his legs, I notice he's fitted a pair of segs to the heels of his shabby trainers. It looks odd. Maybe he bought a packet of the little steel crescents from the cobblers as an investment before the shop shut down.

In the crowd there's a man about my age. I know him. He used to work at Brodworth pit. We called him Elvis. I've no idea what his real name is. He was a bit of rock 'n' roller and had long thick sideburns that almost met under his chin. Someone once said he looked as though he was permanently on the phone. He's still got the thick whiskers but now the phone is grey.

Elvis has one foot on the bottom rail of the safety barrier, elbows resting on the top rail, hands clasped, looking ahead, never sideways. It's a miner's stance and I copy it.

'It's a sad day seein' the old Stute knocked down,' I say.

Elvis doesn't appear to have heard me, then after a few seconds he says, 'That place has been a good servant to the people of Brod'orth over t'years.'

'It has,' I say. 'I remember my dad bringin' me here when I wa' a lad, and then me bringin' my lad here.'

'All them acres of playin' fields,' Elvis says. 'The bowlin' greens.'

'The football pitch.'

'The runnin' track.'

'The cricket pitch.'

'And inside we had changin' rooms, meetin' rooms, a boxin' club.'

'And a library,' I say.

'I can still recite the words from my NCB induction course,' Elvis says, still looking up at the crane, speaking as though he's reading the original document. 'The amenity was provided through levies imposed on coal owners and the running costs were met by the miners through subscription.'

'Aye,' I say. 'It belonged to all of us. It wa' the heart of the community.'

I remember Deb pulling her nose up whenever I went there for a union meeting or to help organise a social event. I couldn't get her through the doors. That all changed when the union asked the miners' wives to set up a kitchen there for the miners' families during the strike. She was one of the first to volunteer and when it all finished, she started going to the library. She was there every day. She couldn't keep her nose out. And then she started going to night class at college with some of the other women she'd met at the library. Something to do with social sciences, I think she said. Anyway, something was switched on. Something above my head.

Elvis asks me what I'm up to these days and I tell him about my training course.

'I'm goin' to call in there,' I say, nodding towards the site entrance. 'See if they're lookin' to tek on any plumbers.'

Elvis tells me he's already made enquiries about labouring jobs but there's nothing doing.

'Brod'orth's goin' to t'dogs,' he says.

I point at the crane driver high up in his little cabin.

'Tha wants to get a job like he's got. Sat up there all day, pullin' a few levers.'

'It'll not be t'only thing he's pullin' up there,' Elvis says, straightening up. 'Well, I'd best be gettin' off t'fish and chip shop. I'm hopin' they've got some sturgeon left. Our lass likes a bit of caviar wi' her scraps.'

I step through the onlookers and enter the building site through a door in the hoarding. The door is such a neat bit of joinery and so well disguised by the abundance of safety signs that it takes me a few minutes to find the handle. As soon as I step through, I'm almost run over by the bulldozer, its path switching direction like a toy earthmover in a sandpit. In a quiet corner well away from the dust and noise, salvage workers have carefully stacked the external stonework – the mullions from the windows, the copings from on top of the walls, the steps leading to the porch, the porch itself. It's all good stuff. Quality materials on the way to a new home. To my left, a couple of blokes are loading sections of the wood panelling from the meeting rooms into a truck, stowing them alongside the curved staircase and the heavy front door. There are scorch marks on the door and I recall the night Gav got arrested.

It happened a few months ago. Some 'druggies', according to an article in the Chronicle, lit a fire in the doorway causing extensive damage to the entrance. The butcher next to the betting shop couldn't wait to tell me he'd heard Gav was there on the night of the fire larking around with his mates. The butcher didn't like to say if drugs were involved. When the police arrested Gav, he admitted he had been there and said they were only messing about with some fireworks. They were bored and one of his mates pushed a banger through the letterbox for a laugh. There must have been two years' worth of junk mail behind the door and it caught fire. Gav and his mates managed to put the flames out by pouring their cans of coke through the letterbox before running off. Gav was fined a hundred pounds.

Now I leave the men loading their truck and walk over to the site office cabin where the site manager is standing at his desk, checking a set of plans under a fluorescent light so bright it makes his white hard hat gleam like a headlight. I tap on the cabin door and lean in.

'Hey up, mate. Sorry to bother you.'

The site manager looks up over his glasses.

'It's okay. What can I do for you? By the way, you need a safety helmet on this site.'

I tap my head as though there might be a hat up there somewhere.

'I know. I was just passing. I'll only be a minute. I was wondering if you were planning on setting on any plumbers once you've got the site up and running.'

'I've set on all the plumbers I need. I've just about finalised all the tradesmen contracts.'

I take a step inside but keep my hand on the door handle in case he thinks I'm being pushy.

'I'm fully qualified. And my lad works with me and he'll be qualified as well, soon. I'd only be asking for one basic wage to share between the two of us to start with, just enough to keep us going and enough to get the lad into the habit of working. He could do with some experience. Something to bring him out a bit. You know what young lads are like.'

I'm hoping the site manager will ask me to come in and sit down. Talk about the possibilities of finding work. If not there than at some other site. But the man places his hard hat on the only spare chair in the cabin.

'I'm sorry,' he says. 'There's nothing. I'm bursting with plumbers. Finding a good one's the problem. It's the same with all the trades these days.'

'We could always give your plumbers a hand. I know what I'm doing and our Gav's a good worker. He's bright and he's a quick learner. You want to see him on a computer. And we only live round the corner.' I realise I'm flipping over the keys on my key ring one by one like worry beads. 'If there was anything going to do with plumbing, anything, I'd take it.'

'I can see you would. You look like a grafter.'

The site manager puts his helmet back on.

'Give me your telephone number and I'll let you know if I hear of anyone asking for a plumber's mate or a helping hand. But I can't promise anything. And, of course, I'd need to see your qualifications. I assume you hold a full NVQ?'

'Course I do,' I say, hoping the man can't see my eyes blink.

As I'm walking back out of the hidden door, a bloke on a mobility scooter comes towards me, working his way through the onlookers, stopping and starting, everyone, including the pensioners, stepping out of his way, no complaints, no apologies, no words.

I wait until the scooter is almost alongside.

'You'll get done for speedin' drivin' like that, Shinny,' I say.

The scooter slows. Shinny's chest expands and his broad square shoulders lift up level with his ears. It's an extreme but weak intake of breath and his neck muscles strain so hard with the effort that a black hollow appears beneath his Adam's apple.

'I wa' always faster than you, Steeley.' Shinny's shoulders lift again. 'Still am. Even on this thing.'

There are plastic tubes leading into Shinny's nostrils. He looks like he should be on a hospital ward, not on the high street in the middle of a crowd. Poor bastard. All this free air and he's struggling to get a noseful.

We both played football for Brodworth Miners' Welfare. Shinny was good. Very good. Could have played professional. Even though he's fifteen years older than me, nobody covered more ground. He was the most naturally fit player I ever came across and he could strike a ball harder than Peter Lorimer. Now I've heard the poor man has to carry an oxygen bottle wherever he goes. It's probably through working at the pit, they say. Pneumoconiosis. But no one would be able to say for certain until he was dead and they cut open his lungs.

The mobility scooter picks up speed and I shout after it, 'You were faster than any of us.'

With a fierce, defiant countenance, Shinny motors across the road where a young lad, waiting at the bus stop with his mates, opens the door of the betting shop and helps Shinny over the threshold. When the lad returns to his gang, they laugh at him for being so thoughtful and he has to let them ruffle his hair as payment.

The sight of old Shinny makes me feel sad, and yet in a way I feel better about the money Jagger owes me. My debt is serious, that hasn't changed. It could mean the end of my working life. But it's only money. It's not oxygen.

I'm still thinking about my old footballing mate when two young mothers with pushchairs cross the road from the doctor's surgery and join us on the pavement. One of them asks me what's going on.

'They're knockin' the Stute down, love,' I say. 'All the lot.'

'It's about time,' her friend says. 'It's a right eyesore,' and they move on.

Saturday

1

Time to practise my soldering again. It seems to take up all my spare hours these days. And I'm still not confident. I take my pot of coffee into the garage and pull my trail bike and two of Deb's cardboard boxes out onto the track so I can get to my soldering bench. As usual, I only lift the door a foot off the floor. Just enough to keep an eye on the trail bike's wheels in case somebody decides to run off with the thing. If I left the door fully open, I'd have every passerby looking in. Not only Colin next door but anybody sniffing around looking for scrap or valuables. Only the young lads that regularly play football on the track would dare get on their hands and knees and look under the door. They're okay. I don't mind talking to them. They're fascinated by the Golden Flash renovation and they ask the best questions.

I light my blowlamp and spend half an hour soldering and unsoldering scrap copper elbows onto a short length of scrap copper, all acquired under cover from the training centre, and I only stop when the copper has been heated up so many times it's turned black and can't take any more. All that practice and still no improvement.

There isn't much bike building to do and I can't test the Golden Flash engine without the kick-start Robert has promised to weld for me. The silencers would benefit from another five minutes of buffing.

And there's a finger mark on the headlight trim, and the carburetor cable could do with oiling again. As I'm cleaning the machine, I see my upper body reflected in the polished engine casing. There's a big round head sticking out of a pair of tiny blue overalls and the monster has a serious look on its face. I'm taking the same care now over the bike's appearance as I did over my own appearance when I first started courting Deb.

I'm still playing with the image, moving my head up and down to see how weird I can make myself look, when the garage door begins to lift up.

'Bollocks.'

Two feet appear followed by two lower limbs. Then a waist. And then the rest of Gav, lifting up the door, ramming it hard against its stops, causing flakes of rust to shower down on my head.

'You'll be breakin' that door one of these days if you're not careful.'

'It'll be right. It's only a door.'

The Flash is covered in flakes of rust and when I blow them away, I become lightheaded and have to hold on to the garage side to maintain my balance.

'I've just been cleaning this.'

'What time do you want me to give you a hand with that little job? I've summat on later this aft.'

This stops me dead. I'd given up hope of Gav joining me to repair the toilet in the flat owned by Jagger, the job that Peggs gave me. The unexpected offer helps me recover quickly and I feel stable enough to stand without support.

'I'm just waitin' for a bloke to come for my cement mixer. I'm sellin' it. And my ladders. And my tampin' bar. And all my trowels. The lot's goin'.'

'You'll need your ladders for your plumbin'.'

'I'll get some more later. I need the money now.'

The old cement mixer parked in front of the garage door looks well beaten. The spillages of concrete and mortar, built up in slumped layers, look like folds of skin on a rhinoceros's neck. On the underside of the drum, rock-hard cones hang down like stalactites. The wheels and axles have almost seized and some days, when my back and neck are really bad, I haven't the strength to push the stubborn machine more than a few feet. For years I've planned to scrap the beast fearing one day it would die on me in the middle of a job. But it never did and with the occasional belt from a lump hammer I always managed to keep it turning. Despite my desire to get rid of it, I can't help but feel a touch of pity for the old servant as it looks back at me like a sad, worn-out donkey.

'He should be here in ten minutes then we can get off if you want. I've just got to clean it up a bit first. It's in a bit of a tackin'. And then I could do with callin' at the scrapyard on the way to pick up a few bits for the Flash. It'll only take a few minutes.'

'Give me a shout when you're ready. I'll be in my bedroom.'

'Hang on, Gav. Before you go in, can you take a photo of the Flash for me to put in the Chronicle?'

'Are you finally sellin' it at last?'

'No, am I hell. I'm going to use it to promote my plumbing business.'

'What? And fasten that old sidecar to it for your tools and your fittin's? It'll look like somethin' out of *Dad's Army*.'

'Don't talk daft. I've all on to finish the bike, nivver mind the sidecar. I ought to have a photo of you sat on it, as well.'

'I'm not havin' my photo in the Chronicle on that thing. My mates'll think I'm a right wassock.'

I wheel the Golden Flash a few yards out of the garage and rest it on its side stand. The bike looks exposed and vulnerable in the open on the shared track like a captured animal about to be released into new surroundings. I comb my hair forward with my fingers to cover my thinning sides.

'Come on Dad, smile,' Gav says, aiming his camera at me. 'Don't look so serious, you'll frighten everybody off. It's not Steele and Son Undertakers.'

I take one hand off the handlebars in an attempt to look cool. It doesn't work and I feel even more uncomfortable so I try to take control of the modelling session.

'Don't get the cement mixer in, Gav. They'll think we're scrap dealers. And move the trail bike out of the way. Nay, don't get all your mother's cardboard boxes in. It'll look like we're flitting.'

'I say, who's doin' this?'

I attempt a smile but I've no idea how to pose. I keep opening and closing my mouth like somebody trying out a set of false teeth. We review the photographs together, me pushing the camera away so I can focus on the tiny screen, Gav bringing it nearer for the same reason.

'There's one or two good 'uns there, Gav. But it's supposed to be Steele and Son Plumbing so we really ought to have one with both of us sittin' on the bike, not just me. Otherwise, everybody'll be saying where's the Son.'

'Tell 'em it wa' cloudy. Go on then if you're desperate.'

Gav puts his camera on the wall and sets the self-timer and we settle on the bike, elbowing each other out of the way like kids until Gav tells me to grow up. The Golden Flash looks cool on every shot and I envy the way Gav appears so relaxed and natural. I don't like my own image on any of them. I look like a tired old man. Like my dad. But I have to make a choice and we finally agree which one best represents the proposed plumbing business.

'I'm going to get some business cards printed, as well,' I say. 'When I can afford it.'

'I can make some business cards for you. And I can put that photo on it as well if you want.'

'Bloody hell. That's amazing.'

'What do you want me to print on the card?'

I look down at the ground in anticipation of Gav's reaction, and adopt a voice somewhere between modesty and embarrassment.

'I was thinking about Steele and Son. Golden Flush Plumbing. Fully Qualified.'

Gav roars with laughter.

'Golden Flush Plumbing? Brilliant.'

I know he's taking the mickey and I don't mind. I'm happy. Not only are my business cards on order and they're not going to cost me a penny. More important, Gav has taken a photograph of us together on the Golden Flash to advertise the business. Steele and Son Plumbing might come off after all.

I switch on the cement mixer and whistle to the rhythm of the cleaning bricks as they clatter around and scour the inside of the drum. The bricks have sacrificed their sharp edges over time and now they're as smooth as pebbles. I switch off the machine, tip the waste down the side of the garage and wait for the buyer to turn up with his forty pounds.

2

The lane to Pete's bike shop used to be a busy route. I've driven along it many times, backwards and forwards, early mornings, afternoons, nights. It used to lead to the pit. Now every time I drive down the lane, even though there are weeds growing out of the cat's eyes, I can still imagine being among the mix of serious and jokey miners as we arrive for our shift or set off home, shift done. I can't help smiling as I remember the mickey taking and the black humour. Good times. I know it's a bit romantic to think like that. Who in their right mind goes deep underground into the blackness and dust to claw into a seam of coal five days a week? But the comradeship that came with working so close together in a dangerous, dirty environment was real and I miss it.

There are only a few houses left standing along the lane. They make up a red bricked terrace known locally as Old Pit Row. Most of the properties are empty shells now, their windows and doors sealed by breeze blocks, blind to the changes. The terrace may still be standing but it's lost its dignity. It looks beaten and subdued. A bit different to those dark mornings when hallways glowed with light from kitchens and there were bottles of milk on every front step, the beginning of a day of purpose and activity. I often wonder why nobody ever stole a bottle from the doorstep or kicked over an empty one for a laugh.

Behind Old Pit Row, parallel to the lane, a high steel boundary fence has been erected to keep people out of a new industrial estate housing a massive grey warehouse shed. The fence acts as a filter in the wind, trapping paper, pizza boxes and drink cans along its base. The galvanized fence uprights, pointed and split at the top to prevent intruders climbing over, look like middle fingers warning everybody to keep out.

'I used to go scraggin' down this lane with my mates when I wa' a lad,' I say as we park up in front of the bike shop. 'We'd only be about ten but nobody ever bothered us. Can you imagine doin' that these days?'

Gav has been on and off his phone most of the journey, speaking to various people in a kind of shorthand that makes no sense to me.

'What's scraggin' when it's at home?'

'Nesting. We used to see who could find the most nests and who could identify the most eggs.'

'Sounds fascinatin'.'

'It was. If I found a broken shell and I didn't know what bird it belonged to I used to take it back home and your granddad would tell me straightaway. Then he'd look it up in this little guide book he had about birds' nests and eggs and he'd show me a picture of it and read out what it said – size of egg, typical number of eggs laid, number of broods per year. All sorts of things. He knew some stuff about birds. Still does, when he can remember.'

Now these old native hedges have been grubbed up and the landscape is open and bleak. All that remains is a solitary elder which has somehow survived the chain saw and digger. As we get out of the van, the wind blows a black bin liner into the air and it snags on the branches of the elder. The bag looks like a dead crow strung up by a gamekeeper to ward off predators.

A weak mechanical bell tinkles above our heads as I push open the door of the bike shop. Behind the counter, visible through a doorway leading to the back room, is a line of old bikes, all parked the same way, handlebars turned to full lock, headlights facing us. They stare back at me like a row of rescue dogs pleading for a good home.

Pete, the owner, comes in from the backyard. His overalls are black with engine oil and look as stiff as leather. They're unzipped over an unbuttoned shirt, and his grey and ginger beard mingles with the grey hair on his chest. I don't think I've ever seen him wearing anything else.

'Hey up, Pete. How are we doing? This is our Gav.'

'Hi Gav. I've heard all about you. Your dad tells me you're not into bikes.'

'Am I hell.'

'He likes his cars and his computers, don't you, Gav.'

Gav mumbles something and looks away.

'I suppose you've come for that mudguard and kick-start for that Golden Flash of mine?' Pete says.

I laugh at the puzzled, suspicious look on Gav's face.

'Pete's been after my bike for years, haven't you. You'll have to keep on wanting. I've no intention of selling it now, not when I'm so close to finishing it.'

'I don't blame you. Anyway, I've found a mudguard but I've still had no luck with that kick-start.'

'There's no rush. I'm getting my old one welded. That'll have to do for now.'

'Usual?'

Pete brings out two white mugs from under the counter. The insides are almost black with tea stains and I see Gav take a quick look then turn away.

'Coffee and a sausage roll? I can run to two seeing as it's your lad.'

I seek a smile or a nod from Gav but find neither.

'No thanks,' I say. 'We haven't time.'

Pete disappears into the backyard and I survey the shelves behind the counter, built on either side of the original kitchen chimney breast. The second-hand pistons and barrels and various sized boxes of engine parts fill the shelves like a well-stocked pantry.

'It's a right shop this, isn't it, Gav. There's loads of scrap bikes in the yard, and he's got thousands of spare parts. God, I've enjoyed some Sunday mornings down here. He'll let us have a look round if you want?'

'It's a right dump,' Gav says, flicking through one of the vintage motorcycle magazines on the counter, its pages edged with black finger prints. 'It's filthy. Everythin' stinks of old engine oil, and he's a bit dodgy if you ask me. What's the idea of the ponytail?'

'Hey, be quiet, Gav, bloody hell. Pete's looked after me over all the years. He's helped me rebuild my engine and he's got me all sorts of parts for the Flash.'

'Yes, and how much has he charged you for them?'

Gav tosses the magazine back onto the counter and picks up another one with his finger and thumb as though it's infested with fleas. On the front cover there's a black and white photograph of a Velocette police bike from the nineteen fifties.

'It must have been a right laugh in them days being chased by a copper dressed in a big overcoat like that,' Gav says. 'And look at his bike. He couldn't catch cold on that thing.'

'They used to call them Noddies.'

'I'm not surprised.'

'They had to nod to their senior officers when they were out riding. Show them respect.'

'Toadies.'

Gav drops the magazine back onto the counter and stares out of the window, his nose almost poking through the dusty security bars.

'I can't believe the prices you've paid for some of the junk you've bought from this place. I could have got you a complete bike, any model you like, for a tenth of the money it's cost you to buy bits from here. He's rippin' you off.'

I have to be careful, here. Gav is irritated. He can get the monk on faster than anybody I know and if that happens, I'll end up having to take him home and do the plumbing job on my own.

'He's not ripping me off. It's not like buying parts for a new bike. Bits for old bikes like the Golden Flash are expensive. And anyway, that's not the point. I've enjoyed every day I've worked on that bike. I know it inside out, every nut and bolt.'

'And don't we know. We never see you. As soon as you get home from work you go straight into the garage or come down to this place to spend even more of your money on bits.'

'It's my hobby. You'll find out when you get working. You've got to have something to do in your spare time otherwise it's all graft.'

'You'll never ride that Golden Flash, Dad. Every time you've got close to finishin' it you've had to do it all up and start all over again. It's gone rusty or somethin's dropped off it or you've run out of money.'

I return the abandoned, sad gaze of the row of bikes. Gav's summary cuts me up. I can't fault his logic but

I'm not going to tell him that. Anybody looking coldly at the time, effort and money I've spent over the years rebuilding the Flash would think I was mad or daft or both. But sometimes, some things are better never finished. Sometimes it's as much about keeping in touch with the past as it is about making something new for the future. Right or wrong, and I wouldn't want to get into an argument about it because it could upset me, while ever there's work to do on the Golden Flash, part of me is still a miner.

Gav checks his mobile.

'Have you seen the time? Is he makin' that mudguard for you?'

Pete comes in from the back, places the mudguard on the counter and turns it round for me to inspect.

'I've rung round everywhere but most of the ones I could find were too far gone. This one is pretty good. Somebody's removed the stays but at least they've used a spanner and not ripped the things off. Some people have no respect for metal.'

'That's okay. I can make some new ones. What do you think, Gav?'

'How would I know?'

'How much are you wanting for it, Pete?'

'It's an original and as I said they're hard to come by for the Golden Flash. I can let you have it for forty. I could get double that on the internet. The trouble is you've no idea who's buying it on there. They might just be selling it on to make a profit. But I know you're as passionate as me about putting a classic bike back on the road. I'd sooner sell it to you for half the price.'

'That's great, Pete. But I'm struggling to pay that much for it at the minute.'

'Pay me when you can. Get my Flash finished.'

Pete picks up a sheet of paper from the counter. He's written his name and home telephone number in biro on each line all the way down to the bottom. It looks as though he's been given lines for bad behavior. He tears a strip off and hands it to me.

'If I'm not here, ring me at home.'

'How do you mean, if you're not here?' I say, laughing. 'You're always here.'

'Only for a few more weeks. I'm closing down.'

'You're joking? What for?'

'They're knocking down what's left of this row to make way for another big warehouse. I'm calling it a day.'

Pete shrugs. He looks beaten. I say I'm sorry for him after all these years of good service and tell him he'll be all right. I've no idea why I say that, knowing how hard it'll be for him to find work at his age. We shake hands with a firm grip and I walk out to the sound of the tinkling bell, wondering how long it will be before Pete's rough, oily hands become soft, white and redundant.

3

The van's engine begins to splutter on the way to the little plumbing job, and recognising the familiar symptoms of running out of fuel, I dip the clutch and swerve onto the grass verge edging the quiet country lane.

Gav stares at me.

'You're kiddin'?'

'Don't panic. I've got some in the back.'

As I carefully pour the spare diesel into the fuel tank, the passenger window opens and Gav rests his arm on the frame. He won't look at me, not even slyly through the wing mirror. Running on reserve is getting to be a bad habit of mine. Forever switching between the van and the little trail bike depending on which has the most miles left in the tank.

The smell of diesel glugging into the tank like somebody being sick into a toilet makes me feel bad. I can't remember the last time I filled my van to the brim. Maybe once I start plumbing...

An approaching car blasts its horn and someone shouts Buy British. The sudden noise in the middle of the quiet lane makes me jump and I spill precious fuel and fire back my response.

'Piss off, you silly bastard.'

Gav shoves his head out of the window.

'Well done, Dad. Look well if they turn round and come back.'

The can is now upside down as I shake the last drops of diesel into the tank. We don't see the car return until it mounts the verge and skids to a stop a foot from my van's front bumper. The tinted windows make it hard to see who's inside. Nobody gets out. I tighten and untighten the fuel cap, watching and listening for any sign of movement. Gav slips out of the van and joins me as though it needs two to screw the cap back on.

'Don't look at the car, Gav, for God's sake.'

'Don't worry. I'm leggin' it if there's any trouble.'

For a few seconds there's silence and stillness then the car's front doors fly open and two youths jump out. The driver is a good six foot, eyes hidden behind reflective sunglasses. The passenger is shorter, cocky, red baseball cap back to front.

'What's up, kid?' the driver says. 'Broken down?'

'More like nickin' diesel,' his passenger says.

I've just made up my mind to go for the driver when Gav straightens up and wipes the sweat from his palms down his jeans.

'Jesus. I wondered who the hell it was,' he says.

I stay crouched, unsure of the situation, waiting for someone to smile. It's only when Gav locks hands with the two youths that I relax and stand up.

'My dad's run out of diesel. Again.'

I give a wry grin.

'I didn't run out. I've just had to go into my reserve supply, that's all.'

Gav isn't listening to the excuse. He's impressed with the big silver saloon and he wants to know the figures.

'This is one tidy motor, Jason.'

Jason pushes his sunglasses up into his thick black hair.

'Two point four litre injection, kid.'

Gav steps onto the lane to take in all of the car's style and power.

'Is it yours?'

They're at the limit of my hearing so I move closer, pretending the van's headlight needs a wipe over with a rag.

'This, kid, is our next wage. You and me's taking it to Manchester next week. Ben's not coming this time. He's doing another job, aren't you, kid.'

Ben says, 'Yeah. Big run up to Newcastle. Sport turbo diesel hatchback.'

'And they want us to drop off some stuff at one of their mate's flats on the way back from Manchester. It's all extra cash,' Jason says and he pretends to pull a one-armed bandit. 'It's like printing money, kid. We're in the good books with that computer job we did for them.'

A little blue car goes by, the old couple inside staring straight ahead, too frightened to look at the dodgy characters loitering next to an old van and an expensive motor bumper to bumper on the grass verge. I'm laughing to myself, imagining the pensioners doing a handbrake turn, jumping out of their car in masks, baseball bats in hand, yelling, 'Hey punks – this is our turf,' when one of the saloon's rear windows glides open.

Gav leans into the opening and says, 'I thought you two were doing a job today.'

I can hardly hear what they're saying so I take my rag over to the other headlight. There are two girls in the back. One lights an untipped cigarette and studies the smoke as it drifts out of the window and floats my way. The pungent smell tells me it's not a Woodbine.

The girl pulls a lock of her long blonde hair horizontal and lets the strands fall gently back into place.

'It's been cancelled,' she says. 'We're cruising and posing. Jump in. You can sit between me and Ella. It's as big as a bus in the back of here.'

'You're all right, Charlotte,' Gav says. 'I can't. I've something on. I've got to give my old man a hand with a plumbing job.'

Charlotte hands the joint to Gav who takes a deep drag and passes it back. When she inhales again, the smoke seems to wrap itself around her words, cushioning her voice.

'Please yourself,' she says. 'If we're not good enough for you.'

The other girl, Ella, is talking to somebody on her mobile phone. She interrupts her conversation.

'Don't be boring, Gav. Come on. We're off to Leeds. Jason's treating us.'

Charlotte and Ella shuffle up to make even more room in the back but I hear Gav say no, he can't. His voice has dropped and when he turns round the excitement on his face a few minutes ago has been replaced by disappointment and scorn. I glance down at myself, at the scruffy fuel can and the scruffy rag in my scruffy hands, at the dents and scratches in the van's bodywork, at the oil stains on my jumper and jeans and I feel shabby.

'Get yourself off, Gav. I can manage on my own. There'll be plenty more jobs coming up for you to have a go at.'

My offer sounds hollow and when Gav says nothing, I feel even worse. Jason takes something out of the front footwell. Gav tries to block my view but I've already spied the brown envelope changing hands.

'Right,' Jason says. 'We're off. Catch you later, kid.'

The powerful car reverses off the verge, churning up the grass before accelerating away, the lads leaning out of the windows, laughing and waving, the girls in the back no doubt serene and detached.

4

We pull up outside a big Victorian house and I check the address.

'This looks like it, Gav. It's been converted to flats. Six by the looks of it. See the meter boxes?'

Six white meter boxes are set into the wall in a line under the bay window. A door on one of the boxes is broken and hanging down on one hinge. On two other boxes the doors are missing altogether and dried leaves have built up under the exposed meters.

'It's a dump,' Gav says, acting like a child taken home too early from a party. 'Does anybody live there?'

The flat is on the ground floor facing the back garden, probably the original kitchen and dining room. An old woman parts the net curtains, which look as fragile as a gas mantle, and invites us into the dark hallway. She must be in her nineties. I've seen better clothes in the bag of rags I keep in my garage. Her head is wrapped in a thick brown scarf, tied under her chin the way my grandmother used to do when she had toothache. The old woman is wearing fingerless gloves, one green, one purple, and there are old newspapers stuffed down her black wellingtons. I rub my hands and shake my shoulders as we encounter the cold musty air in the living room. Head-high stacks of yellow newspapers lean against the walls like buttresses, blocking out almost all the light from the window. It's like entering a dungeon.

The old woman leads us towards the bathroom through the narrow corridor between the settee, made up into a single bed with an old brown coat as a blanket, and the dining table with its solitary straight backed chair. She pauses in front of the sideboard mirror, which is covered in dust apart from a narrow sweep of clear glass at head height, and tucks a stray lock of hair up into her scarf. As we wait for her to set off again, I glance at the open fireplace through a gap in the furniture and it doesn't make me feel any warmer. The blue and white tiled surround looks as cold and dark as the entrance to a cave and there's been a forlorn attempt to block off the chimney with scrunched up newspapers. I try not to breathe in the stench of urine in the bathroom as the old woman points to the toilet at the side of the bath.

'I think it's leaking from the back of there somewhere.'

The toilet looks as old as the woman. The cistern sits on two cast iron brackets close to the ceiling. An inch and a half thick lead pipe connects it to the pan and there's a heavy-duty chain with a black rubber handle hanging down in front of my eyes. Water has risen up the wall behind the pan and blown the plaster causing the faded rose-patterned wallpaper to bulge and split. When I tap the wall with my foot, there's a hollow dead sound and chunks of damp plaster break away.

'How long has it been like this, love?'

'As long as I can remember. I've reported it to the landlord dozens of times but he hasn't done anything until now.'

I shake my head.

'Our friend Mister Jagger?'

'That's him.'

I wish I could share with Gav the anger I feel towards Jagger. Get a bit of moral support. But, as with Deb, I've not said anything to him about the bad blood between me and Jagger. How Jagger despised the striking miners and profited from our struggle. And I haven't told him about being stung for the pond, either.

As I check around the pan and the underside of the cistern for leaks, I notice something glistening on the lead pipe where it sets back to the wall. It could be condensation, the bathroom is as damp as a swamp, but when I wrap my hand around the pipe a tiny amount of water collects on my thumb and finger.

'I think it's leaking where it goes into the bottom of the cistern, Gav,' I say and turn to the old woman who is watching me with a gentle smile on her face. 'Don't worry, love. We'll see to it for you. It shouldn't take us long.'

Time to put on my overalls and lay out my dustsheet, a job made more awkward due to Gav sitting on the bath side with his feet dangling above the rotting carpet to keep his trainers dry.

'It's not a dustsheet you want in here, Dad, it's stilts.'

'This is how the flushing mechanism works, Gav. When you pull the chain, water drops down into the toilet pan and the weight flushes everything out and down into the drain. And the trap stops any smells coming back up. They've done away with these, now, unless you've got plenty of spare cash and you want to make your bathroom look like a Victorian boudoir. On modern toilets, the cistern sits right on top of the pan.'

'It's called a close coupled toilet,' Gav says, reading from a plumbing brochure.

'Where've you got that from?'

'Your portfolio. When you said we were going to fix a toilet, I thought we might need some info.'

'Clever sod.'

Gav winks and says, 'Feet are for dancing – head is for thinking,' and he begins to read aloud.

'On a close coupled toilet, waste is syphoned out of the toilet pan rather than relying on the weight of water. The latest models have a dual-flush facility with two buttons on the cistern: a large button for faces…'

'Faces?' I say. 'Faeces, you clart.'

'Faeces, then. And a small button for urine. The buttons feel different to the touch allowing the most appropriate flush to be selected every time, even in the dark. The button design is also a useful aid to those with impaired vision.'

Gav lifts half his backside off the bath, he's always been economical when it comes to physical effort, and puts the brochure in his back pocket.

'Beat that.'

'Okay, clever clogs,' I say. 'What's the point of having a dual flush? Why complicate matters? Why not just have one little lever and one big, single flush like we've got back at our house?'

Gav shrugs his shoulders as if to say who cares, I've won.

'It's all about saving water,' I say.

'What for?'

'The environment.'

'Can you get one with three buttons on for when you've had a curry?'

'You see. All that information you keep filling your head with is stopping you from thinking for yourself.'

'It's not information, Dad. It's knowledge. That's what my computer teacher told us at school. He said we were part of the knowledge society. We are the future.'

The stop tap won't budge so I tie up the ball valve in the cistern and bail out the cold water into the deep cast iron bath at the side. There's no need to worry about spoiling the enamel on the bath. It's already heavily chipped and there are ingrained bands of brown stain around the sides, a visual summary of water levels over the years.

Gav says, 'You didn't tell me I'd need a gas mask.'

'Where there's muck there's money.'

It takes me five minutes to disconnect the flushing mechanism and I lay it out in order on the sodden dust sheet.

'Play about with it if you want. See how it works. That's what we did at the training centre.'

'I'm not touchin' that thing. I might catch summat.'

'You can't go on like that Gav if you want to be a plumber. You've got to get stuck in.'

'Yes. *If* I want to be a plumber. Anyway, I'd let you do all the mucky jobs. I'd do all the drivin' and collectin' all the money.'

Half an hour later the crumpled figure of the woman appears in the bathroom doorway. She's scraping hard brown fat out of a white enamel shaving mug, carefully wiping the knife on a newspaper as though she's buttering a slice of bread.

'Would you two gentlemen like a drink of tea? I've found a spare cup under the sink.'

Gav looks away and appears to develop a great interest in the frosted glass and faded net curtains.

'No thanks, love,' I say. 'We've just had one.'

Sweat is dripping off my forehead and I try to smile. The dustsheet is hardly visible under the increasing number of tools and dismantled parts.

'It looks like it might need some new washers, love. Everything's worn. I'll have a look in my van but I don't think I've got any.'

'Oh dear. Never mind. Leave it. I'll manage.'

What a tough old bird she is, I think. Not perturbed at all by the bad news. I might just as well have said the clock on the mantelpiece is a few minutes fast for all it seems to matter to her.

'My husband was a miner during the second world war,' she says. 'He wanted to join the army but they told him he had a heart murmur and they wouldn't let him in. He was too ill to be killed.'

She tries to laugh but it turns into a cough that becomes so severe she has to rest her boney frame against the door jamb. She looks unsteady and even Gav gets off the bath side ready to catch her if she starts to fall over. The old woman eventually recovers and wipes her eyes with the back of her purple glove.

'It was hard graft but it was work. There was no dole or anything in those days, you know. And no national health service. If a man couldn't find work he had to beg, and if one of us needed to see a doctor my mother had to pay sixpence a week, every week, until it was paid off. I don't know how she and my father managed. I only ever saw my father cry once. That was the day the Labour party came on the wireless and announced they were bringing in the National Health Service and we'd all be a part of it. He said he never thought he'd live to see the day.'

'They must have been hard times,' I say, pulling my damp shirt away from my back, trying to show the old woman I'm listening despite being desperate to get on with the job.

'I lost my husband ten years ago, God bless him. We never had much money but we managed. I've been on my own ever since. Nobody comes to visit me now. No family. No neighbours. Some days I feel like giving up. Take my advice, gentlemen. Don't grow old.'

The old woman delivers her story like a well-rehearsed poem and I wonder how many times she's repeated the words to her reflection in the dusty mirror in the cold front room. She lets go of the door jamb then looks at the shaving mug of brown fat and the dirty knife in her hands as though someone placed them there when she wasn't looking.

'Would you two like a cup of tea?'

Gav's head shrinks into his shoulders and I say no thanks again.

Luckily, I find some washers in a box in my van, and with the help of a smear of grease and a squirt of silicone sealant I manage to fix the leaking cistern. Peggs would be proud of me.

'That's it, love,' I say, trying not to startle the old woman as she snoozes in her chair. 'All working again.'

The old woman opens her eyes wide and lifts herself up.

'Thank you so much. I feel all posh now.'

When I ask the old woman if I can wash my hands, she tells me I'll have to empty the bowl outside when I've done because the sink's blocked. The rancid smell rising from the plug hole makes my stomach heave as I pick up the greasy bowl and empty it down the drain outside.

'You ought to get that fixed as well, love.'

'I'm used to it by now. It's been like that for as long as I can remember. It's another thing I've reported to

Mister Jagger. But it's like the toilet, he just says I'm next on the list.'

Gav asks her how she manages in the middle of winter when it's snowing and icy.

'It's a bit awkward,' she says, 'especially if I've let the bowl get too full. It can get a bit heavy and it once froze solid. But I usually manage to empty it.'

I pull the pleated curtain under the pot sink to one side and shine my torch inside. The u-bend is the original, crafted out of lead with a brass boss soldered into the base and a drain plug with two lugs. To get to it I have to move a row of mouldy jam jars, packed tight with wire-hard paint brushes, and a few old bottles of yellow liquid.

'Getting into that trap's going to be tough, Gav. That plug's not been touched since it was first put in. Fancy having a go? Your first plumbing job.'

To my surprise, Gav has a look under the sink.

'Have you got a big screwdriver in your bag, Dad? I'll use it as a lever and try an' twist the plug off.'

I smile to myself and hand Gav the tool like a surgeon's assistant. Gav rolls up his sleeves and with the bowl under the sink to catch any water he wedges the screwdriver between the two lugs and pushes anti-clockwise. I'm looking over Gav's shoulder and holding my breath and I want to say take it steady. I know from my days at the pit and on the building sites what damage heavy hands can do.

'Back off a bit, Dad. Let me breathe.'

Gav's fingers are careful and with one extra push the aged seal breaks. The stench is overpowering as he pokes a way through the blockage of black sludge and grey hair, and flushes away the slimy residue. I give my son a pat on the back.

'Well done, lad. I didn't think it would come off. Nice job. You'll have to put some tape on the threads before you screw it back in again.'

'I know I will. I've read your portfolio.'

Gav re-seals the plug, I turn on the cold tap, and with the old woman smiling at our side, we watch sparkling clear water swirl down the plug hole and gush away into the drain outside.

'There you are, love,' I say. 'You've got your sink back.'

The old woman turns to Gav and holds onto both his wrists with her weak, gloved hands.

'What a wonderful young man you are,' she says and Gav's cheeks turn red. 'All it needed was someone with a bit of expertise and determination. Thank you so much.'

There are tears in her eyes and she looks as though she'll never let go of Gav.

'Just a moment,' she says.

The old woman totters over to the settee and returns clutching a handbag decorated with blue lace and purple beads. She opens the brass clasp and feels around inside.

'How much do I owe you, young man?'

'Nothing,' Gav says. 'Don't worry about it.'

'Are you sure?'

'Sure.'

'Well, what a refreshing change to have work done by someone who cares. Someone not driven by money. What's the name of your company?'

Gav straightens up and pushes his chest out.

'Steele and Son. Golden Flush Plumbing.'

On our way home, I claim glory for having anticipated the need to carry a box of assorted washers, and Gav runs out of big words to describe his own expertise at repairing lead u-bends.

'An hour and a half for a measly twenty quid,' Gav says, laughing at me. 'You'll never make any money at that rate.'

'They'll not all be as awkward as that one. Poor old lass. What a state to be in. She was crying her eyes out when we left.'

Gav goes quiet for a few seconds then he pats me on the shoulder.

'You want to get in touch with that bloke you've just sold your cement mixer to. See if he'll let you have it back.'

5

'Hey up, Peggs…Victoria Hotel? Course I can. I'll come straight away…Jagger? You're kidding me?…Not a chance…Go on then, seeing as it's you.'

Deb hears me snatch my van keys out of the fruit bowl on the kitchen table.

'Where are you off to?' she says, stirring a pan on the cooker. 'Your tea's ready in ten minutes.'

'Sorry love. Put it in the oven,' I say, jangling the keys in her face. 'I've only got a call-out for a plumbing job. Time and a half. Not bad for a trainee, eh?'

Half an hour later I arrive at the Victoria Hotel and pull on my overalls. The woman on reception looks me up and down until I tell her my nickname is Golden Flash and I'm here to save the hotel from flooding. She smiles and sends me straight up to the Cavendish, a large private function room on the first floor, where I find a red-faced hotel manager holding a plastic bucket over a table in the middle of the room. There's a regular plopping sound as water drips into the bucket from a hole as big as a ten pence piece in the centre of the ornate ceiling rose.

'Is the plumber up there, mate?' I say, pointing to a set of ladders leading up to the loft hatch. 'I've come to give him a hand.'

The bucket is almost full and the hotel manager is ready to swap it for an empty one. Sweat is dripping from his forehead.

'He is. I hope he's not going to make any more holes in my beautiful ceiling, sending plaster all over the blooming place. I've some VIPs coming in here in half an hour and I've all this table to clear up and all the buffet to set up or else I'm in serious trouble.'

I climb the ladder and ease myself through the loft hatch. A few yards away, Peggs is kneeling by the side of a galvanised water tank and he shines his torch to help me cross the joists and join him.

'It's warm up here, Peggs.'

'You'll be able to have a cold shower in a minute if I don't fix this leak. You're just in time.'

'What's the problem?' I say, trying to look into the water tank. The water level is high and Peggs has his good arm inside right up to his armpit.

'It's leaking like a sieve. There's a crack in the seam right at the bloody bottom. I've managed to tie the ball valve up and I've plugged the seam for now with a bit of putty but it's paper thin. I daren't press too hard. I've tried to put some silicone sealant on it from the outside so I'm hoping it's going to hold until I can drain it off.'

Peggs flashes his torch across the joists with his bad hand. The beam is unsteady and it dances on the shallow puddles of water where the ceiling dips slightly.

'Nearly all this ceiling was flooded when I got up here. Another minute and it would have collapsed.'

The ceiling is the original structure by the looks of it, at least a hundred years old. There are rows of thin laths, nailed less than half an inch apart at right angles to the joists. Lime plaster, reinforced with horsehair, would have been spread across the ceiling from below with a trowel and allowed to ooze over the laths where it would have formed a strong, lasting bond. A plasterer once told me the technique is based on the centuries old wattle and daub method of construction. A marvellous thing, the plasterer said, and I had to agree.

'I was just about to smash a hole in it with my hammer,' Peggs says, 'but the manager started screaming at me not to cause any mess.'

I imagine the broken laths sticking through the ceiling like compound fractures and I want to scream as well. Peggs pulls his good arm out of the tank and tries to plane the cold water off his pale skin with his bad arm.

'Anyway, the ceiling didn't collapse, thank the Lord, and the water's almost drained away down the hole. Jagger would have shot me if the ceiling had come down on him while he was having his meeting.'

'His meeting?' I say, my heart skipping a beat. 'He's not going to be showing up here, is he?'

'Yes. It's his do. Apparently, the hotel was going to cancel his meeting because they couldn't get their own plumber out until tomorrow and they didn't have another room available. The manager told me Jagger threw a wobbly and threatened to put a rag soaked in petrol through the hotel letter box if he cancelled. He said Jagger told him he'd get his own plumber out and send the bill to the hotel. And he expected a bottle of champagne to be waiting for him on the buffet table for his pains.'

'He's a gangster as well as a bad-payer, then. Look. I'm keeping my head down if he's coming here.'

'So am I. He's already told me to stay out of the way. Anyway, the main thing it's fifty pounds for an emergency call out. Twenty-five pounds each.'

I go quiet. I've said all I want to say about Jagger and it's not made me feel any better. And twenty-five quid is twenty-five quid.

'Right,' Peggs says. 'I'm going down to the kitchen to drain off the tank. Keep your hand on that putty until it's emptied. I'll have to stay down there until Jagger's finished his meeting. It could be an hour. And you'll have to stay up here. Will you be all right on your own until then?'

'I think I'll manage. I'll keep swapping hands.'

Peggs drags his bad leg across the joists to the loft hatch and I follow on different joists to spread the weight. He shoves away my helping hand and climbs out of the loft onto the ladder.

'And be as quiet as a mouse until they've all gone,' he says.

'Don't worry. I'll not make a squeak.'

Half way down the ladder Peggs pauses and looks up. 'And make sure your phone's turned off.'

Right arm numb. Withdraw. Left arm numb. Withdraw. Repeat. The light's not too bad in the loft with the torch turned off once my eyes get used to it. The warm joists make a good seat and I settle down and listen to the pink, pink, pink of the dripping ball valve and the occasional rapid flutter of a bird as it flies in and out of the eaves.

Within a few minutes, muffled voices drift up from the room below. Damn, I whisper to myself. If I was a bit closer to that spy hole, I'd be able to see what Jagger's up to. Surely that putty'll hold for a few minutes without me pressing on it. And the pressure inside the tank'll be getting less and less because the water level is definitely going down. Go on, Steely. Just a quick peep.

I creep across the joists, pausing and holding my breath when the dry timbers creak. The smell of coffee and hot food mix with the taste of warm dust as I lower my head over the hole and stare with one eye at the table below.

In the centre of the display there's a whole salmon on a silver tray. The fat pink fish is so big it hangs over the sides. Beef and ham slices fan out on silver plates. Chicken legs dressed in little white paper frills are arranged in circles and there are types of fruit I've never seen before. Every gap between the silver plates is filled with green and red salad leaves and there are bottles of red and white wine, a bubbling glass coffee maker, and Jagger's bent bottle of champagne sitting on its own in a bucket of ice.

Two figures appear at the table and I pull away then slowly move back in again. It's Jack Jagger and another man, a sloppy man, sloppy suit, big belly, hitching up his trousers. He has a round bald patch on top of his head, the best three-egger I've seen in years. My hamstring cramps up and I stretch my leg, silent as a stalking cat, and resettle.

Jagger looking over his shoulder.

'Auction's all sorted, Hutchy' he says. 'Big plans to develop the farm. Expensive houses. No riff raff. Got to get this one through. Got to.'

Hutchy hitching up his trousers again, biting a chicken leg.

'Consider it done, Jack. Planning committee like putty in my hands. Just got to work on the new council leader. A woman would you believe. But don't worry. I'll get something on her before long.'

Jagger pouring both of them a glass of red wine.

'Don't want any objections from Lord Havem.'

Hutchy brushing bits of chicken off his shirt where his belly bulges through his buttons. 'Don't worry about

Lord Havem. He owes me a few favours.' Hutchy shaking his head at Jagger. 'Lord Havem for a neighbour, eh. Moving up in the world, Jack.'

I swear to myself. Didn't Robert say his neighbour is called Lord Havem?

The noise level rises as more guests arrive. When Jagger and Hutchy split up and mingle, I creep back to the tank, settle myself on the ceiling joists, and wait in the gloom for the event to end.

Sunday

1

The van's heater is still blowing cold air as we pull into the car park behind the cafe. I unload the mop, brush and bucket of cleaning equipment and Deb unlocks the café's back door and puts the radio on. As usual I'm trying to be clever and carry everything in in one go and I drop the bottle of bleach as I'm back-healing the door shut. It's a good job it's plastic and not glass like the old Wimsoll bottles I used to fetch for my mother. It's freezing in the café and when I take the containers out of the bucket and set them down on the cold hard floor, they look like a family of penguins huddled together.

'It's like being in a fridge in here,' I say, and I grip the top of the radiator under the big front window expecting it to be as cold as the floor. It's not and I nearly smack myself in the face as I yank my hand away. 'Bloody hell, Deb. That thing wants turning down.'

'Make your mind up.'

The wall directly above the skin-burning radiator is as cold as the glass in the sunless window.

'I'll bet there isn't half an inch of insulation in these walls,' I say. 'Chuffing landlords. All these shops want upgrading. Four inches of mineral wool and you could save a hundred pounds a year on heating. We did it last week at the training centre.'

Deb takes her coat off and hangs it up in the cubbyhole at the side of the electricity meter.

'It'll soon warm up once I get scrubbing.'

'I can give you a hand for half an hour if you want. Then I've got to get back to the garage. Barry's coming round later this morning. He's going to show me how to bend copper pipe. And he wants to see how the Golden Flash is coming on. He hasn't seen it for ages. It must be at least four years.'

'Will he be able to see any difference?'

'Funny.'

Steam condenses on the little round mirror above the sink as Deb fills a bucket with hot water and pours in a capful of bleach.

'You can scrub the floor with this bleach, if you want, get all the drips of paint off while I clean the woodwork. You're better off using the mop. Just make sure you keep squeezing it dry and rinse everything well when you've finished. I don't want it smelling like a hospital ward in here on Thursday.'

Deb is watching me as I tuck my jeans into my socks and start mopping around the table and chair legs.

'You're better off pushing the tables up against the wall out of the way,' she says, 'and then put the chairs on top.'

'I do it like this when I'm doing it.'

'You'll get bits of mop stuck to the bottom of the legs. It looks horrible. It'll be a right turn off for my customers.'

'They're not going to be sitting on the floor to have their snap, are they? It's not a Japanese restaurant, is it?'

'Are you going to help me, or what?'

'It'll take me half an hour to move all these.'

'Talk about being beaten before you start.'

Deb turns the radio up. She likes to listen to it on Sunday morning. They play Tamla Motown and Soul music and she says the dedications make her feel warm. Husbands taking coffee and toast up to the bedroom for their wives. Daughters and sons saying how much they love their mothers. Husbands and wives telling the world how much they mean to each other. It's too sentimental for me. I like the music, but I bat away the soft stuff in case it gets to my heart.

We've got on okay so far this morning and I don't want to spoil it so I do as I'm told and push the tables up against the wall and stack the chairs on top.

'I reckon our Gav could make a fist of this plumbing game,' I say, mopping the floor with my back to Deb. 'He's got the makings of one.' I take a break and rest on my mop. 'You should have seen the job he did at this old lady's flat we went to yesterday.' I want to tell Deb how proud I am at the way Gav tackled the job and the way he treated the old lady with respect, once he stopped fooling around. How good it felt when Gav said he worked for Steele and Son Plumbing. I have the words ready but I can't find a way to say them. I begin mopping again. 'But he doesn't seem right keen. I wish I could persuade him to give it a go. Does he ever say anything to you about whether he might come and join me one day?'

'Not really. It would be good though if he did decide to work with you.'

'I'd be dead chuffed if he did.'

'I don't like to see him having all this time on his hands. It's not natural.'

'And a bit of building site banter would toughen him up.'

'He's going to get himself in trouble if he's not careful.'

'Bring him out a bit.'

'Sheila was saying there might be a job coming up at her place. Her boss is looking for somebody to give him a hand, in the back mainly, preparing the food.'

'At that fish and chip shop?' I say and screw the mop into the bucket so hard the bucket turns. 'You're joking. Can you see our Gav in a smock and a white hat? It'd spoil his hair.'

'I wish you wouldn't come down on him like a ton of bricks every time he tries to do something positive. You're knocking his confidence. You've just said he wants building up.'

'You always take his side, don't you? I'm being realistic. He'd never fit in in a job like that.'

'It could lead to better things.'

'What? Chief wrapper?'

'See. You're at it again. Why don't you encourage him for once? You know he hasn't got your experience.'

'I know what he's like an' I know I'm right.'

'You think you know what he wants because you've made your mind up. You only see what you want to see, that's your trouble.'

'Chuffing hell, Deb. I've volunteered to give you a hand cleaning your café – your café – and I finish up getting my head picked over for being honest. You've been watching too much daytime TV.'

Love songs come and go. The air is full of music and disinfectant. Deb cleans the counter with a damp sponge, working in circles before moving onto the doors, methodically wiping the woodwork, top to bottom. I watch her out of the corner of my eye and wonder how anybody can get so much enjoyment out of cleaning. Then I remember Deb saying exactly the same thing when she once sneaked up on me in the garage while I was cleaning the Flash. I smile to myself as I push the mop backwards and forwards over the new laminate flooring at the side of the tables.

'Who's laid this flooring?' I say. 'It must be the best floor I've ever come across.'

Deb rinses her sponge in the sink and I detect a little smile. When I find a stubborn paint mark between two grooves, I start fooling around, mopping the area backwards and forwards like a mad man, as though I'm trying to create enough friction to start a fire.

'I think I could have been an Olympic curler if they'd done it at our school,' I say, blowing clouds of hot breath into the cold air. 'What do you think?'

'Here, then smart Alec. Curl this.'

Deb comes out from behind the counter, adopts a stylish kneeling pose, and slides a bar of wet soap along the floor. It comes at me a bit too fast and as I try to keep mopping and stay ahead of the soap, I end up crashing into a table clattering the chairs onto the floor. Deb laughs at me and I laugh at myself. Together we re-stack the chairs, glancing at each other when we think the other isn't looking. When I tell her she looks sexy in her tight blue jeans, she gives me a cheeky smile and I push up against her and we squeeze each other's backside.

'Well, well,' she says. 'I didn't think you liked curling that much.'

'I like uncurling more. Come on, lass. We said we'd do it in every room. We need this one for a full house.'

'Hang on,' she says, and she reaches over to the back door and pushes the bolt across. 'I hope nobody walks past and looks in.'

I pull her closer and lift up her jumper.

'If they see something they haven't seen before, tell 'em to throw their cap at it.'

As we kiss, Deb unhooks her bra and throws it over the back of a chair. It's a race to see who can kick off their shoes and pull off their jeans the quickest. I lift her onto the table and she wraps her legs round me then I try to climb on top of her.

'Bloody hell, Deb. This table's higher than I thought.'

'Get a chair.'

'It's ladders I want, not a chair. I knew I shouldn't have sold 'em.'

The table wobbles under the thrusting and groaning but it stays fast for the full two minutes. We climb off the table and untangle our clothes, smiling at each other as we get dressed.

'Hey, that was a bit good,' I say. 'It's more exciting when you think you might get caught.'

'It's certainly quicker.'

'I couldn't wait.'

'Neither could I.'

We return to our separate cleaning duties and the sound of love songs fills the space between us.

2

When Barry's van rattles to a halt outside the garage, I wipe my hands down the front of my overalls and greet my old friend with a warm handshake.

'I really appreciate you helping me out, Barry. I'm beginning to lose my confidence with this plumbing game.'

'No problem. People think plumbing's easy. It's not. But I can help you with the basics.'

Barry takes his tool bag and a length of copper tube out of his van, pauses at the entrance and nods at the Golden Flash resting on wooden blocks in the centre of the garage, resplendent in its gold paintwork and polished chrome.

'Wow. It's looking good, Phil. The last time I saw it you didn't have the engine in. It looks like it's almost finished, now. What a beautiful job you've done. You do yourself proud.'

'There's just a few finishing touches to do. I've got to get the front mudguard repaired and painted, and then that's just about it. And when I get the kick-start back from a mate of mine, I'll be able to fire the engine up. I tell you what, I'm having eggs. I can't wait to hear what it sounds like.

'It should have two stays on it like these here,' I say and I show Barry a drawing of the front mudguard in my BSA manual. 'I'm going to have a go at making them myself, bend them out of copper pipe first to make sure I get the shape right, like a kind of template and then make the proper ones out of steel tube. That's if I can master this pipe bending when you've shown me.'

'They look straightforward enough,' Barry says. 'We can make one of the templates now if you want. Then you can have a go at making the other one once you've got the hang of bending.'

'Okay.'

Barry cuts a short length of copper tube and takes his bending spring and blowtorch out of his tool bag and I shuffle two cardboard boxes out of the garage to create more space.

Barry says, 'Chandeliers?'

I shake my head and don't even bother to confirm.

'The only problem I've got with bending pipe with a spring is my knees. They're shot.'

'You'll be all right,' Barry says, 'as long as you anneal it first.'

'What do you mean, "Kneel it first"?'

'Anneal it, not kneel it. Heat the pipe up. It excites the copper molecules which makes it softer and easier to bend. Watch.'

Barry lights his blowtorch, thankfully well away from the Golden Flash, and plays the fierce flame over the section of tube where he plans to make the bend. Bands of blue and orange appear on the tube either side of the flame like magic and when he plays the blowtorch slowly left and right, the coloured bands move with the flame as though they're attached to it.

He shouts above the roar of the blowtorch, 'I'm waiting for the section to turn cherry red.'

I move in closer. I don't know about the molecules getting excited but I am. When the bit of tube he's heating turns cherry red, Barry switches off the

147

blowtorch and cools the pipe. Then he inserts the spring and bends the tube in stages over his knee, constantly comparing it to the drawing in my BSA manual.

'I don't think that's far off,' he says.

'You made that look dead easy.'

'It is with the right technique. You have a go now. I'll talk you through it.'

Nervous saliva gathers in my mouth and I smile to hide my embarrassment. This is harder than being at the training centre. In the workshop, you can hide behind the other students when it's time to try out a new skill. And you don't have to worry about the trainers interfering because there are never enough of them around to watch over you.

'I bet I make a right cobblers of this.'

'Have a go. You might surprise yourself.'

Under Barry's guidance I anneal the tube and pull a bend to copy the angle of the second stay.

'That's pretty good,' Barry says. 'The shape's nearly there. A couple of ripples but not bad for a first attempt. How's your knee?'

I feel around my kneecap as though confirming it's still in one piece.

'Fine. I never felt a thing. It felt more like bending a piece of lead pipe.'

'Everybody makes ripples the first time. You'll master it.'

Outside in the daylight I look down the line of my bend.

'It's rubbish.'

'It's a lot better than some of the bends you'll come across when you start plumbing. Especially some of them under the floorboards.'

'It doesn't matter, does it? Under the floor? Nobody's going to see them.'

'It might take a few minutes longer to do it right but that bend could be under somebody's floor for thirty years or more. It's your handiwork. Your signature. It wants doing right.'

'I'll be under a floor in thirty years. But I know what you mean.'

'Do it right, neat bends, well clipped, and you'll actually save time in the long run. You'll find out when you come to work on a shoddy installation. There'll hardly be a clip in sight, just the odd one hammered in to keep everything strapped down. It'll all look fine until you cut into the pipework and then it'll go off like a giant mousetrap.'

I'm listening but I don't want to appear too attentive. I don't want Barry to think I'm a swot. I'm too cagey to analyse why I think learning has to be an accidental process and not a methodical one. But it gives me a good excuse if I make a mistake. I suppose it's a survival tactic. That's why I'm playing around with the bending spring now, straining my face and biceps like a strongman, pretending I'm bending a solid iron bar.

'You don't want to end up being a bodger, do you?' Barry says. 'I bet you wouldn't do a bodge job on your Golden Flash. You wouldn't want to be doing seventy miles an hour down the motorway thinking, "Did I tighten that front fork up?" would you?'

I stop playing around with the spring.

'Would I hell.'

'What's the difference?'

'I'm doing my bike for me, not for somebody else.'

'When you're plumbing, that's for you, isn't it? It's still your handiwork.'

I feel bad. Here's Barry trying to show me a basic skill and I'm putting up a defensive wall. Come on, Steeley. What are you frightened of man?

'Barry, I'd love to be a decent plumber, I really would. But I'll never be any good. All them books and all that theory. It just goes straight over my head. It's like a foreign language. I've had to get our Gav to translate virtually every question for me.'

Barry gives a weary smile as he takes his spring back.

'It's up to you. It's going to be hard enough as it is without cutting corners. You really ought to find a qualified plumber to work with for a year or two. A few years ago, I would have taken you on myself.'

Only when I'm feeling optimistic do I dare believe that I might one day get the chance to work as a plumber's mate with a craftsman as skilled as Barry. I grasp the compliment and hang on to the hope that he might change his mind one day and take me on after all.

'I could give you a hand. I wouldn't want paying or anything. Not until I'd learnt a few things off you. Got the hang of it. And I could bring our Gav along with me. He's smart. He'd pick it up in no time. I'd pay his wages so it wouldn't cost you anything.'

'It's too late now. I'm not taking on any more work. There's too many at it and everybody wants it doing for nothing. Customers don't seem to want a quality job doing any more. It makes you wonder what kind of quality they produce in their own workplace. No. I'm winding down. I'm thinking about doing a bit of repping or something, if I can get used to a shirt and tie and the M62.'

Barry cleans his calloused hands with a rag.

'You've done all right there, Phil. You've got a feel for it. You just need to believe in yourself and keep practising.'

The ripples on the inside of my bend look unsightly and even as I'm running my thumb over them, I can't wait to have another go.

'Cheers, Barry. That's the first time anybody's ever told me I've done anything right at work.'

I pull a few more bends of varying angles, each one with fewer ripples than the last, then Barry packs away his gear.

'We can do a bit more another day and then have a look at machine bending and soldering, if you want.'

My confidence has returned. If I can master these basic plumbing skills I might survive.

'That's brilliant. I'm going to write this spring bending down in my portfolio this afternoon even though I know the training centre'll put a line straight through it.'

'Right,' Barry says. 'I'm off.'

'Hey, don't forget your copper pipe. There's nearly a full length left over.'

'You're okay. Keep it. Use it to practise your bending.'

3

Tap, tap, tap on the table top. I'm sitting on the settee staring into the unlit gas fire, tapping my ball point pen at a piece of paper on the coffee table, leaving little black dots in a random cluster. I could do with a bit more elbow room but Gav is sitting next to me with his feet up on the table and he's fast asleep.

Deb is on the armchair with her feet tucked under her. She's looking through a food magazine and every time she turns a page it sounds like a little wave coming ashore. The café's menu board at her side is pressing against my right shoulder and I try to push it away but there's nowhere for it to go – the big suite takes up almost all of the floor space in the little front room.

When we got ourselves into debt and lost our house through repossession the suite was one of the few items of furniture we managed to save. I thought I was being crafty hiding it in my dad's garage out of sight of the bailiffs, but sometimes, like now when all three of us are in the room, I wish I'd let them take the big lump of a suite and hidden something else in the garage instead. Maybe my acoustic guitar and record collection. Or perhaps Deb's cabinet full of miniature lighthouse ornaments. We never thought the bailiffs would take them but they did.

I screw up the dotted sheet of paper and lob it into the wicker basket on the hearth. The movement disturbs Gav and he wakes up, checks his mobile phone then shuts his eyes again.

After a few more minutes of pen-chewing and head-scratching I nudge Gav's feet.

'Give us a hand with this, Gav. I'm advertising my trail bike. I don't know whether to aim it at a sensible, middle-aged, boring old fart who needs a run-around to go and pick up his pork pies from the market or at some young tear-away who wants to blast up and down the muckstack frightening all the neighbours.'

Nothing. Gav moves his feet a few inches away from my new blank sheet. Deb turns another page and creates another little wave.

'Should I put, Needs a Respray? Or do you think that'll put people off?'

Gav opens his eyes and checks his mobile again. I feel like telling him not to worry, it's still there.

'You think it's hard selling your bike,' he says. 'You want to try finding a job.'

Through the party wall, I hear heavy footsteps thudding up the stairs.

'It's a good job Colin's only a skinny little bugger, otherwise he'd be bringing this whole terrace down.'

I feel better for sorting out the neighbour but it doesn't make writing the advertisement any easier. I've chewed the black top of my biro so much it's gone grey.

'Should I put the mileage down? I think it's been clocked. What about, Smokes A Bit. Might Have Pneumoconiosis?'

No response.

'One hundred pounds ono. Price includes scintillating conversation with wife and son.'

Still no response.

I crush my second attempt and throw it so hard at the wicker basket it bounces off the rim and spins around on the hearth like a sprayed fly.

Deb lowers her magazine and stares at me over the top of her reading glasses.

'What's up with you, Phil?'

Before I can think of a reply worthy of such a deep question, Gav butts in.

'My dad's having to sell his trail bike because he's run out of money for his training course.'

'Have I hell.'

'What, like you didn't run out of diesel yesterday?'

'Your dad had better not have run out of money,' Deb says as though I'm not there. 'He's got half the café rent to pay next week.'

Deb raises her magazine and returns to her menu hunting. Gav kneels on the arm of the settee and plays with his fringe in the mirror on the side wall.

'I don't know why you don't get rid of that Golden Flash, as well, Dad. I'd have got rid of it years ago if I'd been you and done something useful with the cash. Made some money out of it.'

'Money's not everything, lad. You'll find out one day.'

Gav runs his fingers through his hair and checks how it looks from both left and right.

'All you do is mix concrete all day long and then mess about with your motorbike. And you keep on about the day when you get your little pit pension as though it's going to change your life.'

'It will. It might not be much to you but that pension took some earning.'

Deb slaps her magazine into her lap.

'I'm sick of you two bickering at each other. I've come home for a rest from the café for five minutes and all I get is you two at each other.'

Gav pushes himself up off the arm and throws his weight into the seat cushion.

'Why are you attacking me, Mam? It's my dad who never helps you in the café. I help you.'

'Aye. I know you do. When I ask you to. I have to go down on my bended knee before either of you'll do anything. And I've got all the washing and ironing to do, all the cleaning to do, all your meals to get ready.'

Deb goes quiet and I know there's something brewing.

'Is it the café that's bothering you, love?'

As soon as the words come out of my mouth, I know it's a mistake. Deb throws her hands up.

'Of course it's the café.'

I try to put my arm around her shoulder but she tells me to get off.

'Why didn't you say something?' I say.

'Say something? Haven't you got eyes in your head?'

I look at Gav for some moral support then down at the floor.

'It's going to take me ages to get it the way I want it,' Deb says. 'Ages. I'm desperate to get all my new stuff in and get it all set up so it can start paying for itself. But it's a total mess. Everything I do just ends up creating more work and costing more money. I start on one thing thinking it'll be straightforward and then it turns out I need to fix something else before I can do that and on and on it goes. Me and Sheila tried to screw a nail in one of the chairs this morning to stop it from rocking but as soon as I touched the leg it broke off.'

Deb's magazine has slipped off her lap onto the carpet. I pick it up and carefully hand it back, wary that she might throw it at me.

'It's not a nail, love,' I say. 'It's a screw.'

'Well, whatever it is, it didn't work. I bought them off the previous owner thinking I was saving money but they all want replacing. And the whole place wants redecorating. I've got all the ceilings to do and all the walls to patch up and wallpaper. On top of that, all the woodwork needs rubbing down and glossing. Then I've got all the outside to do. There's only Sheila willing to give me a hand. It's going to take me forever. I was hoping to have it looking something like for Thursday. It's going to look a right mess for the women.'

'I'll sort the chairs out for you, love. Give me a shout when you're going back up.'

'And what about all the rest?'

'As soon as I've finished my training. I promise. I can't do everything.'

Gav says, 'I can give you a hand with the decorating if you show me what to do.'

'You're always too busy. Just like your dad.'

'I'm busy trying to find a job, that's why. It's soul-destroying keep getting knocked back. I never hear a thing every time I apply for a job because there's another hundred like me applying for the same thing.' Gav backhands the cushion on the settee and stands up. 'I want a job. I want to earn some money and be independent. I don't want to be staying here all my life relying on you and my dad forever.'

I'm relieved the attention has shifted from me and I lift my feet out of the way without complaining when Gav pushes past.

'And we don't want you to be staying here all your life, neither,' I say, gently prodding Gav in the ribs. 'You're costing me and your mam a fortune.'

Gav goes up to his room without replying and Deb sinks back into her armchair and returns to the page she was reading. The few creative thoughts I had about advertising the trail bike have dried up and the living room presses in on me. I might as well be miserable in the garage as miserable in here. The wording on the top of the menu board catches my eye as I brush past Deb. It says, TODAY'S SPECIAL, and I think, God help us tomorrow then.

I take my coffee down to the garage and sit on the milk crate, staring beyond the Golden Flash, not focusing on anything, only moving to lift the coffee mug to my mouth. What's it come to? Always bickering with Deb and Gav, knowing I'm the cause of the friction but unable to stop myself. Nowhere else to vent my anger and my frustration except on my own family. Feeling like an outcast in my own home.

I shut my eyes for a few seconds and when I open them nothing has changed.

Is our Gav right? Am I only good for mixing concrete? No more than a labourer, a skivvy? Waiting for my pit pension, yes, okay, my little pit pension, like a dog standing up at the window waiting for its owner to come home with a bone.

My coffee's gone as cold as the air in the garage when the door springs up and in steps Gav. I chuck the dregs out onto the track and as I slump back down on the milk crate with nothing to say, Gav hands me a pack of cards.

'I've got them business cards done for you.'

Gav's words are as bright as the sun breaking through black clouds and I jump up and fan out the cards, wide-eyed as though each card is the Ace of Spades.

'They're absolutely tremendous, Gav. You've done a right job. Very professional. I like the way you've wrapped the words round the photo. We look as though we mean business on the Flash, don't we?'

'When you said you were strugglin' to pay for your training. How much are you short?'

'I thought I'd got enough but somebody's not paid me for a job.' I've accepted the size of the debt and the zero chance of recovering it. No need to make it worse by telling Gav. 'It's not much. I'm not worried. I'll find it somehow. I've got until Wednesday to pay up.'

The cards really do look great and I sit back down on the crate and check and recheck them and I can't help shaking my head at my son's ingenuity.

'Come on,' he says. 'How much?'

Gav reaches into his back pocket and brings out a thick brown envelope with a bunch of notes sticking out of the top, hundreds of pounds by the looks of it. I almost fall off the crate.

'Bloody hell, Gav. Where've you got that lot from?'

I don't like to ask if it's the same brown envelope that I saw his mate with the flash silver saloon hand over.

'I've done a few jobs with my mates.'

'I wouldn't mind a few jobs like that.'

Gav licks his thumb and starts counting the notes.

'Come on. How much?'

I calculate that if I say it quickly and quietly and remain seated it'll not sound much.

'Five hundred.'

'How much!'

'Five hundred,' I say, a little slower and a little lower.

'Bloody hell, Dad. I'll have nowt left.'

I can't believe Gav is even thinking of lending me all that money. How can he afford it? He doesn't even work. But he's got it from somewhere and look at him now, flicking through the notes like a bookie.

'Less the forty quid I got for my old building gear.'

Gav peels off five hundred quid in twenty-pound notes.

'And I want it all back.'

I scramble up off the milk crate, eyes locked on the money.

'I can't borrow all that off you, Gav. I don't know when I'll be able to give you it back.'

'Don't worry about it. As long as I get it back.'

'Gav, that's fantastic. You're a star. An absolute star.'

My stomach tingles and I can see my plumbing qualification with its official stamp and my name in gold letters in front of me.

'You've not said owt to your mother, have you?'

'Have I hell. She'd kill me.'

'Me an' all.'

Gav is half way up the garden path when I shout after him.

'Hey, Gav. Do you fancy going down to the club tonight? I'm going to see if your granddad wants to go down for a pint. It's his birthday. I'm going to treat him with the money I got from my old building gear.'

Gav looks at me as though I've asked him if he still likes rusks.

'Bingo and dominoes? I don't think so. I've got better things to do with my time. I'll drop you both off if you want, but I'm not picking you up.'

4

Deb's cardboard boxes make a great set of bongos and I bash out a funky groove then reach over to my metal toolbox and complete a magnificent buzz roll. There's a fine file in the toolbox – just what I need to sharpen my lead knife. I push the file at an acute angle along the hooked blade and when both sides of the crescent gleam, I lick my finger and touch the cutting edge.

'Right Mister Jagger,' I say aloud. 'Debtor. Corrupt Developer. Rogue Landlord. I've a feeling this is my lucky day.'

I park my van on a side street well away from Jagger's house, don the old, shapeless jacket I keep between the seats for rainy days, and pull my skull cap down over my ears. With my collar up, head down and knife wrapped safely in a rag in my back pocket, I amble towards Jagger's house, keeping to the pavement on the opposite side.

When I get near the gates, I expect to find them locked as usual but this time they're wide open. There's a builder on his knees with his back to the road laying brick pavers on the drive. Jagger's 4x4 pick up and the white van I saw last week are parked side by side in front of the double garage. I kneel down and pretend to fasten my shoe laces, all the time assessing the situation. Jagger on a sit-on mower cutting his long back lawn fifty yards behind the house, disappearing and reappearing in the gap between the garage and the house. Twenty yards further up, Heavy and Wiry throwing a stick for their grey mongrel to retrieve.

It's risky but possible. My heart begins to race. I half jog back to the van, throw my old jacket into the back and pull on my training centre overalls.

The builder still has his back to the road and Heavy and Wiry and their faulty dog are still acting around at the far end of the back garden. I hear the mower and see Jagger again through the gap between the house and garage. The noise is getting louder.

'Right. Come on, Steeley,' I whisper. 'It's now or never.'

I lift the front of my skull cap for a few seconds to let the air cool my head and then I call out to the builder.

'How do, mate. It's the Water Board.'

The builder looks round briefly, nods, then continues to tap a paver on the bed of sand with the handle of his trowel. The mower reappears in the gap and I put my head down until it disappears. I try not to rush my words.

'We're doing some emergency repairs to a burst water main up the road there and I need to check where the stop tap is in case we have to turn it off. Do you know if the owners are in?'

The builder concentrates on his work, too busy to look up.

'I think the woman's gone out,' he says. 'The bloke's in his back garden cutting his grass.'

'Cheers, mate. I'll see if the tap's in the front garden. Most of the others up this road are. I'll let him know if we have to turn it off.'

'You'd better do. It's nearly time for the kettle to go on.'

Not knowing the builder's circumstances, I'm tempted to ask him if he's been paid upfront for the work and make a cynical remark about Jagger's payment methods. But I think it best to keep my mouth shut and instead step onto the front lawn and wander between the trees and shrubs in search of the imaginary stop tap.

The pond at the side of the monkey puzzle tree looks good, even as a paddling pool filled with a few inches of water. At one end a model sailing boat flying a tiny St George's flag nudges into two yellow plastic ducks, and nearby a child's bucket and spade have been abandoned in a little pile of sand. Where I carefully bedded the York stone flags over the edges of the butyl rubber liner, the joints have weathered and already the pond blends in with its surroundings. 'Yes, Jagger,' I say to myself. 'Well worth the five hundred quid.'

The builder starts laying a new row of pavers, tapping them with his trowel handle in a steady rhythm. I scan the scene. The back garden – the gap – the builder – the back garden – the gap – the builder. Round and round the danger triangle. All clear. I take the lead knife out of my back pocket and stab the sharp hook into the liner just below the stone flags. Then, crouching, looking back through the trees and shrubs towards the back garden and drive, my knuckles acting as a feeler gauge, I run the knife all the way around the pond edge until I'm back to where I started. I grab the liner with both hands and heave. It won't budge to start with no matter how hard I pull so I grab it in a different place and once I get it moving it pulls out easily. Immediately, the water begins to drain into the bed of sand, faster than I imagined, and the little boat and ducks stir and bump into each other.

The sheet is heavy and slippery and I fold it and refold it, treading on the squelching rubber until it's small enough to fit under my arm. All the time I check the danger triangle. The mower is still active, the whine of its engine getting louder as it moves closer to the house. Then it shuts off. I dodge behind the monkey puzzle tree and make myself thin. Sweat stings my eyes and cold water runs off the liner and down my arm and leg. The rubber gets heavier and begins to slip out of my grasp and I have to hug it against my body with both hands. I peer round the tree trunk and through the gap see Jagger unhook the grass box and empty it onto a heap. He looks up. I pull back. The dog is still barking at the far end of the garden. When I peer round again, Jagger is back on his mower and as it disappears, the headlights flash through the shrubbery like searchlights. The builder continues to tap-tap his pavers with his back to me. I hold my breath one more time then sneak down the drive and scarper.

5

Gav follows me through the garden gate and into my mother's kitchen. She's sitting on a chair doing her ironing in front of the portable TV which is set up on the worktop at the side of the bread bin. The picture on the little screen is fuzzy and it looks like my dad's taped a metal coat hanger to the antenna to try and improve reception.

'Now then, Mother.'

'Hello, you two.'

'Is the birthday boy in?'

'He's sat in front of the telly again. I'm having to watch Songs of Praise on this thing. It's from Rotherham.' My mother stands the iron on its heel and a burst of steam shoots out of the sole plate. 'He's not shifted all day apart from turning the gas fire up and down.'

'I'll see if he wants to go down to the club for a pint for his birthday. That'll cheer him up.'

'He needs something to cheer him up. I might as well be on my own for all the conversation I get from him. And I have to keep reminding him what day it is. I've told him umpteen times it's his birthday but it goes in one ear and out the other. Have you got yourself a job yet, Gavin?'

Gav takes a toffee out of the raffia bowl on the dresser, throws it in the air and catches it in his mouth first go.

'Not yet, Nan. I'm still looking.'

My dad is sitting in his arm chair, staring at a talent show on the TV with a face that wouldn't look out of place in a doctor's waiting room. He's got his walking stick across his lap and there's a faint whiff of sweaty feet in the air.

'Happy birthday, Dad.'

'Hey up, Phil. Thanks. I'd forgotten.'

I settle into the sofa and put my hands behind my head.

'What are you watching?'

'God knows? It's absolute tripe. If this bloke was on at the club the secretary'd tell him to bugger off home.'

I laugh out loud. It's Elton John.

'Turn it over, then.'

'It's t'same on t'other side. Pigswill.'

Gav comes in unwrapping another toffee and he sits on the floor under the window.

'All right, Granddad. Happy birthday.'

'Thanks, lad.'

My dad's feet are crossed on the hearth, inches away from the gas fire's glowing radiants. There's a hole in his sock and his big toe pokes through like a budgie's head. My mother shuffles in with the aid of her walking frame and hands me my cup of tea.

'Our Gavin's still not found a job yet, have you, love?' she says. 'Poor lad.'

'You know what you want to do, Gavin,' my dad says. 'Buy yourself a pair of tights and go out and rob one of them high street banks. The thieving swines.'

Gav laughs out loud and I'm sure I detect a slight colouring to his cheeks.

'I've thought about it.'

My mother shakes her head and pushes her walking frame back into the kitchen.

'Fancy going down to the club for a pint for your birthday, Dad? I'll treat you.'

'No. I'm not bothered.'

I've seen this face on my dad a hundred times before. When he's in this mood it's like looking into the eye slits in a suit of armour and it would take a crowbar to open his jaws. But if there is a hint of softening in the way he secretly watches you, you know it's only money and a few pounds will cure his depression.

'Are you sure?'

My dad's looking at the TV but I can tell he's stopped watching the programme.

'Our Gav says he'll drop us off.'

My dad taps his walking stick on the cracked hearth edge and narrows his eyes as though he's at the bookies deciding whether to double up or go for a treble.

'Well, I could do with paying my numbers.'

He disappears upstairs and I join my mother in the kitchen and we listen to the landing floor creak and the bathroom door squeak.

'I told you that would cheer him up, Mam. He didn't even use the stair lift.'

My mother pushes the iron across a skirt and a plume of steam rises in front of the TV making the picture even fuzzier.

'Don't let him have too much to drink, will you, Philip. He's drinking more than is good for him these days.' She rests the iron and turns the skirt over. 'He did upset me last week. You know that bottle of wine you and Deb bought me when I came out of hospital when I broke my hip?'

'I do.'

167

'I was saving it for a special occasion. It meant a lot to me that bottle of wine did. Well, it's gone. Your dad's found it and he's drunk it all.'

'He never has.'

'I was cleaning the cupboard and when I picked the bottle up to wipe it, I could see the seal was broken. When I looked, he'd filled it up with water and put it back on the shelf.'

Gav laughs. He must not have seen the moisture in his grandmother's eyes.

'Bloody hell, Mam. I didn't know it was that bad.'

'He never used to drink like that when he was working.'

'He didn't have time then, that's why.'

'I remember many a time your dad coming home when he'd been on the afters. He'd have called at the pub for a pint like they all used to do and I'd have his dinner waiting for him for when he got in and sometimes he'd be that tired, he'd fall asleep before he could finish eating it.'

'I've seen him like that. It was hard graft in them days.'

'Now he seems to drink because he's nothing else to do all day long.'

I pretend to strike Gav in the stomach with my fingers and he recoils and laughs.

'Give over, Dad.'

'Let that be a lesson to you, Gav. Keep off the booze until you've got a job.'

We turn off the main road and drive into the working men's club car park. It's full as always on a Sunday night. Cars have had to park in front of the Methodist church next door and more cars have been left on the main road outside the undertaker's premises. Empty taxis draw up and leave loaded with groups of noisy young lads and lasses.

'Park in front of that van, Gav,' I say.

'He'll not be able to get out.'

'It's okay. He does the bingo. He'll not be going anywhere until closing time.'

I help my dad out of the car and Gav hands him his walking stick.

'I drove past here at quart to seven,' Gav says. 'There were blokes queuin' up outside waitin' for it to open.'

'The doors don't open till seven,' I say, thinking I'm being helpful.

'Sad or what.'

I don't think it's sad. It's only like queuing up to get into a football match or a nightclub.

'They'll have been making sure they got their names down for the darts and the pool table,' I say.

'What a waste of life.'

I give in. Gav's in one of those moods.

'Are you sure you're not comin' in?'

'Am I hell.'

My dad's hearing isn't great and he hasn't picked up on the strained conversation.

'You're comin' in for a drink with me and your dad aren't you, Gav?'

Gav glares at me as though he's been set up.

'Go on then, Granddad. Five minutes. Seeing as it's your birthday.'

The airtight club doors pull open with a whoosh and the suction draws the smell of fried onions, hamburgers and piss out over our heads and into the car park. Old Albert, the steward who signs us in, has been doing this job for years. He looks as though he lives on liquids, more a harmless administrator than a doorman, proud to wear a blazer and tie and sit at the front desk with his committee member's badge on display.

The lights in the tap room are on even though it's still daylight outside, and the air is full and humming with laughter and conversation. Most of the tables are taken by blokes playing cards and dominoes. The snooker table and the two pool tables are occupied by young lads and the sharp smack of ball striking ball cuts through the chatter. I help my dad into his chair at his usual table and with a proud smile on my face I introduce Gav to the men around the table.

'This is our Gav.'

'He's a grand young man, Phil,' one of the men says. Another says, 'And he's doing all right for hissen by t'looks of it.'

Gav goes red and pulls his shirt sleeve down to cover his big, shiny watch. I already feel better. It's the first time he's smiled since picking us up.

I get the drinks in and when I return from the bar my dad is already settled into a team game of dominoes, walking stick abandoned, purpose in his eyes. At the end of the first game, I offer a toast to my dad's birthday and everyone at the table takes the mickey and says the old man should buy a round. My dad pretends not to hear then he tells them not to hold their breath. The celebration only lasts a few seconds and the dominoes are shuffled again.

'I see they're finally knocking the Stute down,' I say, aware I've only got a few seconds to get the players concentration before they pick up their new tiles.

'You could see it coming,' my dad says without looking up.

'Well, here's to the Stute and all it stood for,' I say and I raise my pint in anticipation but nobody picks up their pints and their eyes stay fixed on the potential of the new dominoes. Gav laughs at my awkward raised glass and the lack of enthusiasm around the table. After a few seconds skinny Pod Green who looks like a middle-distance runner until you see him from the side, says he thought he'd seen something about the demolition in the Chronicle. A second player, Fred Short, a former miner about sixty-five with a shiny clean-shaven face marked with tiny blue scars, clicks a domino down onto the table.

'When they shut Brod'orth pit,' Shorty says, 'they might as well have shut Brod'orth, ne'er mind t'Stute.'

'Brod'orth wa' a good colliery,' my dad says, slapping down his domino. 'But they owt to have blown the bloody lot up. That'd have shown 'em. We had to fight for everything we ever got from that pit. Colliers always have. A decent wage. Health and safety. Concessionary coal. We'd have got nothing without a strong union.'

'The union couldn't keep the pits open, though, could they, Dad?' I say, knowing what's coming next and winking at Gav, trying to include him in the banter.

'You're right. They couldn't. If it hadn't been for the union, the pits would still be open today. And ten-year-old lasses would be working on the face a mile underground.'

'It'll get a lot worse afore it gets better,' Shorty says. 'Because the Tories'll not rest until their grubby little hands have squeezed every last gasp of air out of every last trade union. They went for the biggest fish first and they think the rest'll cave in.'

'I agree wi thi, Fred,' my dad says. 'But Labour's not covered itsen in glory, neether. Wilson shut more pits than Thatcher did. And t'last lot nivver supported us.'

'I'll gi thi that,' Shorty says.

'We're used to being shafted by the Tories,' my dad says. 'They're the experts at it. But we didn't expect it from our own party.'

Pod Green places his domino down on the table as though he's creating a work of art and says, 'I suppose if tha goin to get shafted, tha might as well go for a deluxe shaft and vote Tory.'

We all laugh at Pod Green's dry humour. He always says just enough to leave you wondering which side he's on. He's never worked at the pit and probably thinks it's time we got over it.

All the players have gone quiet, now. The game of dominoes is far too important to allow a long-gone pit closure and the demolition of all that was left of the miners' welfare, recreation and social wellbeing to interfere with concentration.

I sit back and look around the tap room and everywhere the same harmless, all-consuming little contests are being played out with dominoes and cards and darts and cues. My dad is happy and so I'm happy. All that changes when I see Gav looking down on me, unsmiling, no attempt to hide his desire to be anywhere but in a working men's club.

He finishes his half and hands me a five-pound note.

'I'm off, Dad. Get my Granddad a pint.'

'You fetch it him, Gav. He'll appreciate it a lot more coming from you.'

'I'm not goin' near that bar while they're hangin' around.'

I turn round to see who he's on about.

'Don't look round, Dad.'

'You mean them three lads?'

'They're a pain. They've been hasslin' me and Jason and Ben for weeks. Wantin' to know what we get up to.'

'Join the club.'

'Right, Granddad,' Gav says as he stands up. 'I'm off. Enjoy your birthday.'

'Thanks, Gav. I am doing already. Hey. Come here.'

He grabs Gav's hand and pulls him so close I think he's going to plant a kiss on his forehead.

'You'll find a job eventually, lad. Don't give up, keep your dignity and don't let the bastards grind you down.'

As Gav and my granddad are talking, the three lads at the bar head towards our table, each carrying two pints of lager and laughing loud enough to spoil the concentration of the blokes at the tables around us. Their evening strategy is clear. Get drunk on the club's cheap lager and then pile into a taxi destined for town where the alcohol is treble the price.

'Look who's here,' the biggest of the three lads says, displaying the tattoos on his hand as he points one of his pint glasses at Gav. 'One of the flash boys. Where's Jason and Ben then? Doing some big-deal-in-the-city-with-the-big-boys?'

The tattooed lad's two mates, a chubby lad with a red face and a short lad with long black hair pushed behind his ears, laugh at their leader's sarcasm. Gav tries not to look in their direction.

'I'm off, Granddad. See you later.'

'Bedtime is it, Gav?' the tattooed lad says.

I tell the others I'm going for a slash and I follow Gav into the reception area.

'I see what you mean about those three lads,' I say.

'They're numpties.'

'Anyway. Thanks for the lift, Gav. And for treating your granddad on his birthday. I know you've got better things to do.'

Gav pushes open the exit door and looks back at me.

'How can anybody do this for a night, never mind a lifetime? What a complete waste of time and money. Is this what I've got to look forward to?'

When I return to my pint and my dad's game of dominoes, my heart is in my boots and the three lads are still hanging around. For a few minutes they watch the game from the sidelines. But they soon get bored with the slow movement of black rectangular tiles and decide to knock on the table whenever one of the players hesitates, laughing at the disturbance they're causing. Shorty tells them to grow up and Pod Green says it's not too late for them to bugger off into the concert room to play bingo with the women.

The three lads ignore the advice and think it's good fun for each of them to stand behind a player and make a shocked face whenever a domino is played as though the player has committed a catastrophic error of judgement. The big lad stands behind my dad with his tattooed hands wrapped around both pint glasses. As the game reaches a conclusion, the tattooed lad leans over my dad's head and then pulls away as though he's inhaled smelling salts. I hear him tell the other two lads that the old man needs to get his nappy changed. They sniff the air and pretend to grimace with disgust.

Fortunately, my dad is busy shuffling dominoes and he doesn't hear their mockery. Shorty sees the hard look on my face.

'Ignore them, Phil,' he says. 'They've started coming in on a Sunday night, taking the mickey out of anybody they can.'

I don't answer him.

The lads' taxi must be due because all three down the last of their lager, abandon their empty glasses on the nearest table, and make for the door. I nod to Shorty and Pod Green and we get up without a word and track the gang to the toilet. Old Albert senses there's trouble in the air.

'Everything okay, Phil?'

'Code one, Albert.'

'Code one? Right.'

Albert takes his red biro out of his top pocket and scribbles something in his notebook.

We stay right behind the three lads as they go into the toilet and I catch the door to stop it banging into my face. A man stumbles out, struggling to fasten up his flies, and that leaves just the six of us inside. The three lads are lined up at the trough, sharing a joke, holding onto the wall for support. Shorty and Pod Green block the exit and I pretend to unzip my trousers at the trough behind them.

'Now then you lads.'

They look round lazily, unconcerned, convinced I'm talking to somebody else. There's a shhhh as jets of water gush out of the sparge pipes. I pretend to zip up, turn on the basin tap, and make eye contact with the three faces who have now worked out that I am indeed talking to them.

'That old man you were pillocking in the tap room back there. Him we were playing dominoes with.'

The big lad with the tattoos doesn't like the threat in my voice. His face hardens and he tightens his belt.

'Who says we were pillocking him?'

The chubby lad with the red face notices Shorty and Pod Green standing guard at the exit.

'We were only having a laugh with the old timer,' the chubby lad says and his mate with the long black hair backs him up. The big lad is still staring at me. He thinks he's tough. I ignore his soft mates and step up to within a foot of his face. He doesn't back off.

'If ever you take the piss out of him again, I'll fucking drag all three of you outside and throw you through that fucking undertaker's window. Is that clear?'

He still doesn't back off. I was ready to let him leave with a warning but he hasn't finished.

'I told you. We weren't pillocking him,' he says. 'And anyway, it's not my fault he stinks of piss.'

I grab his throat and pin him hard against the wall tiles. He's staring straight back at me but his hands stay by his side.

'Listen you little twat. Never take the piss out of him again, do you hear? That bloke's my dad. Take the piss out of him and you take the piss out of me. Okay?' He doesn't answer so I squeeze his throat even harder and lift him higher. 'I said, okay?'

After a few seconds his stare shifts downwards. He's not as daft as he looks. Wrong time to prove his toughness. It's to do with club rules and that means the fight is unequal. One scuffle in here and we would be surrounded by a dozen committee members in seconds. I let go of his throat.

Shorty and Pod Green stand to one side, within head-butting range, avoiding eye-contact, not moving until the gang are out of the toilet. We don't relax until all three get into their taxi. As the cab pulls away, the big lad stares at me. I shake Old Albert's hand and the posse returns quietly to the game of dominoes and pints of beer.

It's after eleven when I help my dad walk a wavy line towards the empty bus shelter at the end of the car park. I don't know who's holding who up. A bread van is parked near the exit and there's a queue of blokes laughing and joking with the driver. My dad fumbles for some change.

'Hang on, Phil. I'll just get your mother a dozen teacakes. She loves 'em. Cheapest in Brod'orth.'

The car park is almost empty now. The cars that were parked in front of the undertakers and the church have gone. Drinkers in loose groups gather outside in the light of the club doors for a smoke and to say goodnight before moving off home, noisy but no bother. I check my watch.

'I think we've missed t'last bus, Dad.'

'Get on my back and I'll carry you home like I used to.'

'And run all t'way.'

I crouch with my arms out as though I'm about to launch myself into the air.

'Come on, Dad. My turn. Jump on. See how far we can get.'

My dad pretends to clout me with his bag of teacakes.

'Don't be a daft bugger.'

We're pushing and shoving each other when a car pulls up at the side of us, engine running. I'm smiling like a fool, ready to give some directions to a lost driver.

'I knew you'd be here,' Gav says. 'Get in.'

Outside the front door my dad checks every pocket but he can't find his key. He puts his hands against the wall and I frisk him like a stop and search. Gav swings the bag of teacakes round and laughs at us. The noise brings my mother to the door and we hear her arthritic hands fumble with the lock.

'Hang on,' she says.

The door opens and my mother moves her walking fame to one side to let her menfolk in out of the cool night air.

'I've brought him back in one piece,' I say.

'And you're only just in one piece yourself by the looks of it. Put him in his chair. He'll still be there when I get up tomorrow.'

My dad's having a problem lifting his leg over the threshold and I'm stumbling like somebody with a clog and a boot on. It needs Gav's sober strength to keep my dad upright long enough to get him through the hallway and settled in his chair.

When I go into the kitchen, my mother is holding the pedal bin open with her mobility reaching aid.

'I've told your dad before. These teacakes are like cardboard. But he has to go and keep buying them. He has to be seen to be jack the lad in front of all those so-called canny mates of his.'

She drops the bag of bread into the bin and covers it with yesterday's racing results.

We kiss my mother goodnight and as we reach the edge of our estate, Gav gets a call on his mobile. It's a short call and when he puts the phone down, he asks me if he can drop me off half a mile from home as he has to shoot off to see his mates about something. I think it's a bit late to be out and about but Gav says it's urgent so I pull my jacket tight around my neck, put my dizzy head down, and keep my feet moving towards our house.

I've only been walking a few minutes when I hear footsteps. I turn round, almost falling over, and have to make a quick side-step to keep my balance. Every shadow thrown by the hedges behind the garden walls looks like a crouching figure. No footsteps. I set off again in a stagger, pleased with myself that I managed to keep my hands firmly in my pockets throughout the whole tricky manoeuvre.

The next time I hear footsteps it's too late. Someone from behind grabs me around the neck and throws me to the ground. The strange thing is it doesn't hurt. It's like falling into bed. I know I'm being punched but I don't feel any pain. My head rolls as the fists strike one side of my face then the other. It's as though I'm taking part in a well-rehearsed wrestling match.

Then the kicking starts and I curl up into a ball. This is getting serious. There's at least two of them and they're not wearing trainers. Each drive lifts me off the pavement, sobering me up in stages. Then the kicking stops. Silence. I stay curled up, sensing my attackers are still standing over me. I'm right. The heavy stomp on my ribcage catches me out and I hear myself groan. Somebody whispers in my ear.

'It's not over yet.'

A car goes by. Feet running away. Then silence. I lay motionless, eyes wide open and only uncurl when a cat appears in the gateway further down and trots across the road. When I try to stand up, I fall backwards into the hedge. The foliage is soft and supportive and I let the leaves cushion me until my head stops spinning and I'm able to draw in a shallow breath of air without my ribs knifing my lungs.

Monday

1

It's half past seven and I've been up since six, soaking my aches and pains in the bath, trying to work out who beat me up last night. Did somebody try to mug me? It happens a lot in Brodworth and it's getting worse if you believe what you read in the Chronicle. But they didn't take anything. More likely it was those three lads I threatened in the club toilets. The chubby one and his mate with the long black hair tucked behind his ears seemed harmless, but they could have been led along by that big lad with the tattoos. He looked as though he had unfinished business. When they said it's not over yet, did they mean they were going after Pod Green and Shorty?

Deb doesn't believe it was a mugging, either. And neither does she think it was those three angry young lads. She reckons I must have been drunk and fallen off the kerb into the gutter. She patches me up and tells me to go back to bed but I'm feeling better for the soak and by nine o'clock I'm fit enough to drop her off at the café and then drive to the training centre.

There's a queue of vehicles outside the locked gates. The place doesn't open until half past ten on Mondays. Garrett says it's to give extra travel time to those students who live a long way off, like Kath, and are coming back to their digs after spending the weekend at home. It's dead time as far as those of us who live within commuting distance are concerned. We'd sooner be in the workshop practising our plumbing skills or getting on with our assessments.

Everybody asks me what happened to my face and I tell them I came off my trail bike last night on my way to the shop to buy some milk for the training centre.

Despite the acute pain in my ribs and the chronic state of my back, I spend most of what's left of the morning under the floorboards working on my practical assessment. Half an hour before lunch, I'm sitting on my bath taking a breather when Peggs walks by.

'Peggs. Come and have a look under my floor. See what you think to my clipping.'

Peggs borrows my torch, straightens out his bad leg and sticks his head through the trap door.

'My God,' he says. 'It's a miracle. That's the best clipping I've seen in here in a long time. Who's done that for you?'

'Cheeky bugger. It's all my own handiwork.'

'Leave it all connected up when you've finished and I'll get everybody to come and have a look at it to see how it should be done. In fact, I'll go and fetch Garretty now and see what he thinks to it. It might put you in his good books.'

I'm showing off my work to Kath and Robert when Peggs returns with the director of training.

'Have a look under his floor,' Peggs says. 'It's top class. It's the best I've seen for ages.'

'Never mind what's underneath the floor,' Garrett says. 'What's this?'

There's a length of copper tube with an S bend at either end leaning against my basin. Garrett takes it out of my bay and holds it at arm's length as though he's found a snake.

'This is not part of your assessment,' he says loud enough for half the workshop to hear. 'You've just been wasting time and good copper pipe by the looks of it. I could charge you for this. It's as bad as stealing.'

I reach for the tube and groan as my ribcage twists.

'That pipe's mine. I brought it in this morning to practise my bending.'

Garrett ignores my outstretched hand and turns the tube around.

'Oh yes?'

'I did. It's for my motorbike. Give us it here.'

I try to grasp the tube again but Garrett whips it out of my reach.

'It must be a strange looking motorbike,' he says.

Students, sensing a confrontation, stop what they're doing and move in closer. Even old Arthur, the part-time workshop painter, puts down his brush, adjusts his beret, and turns to watch.

Young Simon, who has pushed his way to the front of the gathering for a better view, says, 'He calls his bike the Golden Flush,' and he pretends to pull the chain on a toilet.

From the back, ex-factory worker, Jim Warren asks if my bike is chain-driven and another so-called mate, ex-baker, Paul Griffiths suggests I call it a Flash in the Pan. Everyone laughs except Kath, Robert, Peggs and old Arthur.

'It looks like something your farmer friend here would use to catch his sheep,' Garrett says, clawing the air with the bent tube.

No one speaks or moves. Then a quiet voice breaks the silence.

'I think you'll find he's telling the truth.' Everyone looks round at Arthur. 'I saw him take that length of pipe out of his van this morning when he pulled into the car park.'

Arthur rarely says anything, which makes his witness statement all the more powerful. I hold out my hand.

'See. Now give us it back.'

Garrett's face changes. His smirk becomes a sneer and he hands the tube back to me, maintaining a safe distance.

'If ever I catch anybody misusing time and materials in this training centre there'll be trouble.' As the gathering parts to let Garrett leave, he places his hand on a student's shoulder and smiles at everyone. 'Remember. I sign off your portfolios.'

I sit on the side of my bath and check the bends I've made, turning the tube over, rubbing my fingers around the curves. Kath sits down next to me and Robert leans against my bay wall.

'I could deck Garrett,' I say. 'He's only doing this because he thinks I'm not going to pay up and because I keep complaining about the training.'

'Be careful you don't upset him, Philip,' Kath says. 'He might not sign off your portfolio.'

'He's two choices.'

'We all know the training isn't high quality. But you don't have to be the one to tell him.'

'Somebody has to.'

Robert says, 'I try to ignore him if I can. He's on a power trip.'

'I wish I was on a trip. On my Flash miles away from all this. Clear my head.'

'We'll feel better when we've had that ride up to the Biker's Café this evening,' Robert says.

'Can't wait.'

'I wish I had a motorbike,' Kath says. 'I'd join you. My landlady's a lovely wee woman but life can get a bit boring in a bed and breakfast night after night.'

'We could call round and pick you up if you want, couldn't we Robert. If you don't mind squeezing on the back of one of us.'

2

Over the years my waist has thickened and now the leather jacket I'm looking at through the handlebar mirror on the trail bike feels like a tight band around my chest made worse by the pain in my ribs. I bought the jacket the day after fetching the Golden Flash and sidecar down from Scotland in the back of a mate's van expecting to have the bike rebuilt within a few months. Then of course we had the strike. I want to look good on the bike this afternoon with Kath joining us and the jacket is the best I've got. I stand up straight and shove an old pair of Deb's gloves into my spare helmet.

I back the trail bike out of the garage and check the sky. There's more blue than white and the air is still warm. It's been one of those lovely spring days where you open the back door and neither the cold nor the flies come in. And now it's a perfect evening for biking.

Just as I'm securing the spare helmet to the handlebars, I see Deb trotting down the footpath.

'Have you seen anything of our Gavin?'

'No. Not since last night when he dropped me off after we'd been to the club with my dad. Why?'

'He didn't come home last night and his bed's not been slept in. He's not phoned or anything.'

Deb's words are tumbling out and her voice is higher pitched than normal. I pull on my helmet.

'You need to stop whittling about him, Deb. He's old enough to do what he likes now.'

'A couple of blokes came round here this morning, just after you'd gone to the training centre. They said he owed them some money.'

The word money distracts me for a second causing me to fumble the buckle on my helmet.

'It'll be his slack mates. We bumped into 'em on Saturday morning on the way to a job. Jason and somebody else ... Ben I think he's called. Were there two lasses with 'em?'

'I couldn't see anybody else. But if they're his mates, I'd hate to see his enemies. What if it's them who beat you up last night?'

'I thought you didn't believe me when I said I'd been beaten up?'

Deb has her breath back now and her words are more controlled. She nods at the spare helmet.

'Taking somebody out for a ride?'

'I'm off up to the Biker's Café on the A1 for an hour with Robert. He's taking Kath on the back of his Suzuki but he hasn't got a spare helmet so I'm meeting up with them at her B&B, if I can find it.'

'Kath?'

'She's on our course. I told you about her. I think she fancies Robert.'

'She's got good taste. He is a hunk.'

I ignore the little dig and look up at the sun, still a good two hours above the houses. 'It should be a great ride out. There'll be plenty of bikers there on an evening like this.' I check my watch. 'They think they're wide boys, them mates of our Gav's, but they're just kids.'

'Can't you go and have a look for him?'

'Where do you want me to go, Deb? He could be anywhere. I've told you. He'll be all right. He'll come home when he's hungry.'

I start up the engine and Deb steps away.

'You're not bothered, are you? He might be up to his neck in trouble but as long as you're messing about with your motorbikes then everything's all right.'

I grab the handlebars and stare back at Deb.

'What is it with you, Deb? You can't stand to see me enjoying myself for once, can you? You don't want to come out on the bike any more, and now you don't want me to go out on it with anybody else.'

'See what I mean? What's happened to you lately, Phil? You go off your head as soon as anybody tries talking to you.'

Deb is shouting. I can hardly hear her above the noise of the bike and I can't work out how angry she is.

'I'm going off my head because I feel trapped,' I shout back. 'Trapped like a chuffing caged lion.'

'You feel trapped? How do you think I feel?'

I can't hear her and it's not just the screech of the two-stroke engine. It's my debt, my stupidity, my unsigned portfolio, my old mate Shinny, Gav out of work – it all comes down on me like a coffin lid, shutting everything out.

'Not as bad as me,' I say. 'We're worse off now than we've ever been. We should be on top of t'world, not on t'bottom on it, fighting for work, shuffling back'ards and for'ards like zombies. Counting every penny from one week to t'next. Nowt to look for'ard to except old age and poverty? I'm sick of it.'

In my anger, I've fastened the strap on my helmet too tight and it's biting into my neck. I try to release the buckle but the thing won't shift.

'If I'm not being beaten down, I'm being beaten up.'

'It's you. You don't do anything. You'll not spend any money on the house, you'll not buy anything new to wear, you don't want to go anywhere.'

'We can't afford to, that's why.'

The buckle finally gives way. Another second and I would have wrenched the damned helmet off and thrown it at the garage.

'And you hardly ever give me a hand in the café. You've given up. Well, I can tell you this, Phil. I've not given up. My life's not over yet. I'm going to make a success of the rest of my time, with or without you.'

That shuts me up. I hadn't realised Deb thinks I've given up. Well, I haven't given up. And I'm not running away, neither. I just want to clear my head, that's all. What's wrong with that? I know it's a pathetic question and I can't even convince myself I have the right answer.

'Look. I'll have a ride round the estate when I get back. See if I can find him.'

Deb spins round and marches back into the house. I rev the engine hard to mask my frustration and my words.

'Sod off, Deb.'

Colin next door must have heard the clamour and he pokes his head out of his hut to see what all the noise is about. I ignore him and stomp on the gear lever causing the bike to jerk forward, jarring my neck.

The young lads, kicking their ball against the garage doors, scatter as I race along the unmade track, under the hanging knee pads, throwing up clouds of dust and gravel, and disappear down the steep grassy path between the allotments and the fields behind the Stute. The surface is uneven and I curse the deep ruts. Bricks and rubble shift under my wheels and I have to stand up on the footrests to keep the trail bike and my temper under control.

Almost all the Georgian houses on the boulevard where Kath's landlady lives are offering bed and breakfast. Each house has a B&B sign on a post by the front gate and from a distance it looks as though all the properties are up for sale. I ride at walking pace, searching for the right address. I'm beginning to think I have the wrong avenue when Kath steps out from the shelter of a gateway a hundred yards away and waves to me. I try to look cool, not returning the wave or nodding, and accelerate up to the house.

'You've not changed your mind, then?' I say.

'Not a chance. I'm looking forward to it.'

'It's a bit posh round here. I hope I don't get arrested for loitering on a motorbike.'

Kath is wrapped up in two thick baggy jumpers topped by a green fleece. All three layers are at least two sizes too big.

'What do you think?' she says, holding her arms out and turning round to show off the rear view. 'Cool or what?'

'Very sexy. Where did you get them from? Oxfam?'

'My landlady. God bless her.'

As we're talking, I pick up the sound of a Japanese motorbike and a few seconds later Robert's Suzuki appears at the entrance to the avenue. He pulls up at the gateway and lifts up his visor.

'Sorry I'm a bit late. Parent problems. My dad's had a funny turn.'

'Oh dear,' Kath says. 'Is it all the stress of moving out?'

'Probably. It'll be me who's having a funny turn next.'

When Kath puts the spare helmet on, I notice she's tied up her hair and there are soft wayward strands down the back of her neck. There's something about the way Kath dresses. She always looks comfortable in her own skin. Taking pride in her appearance but not looking for approval.

'Here,' I say. 'I should put these on as well. It could get cold later on.'

Kath pulls on Deb's old woollen gloves and wriggles her fingers at us like a puppeteer. The rear suspension sinks when she sits on the Suzuki and Robert has to adjust his big feet to prevent the bike toppling over.

'Have you been on the back of a motorbike before?' Robert says.

'No. This is my first time.'

'Hold tight and just follow my body. When I lean, you lean, and when we stop, don't put your feet down until I've put mine down.'

'Yes, sir.'

I raise my eyebrows and widen my eyes at Kath. I'm impressed with Robert's sudden assertiveness. And a bit jealous.

As we get to within a couple of miles of the biker's café, I start to think about Deb. She'll be on her own, working hard at the café. I feel guilty at being out in the fresh air having fun with Robert and Kath, and then I feel sad and alone. I slow my breathing to suffocate the

191

sick feeling rising in my stomach. I'll call Deb from the biker's café. Tell her she was right to be worried about Gav. Say that I'm worried as well, and ask her if she's okay and hope there's some hint of forgiveness in her voice and somehow try to say I'm sorry without saying as much because I'm not very good at that. Yep, that's what I'll do. Give her a call as soon as we get to the biker's café.

There must be more than two hundred bikes at the cafe, parked in tidy rows with only a few inches of space between each gleaming machine. We park in a quiet space and I watch Kath take off her helmet. She stares at me and Robert as though she's just taken off a blindfold.

'Did you enjoy that?' I say, ruffling my hair.

'It was fantastic,' she says. 'What a rush of adrenaline.'

'You can handle that Suzuki, Robert. I'd all on to keep up with you.'

'I've got a good pillion passenger, that's why. No leaning the wrong way into bends.'

There's shiny chrome and every colour under the sun in the bike park and I take a long, slow breath through my nose as though I'm sensing the air. I love watching the bike riders as they sit on the walls and at the tables with their coffees and fry-ups, laughing and chatting about their riding adventures and the capabilities of their individual machines. But as relaxed as they appear, I know they're on alert, constantly checking their bikes, watching the precious space and the actions of other riders and admirers.

'There's something about riding a motorbike,' I say. 'Even a little bike like this. You can feel it in the air when you look around this café. Jump on a bike and it's a different world. I'm a different man. I'm not bothered about my past and I'm not worried about my future. It's sheer freedom.'

'It does stop your mind from wandering into dark places,' Robert says.

'It's so exhilarating,' Kath says. 'And totally different from being in a car. When we were going around those bends it felt like half of me was on earth and half of me was in space. What speed were we doing down those long back lanes?'

'I think we hit fifty once or twice,' Robert says.

'No good asking me,' I say. 'My speedo doesn't work. Anybody want a coffee?'

On my way to get the drinks, I stop at a quiet corner away from the main crowd and phone Deb. She doesn't answer and I let it go to the answer machine. I knew she wouldn't answer. She'll still be angry and she has a right to be. I leave a message, trying to sound bouncy but not too happy.

'It's only me. Just wondered if our Gav's got back yet? Let me know if he has. Otherwise, I'll have a good look round for him when I get back. I'm sure he'll be alright. See you later.'

I put my phone away, not too impressed with my message or my tone. But it's as close as I can get to saying what I want to say.

The owner of the café, a silver wispy-haired man about sixty, serves me and I ask him if it's okay to leave a few of my business cards on the counter. He nods and points to a stack of cards next to the sugar bowl.

'That's a nice machine,' he says, picking up one of my cards. 'A BSA Golden Flash.'

'Yes. All my own work.'

'Shame about the spelling mistake. You want to send them back to the printers and get them redone.'

I try to explain the pun but the owner doesn't seem to understand. I leave them on the counter anyway. Maybe it'll be a talking point and lead to plenty of work.

As Robert and Kath take a sip of coffee, I hand them both a card.

'What do you think? Our Gav did them.'

Kath turns the card over and smiles.

'So. You decided to go for Golden Flush Plumbing, after all. I like it. It stands out. And so does your motorbike. It looks immaculate.'

'It is,' Robert says. 'I've seen it. It looks even better in the flesh, I mean metal. Well, you know what I mean.'

'And this is your wee boy, then,' Kath says. 'You can't tell.'

'Hey, what's this?' Robert says, tapping the wording on the card. It says here, Fully Qualified. You're not fully qualified until Garrett decides to sign off your portfolio.'

'I know. I couldn't get all that on.'

For half an hour, sitting together on the wall at the edge of the crowd, the three of us are entertained by the variety of bikes and the buzz of proud owners.

When a group of riders on the next table pull on their waterproofs and ride out of the café, I check the sky. The clouds have thickened and the power of the early evening sun has been reduced to a few weak spokes of sunlight.

'It looks a bit black over there,' I say. 'How about a quick blast while there's still a bit of sun out? Then we can head back.'

Kath picks up her helmet.

'Sounds good to me.'

'If you like,' Robert says, 'we can go the back roads and then over the A1 to Delton. We could call at my farm. That's if you've got time. That would give my mother and dad a shock. They think I haven't got any friends outside of farming. Or inside, for that matter.'

I keep close to Robert through the bends, the blue smokey exhaust fumes from his two-stroke engine getting inside my helmet. The two bikes settle into a steady rhythm and I'm enjoying the freedom of a gently winding country lane when a quad bike bursts out of a hedge from the left in front of the Suzuki like an express train at a level crossing. Robert brakes hard, locking up his rear wheel and I have to swerve around him before coming to a stop a few yards further on. The quad bike, ridden by a young helmetless rider, sends up clouds of dust as it speeds off down the bridleway opposite.

I stand with Kath at the side of the Suzuki, visors up, while Robert checks his back tyre.

'Nice emergency braking Robert,' I say. 'You did well to see him. It could have been nasty.'

'More luck than judgement.'

I knew Robert wouldn't take the compliment even when Kath tapped him on the back and congratulated him on his riding skills.

A rambler with two Nordic walking poles emerges from the track brushing dust off his trousers.

'Did you see that?' the walker says. 'I could have been knocked down.'

'I know,' I say, shaking my head and tutting. 'The young tearaway. He nearly hit us. They're all the same, these bikers.'

'Vehicles are not allowed along a bridleway. They're for the sole benefit of walkers and horses. Is nothing sacred?'

The rambler taps his poles together to dislodge the soil from under the ferrules.

'Well, have a good evening and enjoy a responsible ride.'

He strides out as though he's dragging a sledge and disappears behind the hedgerow on the opposite side of the lane.

'Fancy a bit of off-roading?' Robert says, as we watch the quad bike disappear round a curve a few hundred yards up the track. 'I think you can get to the A1 down there and then cross over to Delton.'

'I'm game,' I say.

'Count me in, boys.'

'I'll take the lead for this stretch if you want, Robert. Just in case you lock your brakes again.'

The suspension on my bike is taking some stick. It compresses and rebounds over the rough ground as it works hard to smooth out the ride. Small loose stones, flung up by the knobbly tyres, rattle under the sump and mudguards. We follow the dust and scars left by the quad bike and after half a mile the track leads into a wood. The regular passage of farm vehicles has flattened the ground and hollowed out the foliage, creating a kind of tunnel. A bank of undergrowth on either side of the track forms the walls, and the branches and leaves form the roof. Only the light reflected off and filtered by a million leaves reaches the bare floor. We ride slowly through the flickering light and the screech of the two engines, enclosed by the dense green foliage, shatters the tranquility of the wood.

The tunnel is short and we soon leave the noise and the shadows behind and ride out into low sunlight and open countryside again. I stop at the side of a closed wooden gate leading off the track to the right and remove my helmet. The gate is secured by a heavy chain and strong padlock, and a sign on a post at the side reads:

KEEP OUT

By order of the Estate

Robert puts his side stand down and takes off his helmet. There's no one around and the noise of the bikes has silenced the birds. I watch Kath lift off her helmet and let her hair down the way Deb used to do when we were out on a ride. I've never known for sure whether Deb ever did like going on the bike with me, or whether she only said she liked it because she knew I liked it. Would I have been so accommodating if the roles had been reversed? Probably not. Is that a good thing or a bad thing? I'm not sure. Maybe I'm too thick to understand or too lazy to find out. All I know is, I bought all the motorbiking gear for both of us and the fun didn't last. I'm glad I kept her helmet.

'They certainly picked the best spots, these landowners,' I say.

Half a mile beyond the gate, cows and horses graze on parkland and two swans float on a lake in front of a manor house. The creatures appear stationary, like toy animals on a toy farm. A crow flies across the skyline, its primaries spreading and lifting as it pushes through the air. Where the low sun catches its plumage, the feathers are as bright as split coal.

'I think my neighbour, Lord Havem is related to the lord who owns this estate,' Robert says.

'They're all related,' I say. 'They all married into money. That's where you've slipped up, Robert. You should have married one of their daughters.'

'I don't have the pedigree or the charm. And anyway, I'm married to my farm. Or should I say I was married to my farm.'

The three of us bask in a pocket of still air where the day's weak sun has been trapped in the shelter of a hedge. Kath pulls her outer fleece over her head, exposing her belly and waist long enough for me to admire the texture and roundness of her pale skin. Robert has noticed her bare flash as well, judging by the embarrassed smile on his face and the way he's averting his eyes.

Kath begins to caress the gold and the lead grey flakes of lichen growing on the top rail of the locked gate. I hadn't even noticed them and her care and attention make me feel clumsy. There's a mound of damp green moss growing alongside the lichen and I rub out a cutting with my finger. I bend down and line up my sight until the little valley of moss I've created becomes a forest on either side of the big house.

'Anybody fancy a walk in the park?' I say.

Kath points to the sign.

'It's private land. I thought in England that meant no trespassing.'

'So what? They took it off us.'

'Gamekeepers have guns,' Robert says. 'If we disturb his pheasants…'

We hang our helmets on the handlebar mirrors and climb over the gate. The mood changes as soon as we get on the other side. I put my hands behind my back as though I own the estate and the three of us amble along the track towards the manor house and lake.

'Rhododendron Ponticum,' Kath says, and she leaves the track. We follow her through the rough grass to a thicket of evergreen bushes dotted with red flowers growing behind the fence at the woodland edge.

'They're not a bit of good for wildlife,' she says.

'The flowers look all right to me,' I say.

'Yes, the magenta flowers are fine. They look lovely but the plant itself kills off everything around it. Nothing grows underneath. Even nearby trees die off eventually because their seeds can't germinate. When the leaves are young, they're full of toxins. Nothing eats them. And when they're established, they're too tough so again nothing eats them. They're a pest. I was always getting jobs to dig them up back in Scotland.'

'I forgot,' Robert says. 'We're in the presence of a member of the green fingered brigade.'

'And you have to spray the ground when you've dug them up, otherwise they come back in no time. Lairds and gamekeepers love them because they provide cover for their game birds.'

I lean over the fence, my hand lightly touching Kath's shoulder, and pull off a flower head. I inspect the magenta bloom, turning it over in my palm, nodding as though I'm an expert on rhododendrons.

'Ah, yes,' I say, 'the very same species. There are loads of these bushes in the park at the back of the town hall. And they're full of game birds taking cover, especially on a Saturday night.'

Kath tries to kick me on my backside but I see it coming and almost manage to catch her foot. Our little dance softens all the pain in my neck, back, knees and ribs.

'I loved that job,' Kath says. 'Out in the fresh air. Working with nature.'

'Why did you leave if you loved it so much?' Robert says.

Kath pushes her fingers through her hair as we rejoin the track.

'The council were always making cutbacks. Every year it was yet another round of redundancies. Always asking you on your appraisal if you were interested in leaving. Because I used to speak my mind and stick up for my work mates, my supervisor decided he would make my life hell and try and get me to leave. And he succeeded.'

'Appraisals?' Robert says. 'Ah. The hectic life in the corporate fast lane. At least with farming you don't have to worry about how other people rate you.'

The low sun is hidden behind black clouds now, tinting them grey at the edges, and the sky appears bigger than ever. I take off my leather jacket and throw it over my shoulder as the three of us stroll along the track side by side. Kath smiles.

'You look happy for a change.'

'Who wouldn't walking round here? It's another world. Now I know what those old pit ponies must have felt like when they let them out into the fields for feast week.'

'It was the same in the old days in Glasgow, according to the stories my mam and dad used to tell me when I was a wee bairn. They said Glasgow used to virtually shut down for two weeks in June every year for Glasgow Fair fortnight. Everybody went off to the coast – to Ayr,

Troon, Dunoon, or Aberdeen and sometimes as far away as Blackpool or Whitley Bay. Or they'd escape for the day on board the Clyde steamer. As you say, it must have felt like being released into the open after being in the dark all year.'

'Didn't they call it going down the watter when they made the journey down the Firth of Clyde?' Robert says.

'That's right. How did you know that?'

'It was on the radio the other day. Beamed through the airwaves to my tractor's onboard entertainment centre.'

'We say watter, as well, down here in Yorkshire,' I say. 'As in, get thissen a drink a' watter lad if tha's gor a thirst on.'

'That sounds more Scottish than English,' Kath says.

'They don't say watter everywhere in Yorkshire,' I say. 'In the posher parts like this estate they'd look at thee gon art.'

We stop where the woodland edge ends. The open parkland is too exposed to risk getting any closer to the big house without being seen, even though the grand building looks deserted.

'Hey, guess what? I'm thinking of having a ride up to Scotland when I've finished the Golden Flash.'

'I hope you're going to give me a call when you come up.'

'Definitely. I got it from up there. It was in bits in a box. It'll be like taking it back home. I know it's totally rebuilt but it's still the same old character, the same old soul.'

'A reincarnation,' Robert says.

The dark entrances leading off into the secluded wood on either side of the track remind me of the times early on in my marriage when I'd be out walking with Deb and we'd disappear into the scrub fringing the muckstack near our house for a quickie. One time a spider crawled across Deb's bare spread thighs as we were lying there in the long grass and she just brushed the thing off and carried on. I couldn't believe it. She's terrified of spiders.

I'm imagining being on my own with Kath, lying in the long grass together, waiting for the spider to appear, when she sees me smiling as though she knows what I'm thinking. Even Robert is smiling to himself. Maybe he's been in the long grass with a maiden.

The harsh scream of an engine interrupts my thoughts. At first it sounds like a chainsaw deep in the wood but as the noise grows louder and a cloud of dust appears above the hedgerow, I know it's the quad bike racing back up the bridleway. Our two little bikes look exposed, parked casually at the side of the locked gate, three helmets hanging over the handlebar mirrors.

The quad bike skids to a halt opposite the bikes and the engine goes dead. I'm about to shout at the rider to keep his hands off when he stands up and hollers at us over the gate.

'What are you three doing down there? Can't you read? You're trespassing on my land.'

'Who's this cocky little bugger?' I say. 'Is he old enough to ride that thing?'

'It could be the gamekeeper,' Robert says. 'I hope he hasn't got his gun with him. He might think we're enemies of game. Act like a pheasant.'

The young rider remains standing, looking at us from his high position, and he doesn't sit down again until we're within a few yards of the gate.

'And furthermore, you're not allowed to bring a vehicle of any description down this path. It's a public bridleway not a green lane.'

Somehow, the young rider doesn't come over as aggressive. It's more an air of entitlement. Knowing his worth. It would have been impossible for a miner to say the same words and not sound threatening. I try to work out how old he is. Sixteen? Seventeen?

'We saw you come down on that thing,' I say, 'so we thought we'd come down as well.'

'We thought it led to the A1,' Robert says.

'We weren't doing any harm,' Kath says. 'We were only admiring the view.'

We climb back over the gate and I pull on my jacket, thrusting my hands out of the sleeves to tighten the leather across my shoulders for effect. I nod towards the parkland, the wood and the manor house.

'Is this all yours, then?'

'It is.'

'Yours or your dad's?'

'This is the family estate.'

'Lucky you.'

'We like to think we keep it in good order.'

I walk around the back of the quad bike like a traffic cop.

'I see you haven't got a licence plate.'

'I don't need a licence to ride on my own land.'

'No. But you need one for the road. Is that why you flew over it back there?'

The rider starts up his quad bike and snicks into first gear.

'Off you go, then. Back up the path where you came from.'

'Hey.' I shout above the noise. 'We're not bloody dogs.'

Kath picks up her helmet.

'It's okay. We're going.'

We watch the young lord-to-be accelerate away and when he disappears into the tunnel through the wood, I zip up my jacket and bang a dead fly out of my helmet.

'I wonder how many applications he had to send off before he got that job?'

'You know what they say,' Kath says. 'Apples always fall in orchards.'

'Come on. We'd better be getting you back to your B&B or else your landlady'll be reporting us to Plumbdeep. Won't she, Robert?'

Robert isn't there. He's slipped away from the gate and he has his mobile phone pressed to his ear. When he comes back, his usual soft smile has gone.

'Are you okay, Robert?' Kath says.

'I need to get back home straightaway. My dad's not well. My mother doesn't know whether he's having a panic attack or a heart attack.'

Kath puts her hand on Robert's arm.

'You get straight off, Robert,' I say. 'I'll take Kath back.'

'I'm sorry about this. This is the best evening out I've had in a long time.'

The light is fading. High up to the west the moon looks down on a band of dark cloud sitting above the low sun. Kath climbs on the pillion seat and I switch on my lights and pull the zip on my jacket tight under my chin. We ride back up the bridleway over cow pats, dried and curled at the edges as thin as roofing felt, and wave goodnight to Robert as he heads east.

Along the undulating country lanes, we ride into drifts of cold air where unlucky moths end their night as yellow slime on my visor and jacket. It begins to rain and the drops hit me like gravel, chilling my bones in seconds. I can feel Kath's arms tighten around my middle.

Outside the B&B, I take off my helmet and the cold air grips my head and tightens my scalp. Kath dances on the spot in an attempt to warm up.

'That was brilliant,' she says, shaking her shoulders and arms. 'You certainly know you're alive when you're on a motorbike at night.'

I stuff Deb's old gloves into the spare helmet and fasten it to the handlebars. Kath's landlady opens the front door and a warm glow turns the lawn amber. The hallway, with its bunch of flowers in a vase on the table and its hat stand heavy with overcoats, is a scene of contentment. It reminds me of when I was a nipper. Playing in the garden at night in the snow with my brothers and sisters. Coming back into the house, hands and feet thawing out, socks for gloves steaming in front of a blazing coal fire and the coal house stocked to the roof with hard-earned fuel.

The landlady's smile is as warm as her house.

'Would you two intrepid travellers like a cup of tea and a piece of cake to warm you up?'

Kath shrugs her shoulders at me and smiles. I smile back and shake my head.

'No, you're all right, thanks, love. I'd better be getting off. It looks like we're in for a storm.'

'Not to worry. Goodnight then.'

The landlady goes in, the lawn darkens, and only a semi-circle of light remains above the door.

'Right, Kath. See you at the training centre tomorrow.'

'Yes. Last couple of days. Are you going to the end of course do tomorrow night?'

'I don't know. I might do. Are you?'

'Definitely.'

I start up the bike and Kath steps away still shivering.

'Thanks for a great ride out, Philip.'

'You'd better go in and get warmed up. See you tomorrow.'

The sound of the exhaust reaches a crescendo at the tip of each gear change as I leave the B&B behind and pick up speed.

I ride out of the city suburbs onto the darker, quieter roads and without Kath's body pressing against me, the cold air quickly chills my unprotected back. Eventually the flat black outline of hedges and trees against the night sky on either side of the road gives way to Brodworth's well-lit streets, buildings, and lines of parked cars.

There's no sign of Gav's car at the front of the house or on the unmade track round the back. I spin the bike round and ride into the estate. The gang of lads drinking cans of beer inside the bus shelter haven't seen anything of Gav. No one at the fish and chip shop has seen him, either. I ask a neighbour out walking his dog near the gable end of our street. He shakes his head and the dog cocks its leg against a bush growing through a crack in the pavement. I give up and tuck the trail bike down the side of the Golden Flash.

Tuesday

1

The sun is still hidden by the muckstack and I'm revising in the garage before setting off to the training centre when I hear a screech of tyres on the shared track. I can hear the idiot's wheels spinning on the loose surface and taste the dust being thrown up as it skids to a halt right outside my damn garage. I snap shut my plumbing manual, yank up the garage door and get ready to give the driver a rollicking. It's our Gav. My anger turns to frustration and I'm about to shake my head when I remember I'm in his debt.

'Where have you been? Your mother's been whittling about you.'

'Here an' there. Dad, that money I lent you on Sunday. Have you still got it?'

'No. I've blown it at the bookies. Of course I've still got it. I'm not paying up until tomorrow.'

'I could do wi' it back.'

'Bloody hell, Gav. That was quick. I've already promised them they'll have it tomorrow. Everything's arranged. You know my portfolio depends on it.'

'Can't you tell 'em you'll pay up later? I should be able to lend you it again in a couple of weeks.'

There's no panic in Gav's voice. He's making it sound as though he's only talking about a few pounds, no big deal. But he can't keep still and whenever a car turns off the main road he freezes until the vehicle passes the entrance to the track and disappears into the estate.

'They'll not let me pay later. They've given me an ultimatum. I either pay up tomorrow or it's goodbye qualification. But anyway, listen. I might not need it. I'm going to see if I can get summat knocked off because the training's been tripe. If I can get five hundred quid knocked off then I'll not have to pay my final instalment and I'll not need your money. I'll be able to give you it all back tomorrow afternoon, every penny of it.'

Gav is staring at something over my shoulder and he looks edgy again. I turn round and see a blue estate car parked at the entrance to the track, its noisy diesel engine ticking over as though the driver is looking for an address. It's only when the car does a u-turn and reveals its taxi licence plate that Gav comes back to me.

'I need it today, Dad. Can't you sell your Golden Flash to that Pete bloke mate of yours at that scrapyard? He said he'd buy it off you.'

'I'm not selling my Flash to nobody. You know I'm already trying to sell my trail bike. Can't you wait until tomorrow? It's only a day.'

Gav curls his top lip and sets off up the garden path. I don't like the way he's acting so I follow him into the house.

Deb is sitting at the kitchen table cutting pictures out of an interior design magazine. She stops mid-cut, scissors agape.

'Oh. You're back then. Where have you been since Sunday? Couldn't you have given me a ring?'

Gav lifts himself up onto the kitchen units and unties and reties the laces on his trainers.

'I've told you not to sit on there, Gavin,' Deb says. 'They're not meant for your weight. Your dad fitted them.'

'Charming,' I say and I sit down opposite Deb and pretend to read the paper.

Gav jumps off the worktop and leans against the sink with his hands in his pockets.

'I had to go an' see somebody about summat.'

'What? Just like that? Nearly midnight and you shoot off. Here one minute, gone the next? Why didn't you tell us where you were going? We've been worried about you.' Deb shakes her head and starts snipping again. 'Two men came round here looking for you yesterday.'

'Mam. All them things you've got in them boxes in the garage. Are they worth much?'

'They are. There's hundreds of pounds' worth of lamps and light fittings in there. And ornaments. Why?'

'They're goin' to get damaged if you're not careful. Now that my dad's sellin' his trail bike there'll be all sorts of weirdos turnin' up to have a look at it, sniffin' around the garage, pikin' at your boxes, wantin' to know what's in 'em.'

I lower the newspaper just enough to weigh up the expression on Gav's face. I know good acting when I see it. Deb continues to snip around a photograph of a flame-effect electric fire, turning the magazine around instead of the scissors to get a neater cut.

'Those boxes had better not get damaged or there'll be big trouble.'

'And another thing. My dad'll be startin' his Golden Flash up before long. He's nearly finished it. There'll be black smoke putherin' out all over t'place.'

Deb and Gav are talking about me as though they've forgotten I'm in the same room. I shake the newspaper and fold back the pages to remind them I'm still there. Deb relaxes her grip on the scissors.

'How come there's all this concern over what's in my cardboard boxes all of a sudden? You've not taken the slightest bit of interest up until now.'

Gav runs his fingers around the top of his T-shirt shirt and stretches the neck.

'I just think they might get damaged that's all if you leave them in t'garage.'

'Where are you going to put them? There's no room in here and I can't take them up to the café yet because they'll be in the way. I'm decorating all this week.'

'I can squeeze 'em in my bedroom. They'll be all right in there until my dad sells his trail bike an' finishes his Golden Flash.'

Deb chuckles as she files her cuttings and puts her coat on ready to go up to the café.

'Your dad'll never finish that Golden Flash. It'll end its days round the back of the garage under that old carpet with that sidecar thing. Anyway, let me think about it. I don't want to move them if I don't have to. They're fragile.'

2

There's been nothing to do at the training centre today. Virtually everybody's finished their assessments and everybody bar me and two or three slowcoaches have had their portfolios signed off by Garrett. Only one more day to go. I'm feeling totally relaxed now. Money in my pocket. Qualification in the bag. I've just got one very important job to do and then it's off to the leaving do.

I trot down to the garage with a purpose. There's no time for tea – I've a kick-start to fit. The two young boys are back again, belting the ball to each other on the shared track, every now and then slicing it into a garage door or into the undergrowth leading to the muckstack. Despite their difference in height, the two boys have a similar kicking style with good back lift and a follow through that my old mate Shinny would envy. Fortunately, the ball is nearly flat and it drags through the air like a seat cushion, otherwise every window in the terrace would be smashed.

The boys lose interest in their game as soon as I lift up the door and they run towards me, side-footing the ball to each other, each pass decreasing in length as they get nearer.

'Now then. What are you two up to today?'

'Nowt,' they say in unison.

I lift the blanket off the Golden Flash and collect the kick-start from the bench.

'What are you doin' on it today?' the short lad says.

I pull a scared face and pretend to bite my fist.

'I'm starting the engine up. For the very first time.'

'What. You're bringin' it to life?'

'I am.'

The boys stare at each other, eyes and mouths wide open.

They put a foot inside the garage, lower their voices and tell me they're both going to build a motorbike when they leave school. I try not to smile. Their whispered words sound like a secret password confirming their allegiance and seeking access to the inner sanctum.

The splines on the welded kick-start mesh with the splines on the gear box shaft and as I tighten the pinch bolt, I say a quiet thank you to Robert. The tall lad giggles and says, 'It'll be like that there Frankenstein bloke. You've put bits of dead bike together an' now you're goin' to bring it to life.'

'Look well if it breaks out of t'garage and starts tearin' up and down t'track,' the short lad says and he starts pacing, heavy booted and stiff-legged, arms straight out in front.

'If it does,' I say, 'just let its tyres down. That'll fox it. Right. You'll have to stand outside now. This could be dangerous.'

They step out of the garage and I make a final quick check over the bike before taking a deep breath.

'Right,' I say to the engine. 'Come on you beauty.'

Tickle the carburettor. Smell the petrol. Feel it chill my finger end. Tentatively push down the kick-start. Feel the piston compress the volatile mixture. Kick. The engine kicks back. Pain shoots through my knee. Try again. Another tickle of the carburettor. This time stand on the kick-start and push down with all my weight.

A sudden explosion of noise. The engine comes to life. Grip the handlebars hard with fear and excitement. Twist the throttle on and off. Hear and feel the motor respond to my wrist. Know the whole terrace will be rattling to the sweet sound.

I'm laughing and crying at the same time, shouting into the noise. Done it. Love Deb. Love Gav. Stuff Jagger. Stuff work. Stuff everything.

The bearings I gently tapped into place after heating the crankcase in the oven while Deb was at her mother's haven't seized. The pistons I carefully scraped and polished for hours at the garage bench haven't smashed through the block. The delicate shell set I fitted to the connecting rods with shaking hands one Sunday morning haven't slipped.

Thirty seconds of life is enough and I shut off the throttle and allow the engine to splutter and cut out. The only sound in the garage is the tick-tick-tick of metal parts expanding and contracting, and for the first time the smell and smoke of the big twin four-stroke fills the air. The two lads stare at me and we shake our fists at each other and shout, 'Yes. Yes.'

The lock on the garage snaps shut first time and I almost skip up the path. The pain from my beating has gone and my feet feel so light I could join the boys in their game of football. I even greet Colin next door as he saws a plank of wood by the back door, pointing out to him what a grand evening it is.

The house is quiet. Deb will be at her mother's and Gav could be anywhere. I scrub the oil from under my fingernails and go upstairs to change into my best clothes. Green shirt, black tie, grey trousers, brown belt, brown checked jacket, black shoes. I can no longer fasten the top button of my shirt and I have to pull my tie tight to hide the gap. My trousers don't reach my waist any more, they're more like hipsters now, and although I'm no dedicated follower of fashion, I know it's not the style to let your trousers gather over your shoes the way mine do. And the jacket? Well, it fits where it touches.

When I stand in front of the hall mirror, I look worn out and poor like one of those labourers digging trenches in the road dressed in their old suits. I hope it's dark when I get to the pub.

The jar at the side of the TV is on my side this time. The six bright pound coins rise to the top and I set off towards the town centre to catch the bus into the city.

The steep grassy footpath is muddy and I have to step from one raised house brick to another, arms out, plotting a dry route past the allotments and the Stute. When I reach the high street, I glance across the road towards Deb's café and I'm sure I see something move behind the big front window. It's seven o'clock. Deb always locks up at five on Tuesdays and goes to her mother's to do some cleaning. Something's not right. I quicken my step and squint to get a clearer view but the reflection from the window makes it difficult to see inside.

Something moves again. There's definitely somebody inside. The café's being burgled. I jog across the road between a gap in the traffic, working out what to do. Go round the back. It'll be those little buggers on the bikes. No. Try the front door first. They could have smashed the lock and gone in there. Even in broad daylight.

I turn the handle slowly and let the door creak off its seal. My heart bangs into my ribcage. I hold my breath.

Somebody's talking. I fling the door wide open and rush in hoping to scare the living daylights out of the intruders. I'm confused. Everything is covered in white sheets and the radio is on. Two young women dressed in pristine white overalls spin round and scream as the door bangs against the wall. One of the women is balancing on a plank of wood between two stepladders and the shock almost causes her to fall off. I'm still trying to work out who they are and what's happening when Deb's head pops up from behind the counter.

'What the hell are you playing at, Phil? Are you trying to give us all a heart attack?'

'It's you. I thought you were up at your mother's. It looked like somebody'd broken in.'

'What, and put Radio Two on?'

There's a groan from behind the counter then a head of short, spikey hair dyed jet black rises slowly at the side of Deb. It's Sheila from the fish and chip shop next door.

'That's hard work, getting up,' Sheila says. 'I haven't been on my knees since my honeymoon. Evening, Phil.'

'Bloody hell,' I say. 'How many more have you got down there? It's like watching Punch and Judy.'

'I'm only staying for an hour,' Sheila says, lighting a cigarette. 'Deb said she could do with a hand. We're having a great time, aren't we girls. It's like being back in the soup kitchen. The women putting the world to rights.'

'Grafting and chatting,' Deb says. 'And loving every minute of it.'

Sheila says, 'I've told my boss he'd better not be docking me any pay or it'll not just be his chipolatas that's going in the fryer tonight.'

My shoulders relax. The café's tables and chairs have been pushed up against the wall and covered with a dust sheet. A paste board has been set up in the middle of the floor, and placed to one side there's a big clear plastic bag stuffed full of the remains of the old woodchip wallpaper from off the ceiling. There isn't a scrap of litter anywhere.

'What are you doing?' I say.

'What's it look like we're doing?' Deb says. 'We're decorating. This is Charlotte and Ella. They're our Gavin's friends.'

'Hello,' Ella says. 'We saw you on Saturday with your Gav when you ran out of diesel.'

Deb chuckles and says, 'Not again?'

'We were with Jason and Ben. In the silver car.'

'I remember you. And I didn't run out of diesel. I had a full can in the back.'

I watch Charlotte regain her confidence on the plank and return to the strip of sky-blue wallpaper she's pasting to the ceiling. Four women. All working hard. I'm outnumbered and in the wrong place. Time to assert my inside knowledge of the building trade.

'I hope you've put plenty of PVA on there first. It'll come off again if you haven't.'

Deb blows dust off the fold of sandpaper she's using to rub down the skirting board.

'Oh,' she says. 'We're an expert now, are we? Too busy to help out but plenty of time to criticize.'

The two girls smile and Ella holds up the container of bonding agent they're using. It's the best brand.

'We've checked the floor upstairs,' Charlotte says, 'and there's no sign of any water getting in through the roof so the ceiling should be okay now.'

I feel like a little boy as I look up at Charlotte working away on the raised plank.

'That's because I've been up on the roof and put some new tiles on.' Now I even sound like a little boy.

'They're on a decorating course at the building college,' Deb says. 'And very capable and polite students they are too.'

Charlotte pastes the new seam and wipes off the excess. She looks satisfied with her work. The two sheets of sky-blue wallpaper match perfectly.

'They're doing a great job, aren't they?' Sheila says. 'I wish they'd come and do my front room. The wallpaper's got that many coats of paint on it, the walls are nearly touching each other.'

'We're going to set up our own business when we've finished the course, aren't we, Charlotte.'

'Yeah. We've done a business plan at college and we think there's enough work out there for us to make a go of it.'

'A landlord we know has already promised us plenty of work,' Ella says. 'He owns flats all over the place.'

I don't like to ask if his name is Jack Jagger by any chance. The two young women are fresh and bubbly and I don't want to say anything that might shake their optimism. I check the dustsheets to see if the young decorators have left a stretch of floor exposed but there isn't a bare square inch. I squint at the ceiling and make a show of inspecting the seams as though I'm an assessor from their course. The joints are virtually invisible.

'Not bad for two lasses.'

'Take no notice of him,' Deb says. 'He thinks he's the only one round here who can do anything right.'

'No. It looks good,' I say. 'I was going to do it but I'd have struggled with my neck.'

I try to look left and right to illustrate my lack of mobility.

Deb says, 'They're going to do the rest of the wallpapering for me and then they're going to show me how to do a professional job of painting.'

I raise my eyebrows, one in jest, one in fear.

'How much are they charging?'

'We don't want anything,' Ella says. 'Gav rang us and asked if we could give his mother a hand because she had so much to do on her own. And it's good practice for us.'

Deb wraps the sandpaper around a block of wood.

'There's plenty more sandpaper if you're looking for something to do. But you might get your shiny shoes mucky.'

My shoes do sparkle a bit more than usual. Trust Deb to notice.

'I can't. We're having the end of course leaving do at a pub in the city. Everybody's going.'

'Don't let us stop you, then,' Deb says. 'I think we'll manage on our own, won't we girls?'

I check my watch as if to convince the decorating team, and myself, of the importance and urgency of my appointment.

'My bus is due any minute.'

'You'd better run off and catch it, then,' Deb says.

Charlotte and Ella wave me goodbye and Sheila blows a ring of smoke my way.

3

There's a live football match on the big TV above the bar when I arrive at the Bull's Head. Twenty or thirty people are gathered under the screen watching the game, singing and shouting, some with their drinks held in the air as though they're the players showing off their trophies to adoring fans high up in the stands. Wherever I look there are lights and mirrors and within the mirrors there are even more lights and mirrors. It takes me a few seconds to work out that the figures sitting in one of the alcoves across the room waving at me are not reflections of reflections but actual people.

Kath is wearing a denim jacket and her hair is undone and loose around her shoulders. Robert looks as though he's borrowed a gamekeeper's tweed jacket. It could have done with a belt round the middle. The man must have been at least three stone heavier than Robert. Young Simon and his little group are standing at the side of the table, all dressed in well-ironed open neck shirts, hair gelled, bottles of lager in hand, looking around the room as though they're planning a robbery.

I wave back but decide not to go straight over in case somebody asks me to join a round. With only enough money in my pocket for three pints and the bus fare home I go to the bar and order my own drink.

The circular bar dominates the centre of the room, its wrap-around mirrors, lit by dozens of tiny spotlights like an actor's dressing room, reflect the backs of the bar staff, multiply the number of glasses and upturned optics, and make the whole room appear twice as exciting. It could have been plucked straight out of a fairground.

There are three young barmaids behind the bar, dressed in short black skirts and white blouses, and a fourth barmaid, older, about my age. She's wearing a low-cut red dress, obviously designed to bring in the punters, and through the mirrors her round backside and confident stance are multiplied a dozen times.

I manage to shout my order to her above the noise of the football crowd and when she begins to fill an angled glass with frothy beer from the pump right in front of me, I have to work hard to keep my eyes off her cleavage and tight red dress. She's enjoying the attention and I decide it'll be good fun to engage in a bit of harmless flirting.

'This bar's a bit grand, love, isn't it?' I say, putting my foot up on the bright brass skirting rail. 'It's like one of those fancy floats you see parading through the streets at a carnival.'

I'm not sure she hears me but she doesn't ask me to repeat myself and I reckon I detect a little smile as she tops up the overflowing glass.

'And you look like four beauty queens,' I say, feeling quite pleased with the chat-up line.

She smiles a tired but soft smile as though I'm the tenth bloke this evening to say those exact same words to her. When she places my drink on the bar she looks straight into my eyes.

'And which one of us would you vote for?'

She's got me in a corner and I laugh.

'You, of course.'

I pick up my pint ready to move off in case she thinks I'm one of those chatty sales reps that hang around the bar looking for a good time while far away from home. The amber liquid looks good under the spotlights and it glows when I stroke the condensation off the glass.

'A beautiful queen and a beautiful pint. If this tastes as good as it looks, me and my class mates could be in here all night.'

The barmaid hands over my change and I'm sure she touches my hand on purpose.

'Class mates?' she says. 'Are you at a college or something?'

'You could say that. We've just finished an eight-week training course. We're all qualified plumbers now, out celebrating. There could be twenty of us if everybody turns up.'

'Plumbers? What a coincidence. I've been going to call one out for weeks.'

I take a drink, eyes wide open, looking over the top of my pint, waiting for the punchline. The barmaid serves the next customer, only smiling at him at the last second before returning my stare. She leans on the counter and I get the full frontal.

'The automatic flushing in the gents' urinal isn't working properly. My husband's had a play around with it but he's not technically minded. He's had the lid off and shone a torch inside but he said he couldn't find anything wrong. He said the mechanism looked like a pig's trotter to him and he was frightened of touching it.'

I shake my head at the lack of gumption of some people, and watch the barmaid ask one of her young colleagues to serve the next customer.

'A pig's trotter?' I say. 'That's a good one.'

'I told you he wasn't technical.'

'It'll be the bi-valve. It's got two little plastic lever things on it sticking out.' I'm trying to impress her but I can't for the life of me remember the name of the levers. 'It'll just want adjusting. If you've got a pair of steps and an adjustable spanner handy, I'll do it for you now if you want. I'm cheap. A pint of beer to you.'

I ignore the nudging and stares from the crowd and carry the light aluminium steps over to my table and wave the adjustable spanner at my fellow plumbers.

'I've only been talking to that barmaid for five minutes and she's given me a plumbing job. A lucky omen or what?'

Young Simon lifts up his bottle and holds it an inch from his lips.

'I wouldn't mind her giving me a job, neither. Hand job or blow job. I'm not choosy.'

He swallows his lager in one go and bangs the bottle down on the table as though he's just set a new gulp speed record.

Kath says, 'She looks like she's been around the block a few times, Simon. She'd eat you alive.'

Young Simon wipes his lips and grins.

'I'd let her. What a way to go.'

The gents are empty and I climb the stepladders and as I'm checking the cistern above the urinals, the door swings open and the sound of the pub enters the little room. A man my age wearing an earring and a patterned waistcoat comes in and without saying a word unzips his pants and starts pissing at the side of the stepladders. His head is an inch away from my knee and after a few seconds he looks up at me with a glassy, slightly curious expression on his face.

'It's no good stashing your crack up there, pal,' he says. 'That's the first place the coppers will check.'

From my lofty position on the steps, I can't tell whether the man is trying to be helpful in a dull sort of way or trying to be funny. Either way, he seems harmless so I play the same game.

'I'm not stashing anything, mate. I'm trying to find out where they've hidden the soap. There's never any in these places.'

The man pulls up his zip and as he goes out, I see him take a sneaky look at the soap dispenser above the basins.

A few inches below the surface of the water, my fingers find the bi-valve. It feels a bit slimy and I have to admit I can see how a non-technical person could mistake it for a lump of flesh and bone. When I try to attach the adjustable spanner, the jaws slip and the bi-valve breaks off. Or what I think is the bi-valve. It turns out to be a pig's trotter after all. The flesh has a waxy, soapy texture and must have been rotting in the water for weeks. I clear the blockage, confess to the barmaid that her husband isn't as clueless as we both thought, and claim my free pint of beer.

When I relay the story, Kath and Robert laugh at my fallen pride and we drink a toast to technical prowess.

More students arrive, some on their own looking lost, others in pairs and small groups, and by half past eight almost the whole class is here. Empty pint glasses and beer bottles begin to stack up on our table. There are a few empty whiskey glasses as well, all downed by Robert who has been buying himself chasers in between rounds, intent on getting drunk on the last night. He's staring into his pint pot, eyes tired and watery, his face flushed by alcohol.

'I thought I'd be full of optimism when I'd finished this plumbing course,' he says. 'But I don't feel any different.'

He pours the beer down his throat and then plays with his empty glass, turning it round and round, trying to keep it in the centre of his circular beer mat.

'You'll be right,' I say. 'We'll all be all right. It's only work. Hey, by the way, Robert. That kick-start you welded for me fits perfect. I put it on this afternoon and kicked the bike up. Two kicks and it was away. You ought to have heard it. It was unbelievable. I thought the garage was going to explode.'

'At least I've done one thing right.'

'Well done, you,' Kath says and she strokes Robert's shoulder.

There's a roar from the crowd watching the football match and I jump up to see who's scored. The camera follows the ecstasy and the agony of the two sets of supporters, the noisy scene replicated in the crowd beneath the TV and reflected all around the room in the spot-lit mirrors. When I sit back down, the table's gone quiet.

'Hey up,' I say. 'Come on. It's supposed to be the last night, not the last supper. Cheer up. Here's to the future, whatever it might bring.'

Robert stands up to collect the empty glasses and he has to grab the table to keep his balance.

'It'shmy turn,' he says. 'Does everybody want the shame?'

Young Simon and his mates have formed a separate round and they shake their heads.

I put my hand over my free pint.

'Not for me. I'll skip this one.'

I'm tempted to have another pint but I can't afford to get into a round. If I stop now, I'm square with everybody. I'm no sponger. I've no time for spongers, those crafty drinkers who never buy the first round and never refuse a drink on the last round. It's like letting somebody put their hand in your pocket and take a fiver out, time after time. But I'm not a penny-pincher, neither. Shaking my purse and counting my change at the bar. I'd always buy my mates a pint if they were short that week. And they would always buy me one if I was hard up. That's the rule. It has to be. Otherwise, nobody would ever go out.

When ex-baker Paul Griffiths, sitting between me and Kath gets up and joins Young Simon's group, Kath moves closer until our legs are touching.

'Good evening, Philip.'

'And good evening to you, too, Kath. You look very nice tonight. Very nice. I bet you didn't get that dress off your landlady.'

'No, I didn't. I brought it down with me from Scotland on Monday especially for tonight. You look good, as well. Just as handsome as you do in your motorbike gear.'

'Not as comfortable, though. I feel like one of them PG Tips boardroom chimpanzees in this get up.'

I'd already loosened my tie in the toilet and now I take it off and stuff it into my pocket.

'That's better. I can breathe again.'

'I thought you were going to spend the whole night with that barmaid. I think she fancies you.'

Kath's observation takes a few years off me. I hope the barmaid fancies me. A little bit of flirting doesn't do any harm, does it? But maybe Kath is having me on, flattering me. Either way, it makes me feel good.

'I was just having a bit of fun with her, that's all. She knows exactly what's she's doing. She's completely in charge.'

I want Kath to respond. Find out her thoughts about me teasing the barmaid. Is she a touch jealous? I'd be a touch jealous if Kath had just spent five minutes talking to a good-looking barman. But she changes the subject.

'Robert doesn't sound too good, does he? I'm a bit worried about him. Is he all right?'

'He's had too much to drink, that's all.'

'No. I mean about leaving his farm.'

'He'll be right once he moves out. He'll have to be. I just hope he doesn't take his guns with him.'

Kath won't lighten up. I'm not dismissing Robert but come on, it's the last night.

'I wonder what he's going to do,' Kath says.

I give up and take a drink to flush away my levity.

'I think he's looking for somewhere to rent,' I say. 'He told me one of his relatives said they can stay with them for a while until they find somewhere permanent. It's in a block of flats in Leeds somewhere.'

'That's going to be a big change for them all.'

'He was hoping to stay on at his farm for a bit but it all depends on who buys it.'

Despite not wanting to add to Kath's concerns about Robert, I can't help telling her about the things I overheard in the hotel loft.

'There's something fishy going on by the looks of it. I'm sure it was Robert's farm they were talking about. If it's the developer I'm thinking of, he's a right bastard. He'll want Robert out quick-smart.'

Kath's face changes from caring to a mixture of anger and sadness. Well done, Steeley. Big mouth.

The crowd beneath the TV roars and fans jump and hug one another. Somebody must have scored. I've no idea who. I've lost interest in the game.

'That's happened a lot in Scotland,' Kath says. 'The developer will convert the old buildings into a designer home or build expensive holiday lets or something similar. It's wrong. The land should be farmed for the benefit of everyone. Or the council should keep it and build affordable housing for local people such as Robert and his mam and dad. It shouldn't be there to profit one individual.'

I sit back startled at how quickly the conversation has gone from me chatting up the barmaid to Kath sorting out the world.

'Listen to Kath Marx here.'

'It's true. We all just sit back and let it happen. We should be marching on the streets against things like that. Anyway, don't get me started.'

Kath takes a drink of beer and changes the subject again.

'I really enjoyed that bike ride yesterday.'

'I did, as well. It was a breath of fresh air. And I enjoyed the little stroll we had down that footpath to that wood. It reminded me of my courting days.'

'It was a pity the wee laird on his quad bike turned up. I could have stayed in those woods all night.'

I try to stop myself thinking about what might have happened if Robert had got the call to go home half an hour earlier, leaving me and Kath on our own near the wood. I'd got closer to Kath than I intended. Did she know? Did she feel the same? How easy it would have been to cheat on Deb without really thinking about the consequences. It would have been the first time.

So close. Too close. What the hell was I playing at? When my mates talk about cheating on their wives, not quite bragging but definitely egos swollen, I wonder what's the point in them getting married. And what about the wives? For all I know Deb could be cheating on me? What would I do if she told me she'd been with somebody else? I feel slightly scared at the thought. I hope Kath can't read my face. This is all getting a bit too deep for a leaving do.

'You're a cool cat, Kath. Nothing seems to bother you. You don't let anybody tell you what to do, you don't follow anybody, you always come top in theory, you can solder better than any of us, and you drink pints.'

There's another roar as the final whistle sounds and the crowd worshipping the TV begins to break up. Robert returns from the bar with the drinks.

'Are you sure you don't want a drink, Phil?'

The spell is broken and I can no longer feel Kath's leg against mine.

'No. I'm fine, Robert.'

I sip what's left of my warm beer, making it last. Everyone else has a good swig of fresh beer and Young Simon's sub group down whatever is in their dark bottles in one go.

'We're off to the Clickers nightclub,' Young Simon says. 'We've heard it gets full of talent on Tuesday nights. Fancy it?'

The loose change for the bus ride home feels sharp and uncomfortable in my pocket.

'Not for me. I've got to catch the last bus.'

'Come on, you old goat. It's the last night. Let's go clubbing and find a bit of life.'

Robert lifts up his swaying head.

'A bit of flife? A bit of flife? More like a bitter life. Time for a taxi home to my pigs and strife.'

Kath helps me lift Robert up, nudging him upright and forward. As we go out through the main door, I exchange looks and smiles with the barmaid.

A few yards from the taxi rank Robert pulls away from me and Kath and throws up under the railway bridge. Kath steps out of the way but my feet aren't quick enough. Robert says he feels better and by the time we get him to the taxi rank he's fit enough to tell the driver where he lives.

There is a short queue outside the Clickers, mainly tanned young lasses in short dresses, no coats, arms folded tight, keen to get out of the chilly night air. I nod to the two bouncers but they ignore me and stand as planted as a pair of anvils.

'Right then, Kath. Have a good night.'

'I will. You're sure you're not coming in?'

'No. I'll get off,' I say, looking down at my ruined shoes half hidden under my sloppy trousers. 'I don't want to be the oldest swinger in town.'

Under the neon light of the nightclub sign, Kath's hair looks as bronze as the buttons on her denim jacket. I want to lean over and kiss her goodnight but I hesitate and it's too late.

'See you tomorrow, then,' Kath says.

The two bouncers part like gentlemen to let her in. They seem friendly enough until they close up again, legs apart, hands in front of their groins, humourless immobile lumps of iron again.

As I turn to go, a small gang approaches the club door led by a purposeful Young Simon, his chest puffed out, eyes staring straight ahead, jaw jutting as though he's the leader of a hunting pack.

'Have you decided to come in after all?' Young Simon says. 'I thought it was past your bedtime.'

'No, I can't,' I say, winking. 'I've some business on.'

Young Simon narrows his eyes.

'You're going back to the Bull's Head, aren't you? To that barmaid and her big knockers, you black prince.'

I sniff the crisp air and tap my nose.

'That's for me to know and you to find out. Always cover your tracks.'

Young Simon rubs his hands.

'I'm hoping there's plenty of young minge in this place. If not, it could be Kath's lucky night.'

I spend most of the time on the bus staring out of the upstairs steamy window thinking about Kath and the bike ride in the woods. It's only when I step out of my clothes and slip into bed with my back to Deb that I think about the five hundred pounds I hid behind the gas meter in the cellar and why Gav suddenly asked for it back.

Deb is quiet. Too quiet.

'Have you had a good night, then?' she says.

I pull the blankets over my ears.

'Not bad. The pub was all right. They've all gone to a night club.'

'Did you meet up with your pillion passenger at this do, then?'

I raise my head off the pillow to hear better. The curtains are open and the street lights give the wardrobe a silver sheen.

'What are you on about?'

'Her you were with at that bikers' café yesterday. You're not the only one with a motorbike round here, you know.'

The mattress moves and I know Deb is sitting up, staring at the back of my head. I half turn.

'That's Kath. I told you about her. We were with Robert.'

'Was she there with you tonight, as well?'

'Of course she was there. It was the leaving do. Everybody was there.'

'Well you're playing with fire, Phil, because I'm telling you, if ever you start messing about with somebody else, that's it, we've done.'

I want to spin round and show how offended I am but my tender ribs and stiff neck slow me down and weaken the effect.

'I'm not messing about with somebody else. Jesus. She's on my course. She's a classmate, that's all.'

'So, you've been seeing her for two months, then? How many more times have you been out with her?'

I sit up and laugh.

'You're paranoid, woman. And anyway, what about you making eyes at Robert when he came round to the garage to look at my bike? Calling him a hunk. It's okay for you to have a bit of fun but not me.'

Deb turns away and as she digs her shoulder into the pillow, she yanks the blankets away from me.

'I can't believe you're accusing me. I've told you. She's a classmate, that's all. She's like one of the lads. She makes me laugh. She doesn't criticize me and she listens.'

Deb spins round.

'I listen to you. I'm fed up of listening to you. But it's all one way. You want to try doing a bit of listening yourself.'

'I've done nothing wrong. I wish I bloody well had. I might be feeling a lot better tonight if I had. Sweet chuffing dreams.'

Wednesday

1

I'm in a line of rush hour traffic on my way to the training centre for the last time and I can't stop thinking about how agitated Gav was when he asked for his money back. Why the urgency? After just two days? He must have been exaggerating, the lad. He's always exaggerating. Just like his mother.

A few miles further on I pull into a lay-by, take the money out of my pocket and slowly flick through the roll of twenty-pound notes. Whichever way I count, the amount remains the same, as does my guilt.

I ring Gav's mobile. No answer. I ring home. No answer there either. When I look in the rear-view mirror at the dark bags under my eyes, my face transforms into Gav's worried expression. I've just enough time and diesel to return home and ask Gav once again why the urgency and this time listen to what he's not saying. Indicator on, wheels ready to make a u-turn, no gap in the traffic. Then a possible opening. I rev the engine ready to cut across the busy road but a motorbike pulls out to overtake a slow lorry taking up the free space I need to get out. My shoulders slump and I take a long, slow look left and right. Still no way out. Blank faces behind protective glass avoiding my eyes. Traffic coming down the hill like an endless train. I abandon the plan, switch indicators and when a car finally flashes to let me out, I continue my journey to the training centre.

Peggs is standing in the centre of a circle of tool bags, ripping new tools out of their packaging and lobbing them one by one into the bags as though he's playing a game at a fair. He's so engrossed he doesn't hear me enter the workshop.

'There's a lot of tool kits there, Peggs.' I say, my voice echoing in the empty workshop.

'Bloody hell, Phil. I nearly shat myself then.'

'How many have you got coming in this time?'

'Twenty-five. They've upped the numbers again. It'll be total chaos next week.'

It feels strange looking around the empty workshop and the lifeless bays. All those practical tasks and assessments we sweated over during the last eight weeks. All gone. Decommissioned. Guillotined. Just short bits of twisted copper pipe dumped in the scrap bin.

Peggs nods at the portfolio under my arm.

'Have you finally managed to pay up then and get it signed off?'

'No. Not yet. I'm going to see the MD in a minute. I've got the money on me but I'm going to try and get something knocked off first. You know my opinion of this place.'

'You want to threaten to write to Trading Standards. Some of the students on previous courses did that when they weren't happy with the training,' Peggs says, and he flings a hammer towards a tool bag but it spirals off course, taking a chunk of plaster out of the wall. 'It seemed to work for them.'

'I'm all right threatening to write to Trading Standards,' I say. 'I've never written a letter in my life. I wouldn't know where to start.'

'Use scrap.'

I retrieve the stray hammer and drop it into the intended bag.

'What are you on about, use scrap?'

'SCRAP. Situation. Complication. Resolution. Action. Polite. I saw it on a video once. I always use it when I want to complain about something.'

I'm no wiser. I suspect Peggs is making it up but I let him go on.

'S is for Situation – I've just finished one of your courses.

C is for Complication – It's shite.

R is for Resolution – You need to reduce the price.

A is for Action – I want a refund of x hundred pounds.

P is for Polite – Please.

And tell them you're sending a copy to Trading Standards.'

This is typical Peggs. Uncomplicated, make it fit, use it for everything – the silicone sealant of letter writing.

'I'll see,' I say. 'By the way, you know that last assessment I did?'

'The one Garretty pulled to pieces?'

'Yeah, that one. Do you think he sabotaged it?'

'I wouldn't put it past him. He's done it before. He did it to a lad who came in here on prison release last year. He made him look that big,' Peggs holds his palm at knee height, 'just because he knew he wouldn't dare argue back and risk being taken off the course by the probation officer. And he did the same to a bloke from Hull. He was unemployed and the social services were paying for his course. He was a big bloke, six foot three and more, but Garretty reduced him to tears. Same thing. He knew he wouldn't dare argue back. He came in here like this, and he went out like that.' Peggs pulls his shoulders back and stands upright then slumps forward, round-shouldered to illustrate the student's dramatic change in self-esteem. 'He failed both of them. Anyway, he's here now. Why don't you ask him?'

Through the window I see Garrett's car pull up and park next to my van.

'If he comes in here, Peggs, you go for a walk.'

As Garrett approaches the open roller shutter door, he starts singing his favourite song, Fly Me To The Moon, deliberately off-key. He strolls into the workshop, hands behind his back, inspecting the condition of the stripped bays, pretending to be unaware I'm there even though I'm leaning against a bench in full view. When he gets closer, he steps back in mock surprise.

'Mister Steele? What are you doing here?'

I take the roll of notes out of my pocket and watch it expand in the palm of my hand.

'I've come to get my portfolio signed off. I told you I had the money.'

Garrett comes within a few yards, hands in pockets.

'I knew you had it. I never doubted it. I told you you'd get there in the end as long as you listened to what I was telling you. You thought I was getting on to you, didn't you? But I kept you on your toes.'

Garrett's grin doesn't soften my face.

'You did that all right.'

Garrett takes a step forward and holds his hand out.

'No hard feelings.'

I slip the money back into my pocket and grip Garrett's hand. And squeeze.

'Steady on. You're crushing my bloody hand.'

'If I thought you'd sabotaged my last assessment I'd be squeezing your bollocks right now, never mind your hand.'

'What are you talking about, sabotaging your assessment? Let go, you're breaking my fingers. I never sabotaged your assessment.'

Garrett tries to unlock my hand and I squeeze one last time before letting go.

'You're bloody mad, man,' he says, rubbing his fingers. 'You've nearly crushed my hand.'

'I'm not mad, I'm calm. If I was mad, you'd know about it.'

'Everything I did was done to make sure you all got through your assessments. I pushed you all the way because I wanted you all to have the best training there is. Standards and quality. That's all I was ever concerned about. You might not have appreciated it at the time but that's why I kept pushing you.'

My own hand is throbbing but I hide the pain.

'I didn't appreciate it at the time and I don't appreciate it now.'

Garrett goes up to his office above the toilets, flexing his fingers, inspecting them for damage. He's not singing now.

The blinds in the MD's office are down and his car is parked in its private space in front of his office.

'Is he in?' I mime through the glass partition in reception and Hazel mimes back, 'Yes. He's free.'

'I wish he was,' I say to myself and stand tall and knock on his door.

'Come.'

As I grab the door handle, my mobile phone rings. I glance at the screen. It's Deb. I switch it off.

The MD looks up from his computer screen and smiles at me without letting go of the mouse.

'Hello, Phil. You can pay the girls in reception. They're expecting you.'

I stay silent, passing my portfolio from one hand to the other, shifting my weight like a schoolkid in the headmaster's office waiting to be caned.

'Is everything all right?' the MD says.

'I want some money back.'

The MD lets go of the mouse, slowly spins his chair round to face me and put's his hands behind his head.

'And why's that?'

I try not to focus on the damp armpits of his blue shirt.

'I don't think this course is what you say it is on your website. I think you should knock us some money off.'

'Us? Who is us?'

Here we go. Divide and rule, like Thatcher did.

The MD's parry makes me look away.

'Me and a few others.'

'Look,' the MD says bringing his hands down from behind his head and crossing his arms. 'I've heard you've been complaining about the course. No one else has complained to me.'

A panel of red lights blink on the big massaging chair in the corner of the room.

'Only because they don't want to cause any trouble. We've been ripped off. We're supposed to have one trainer for every four students. That's a joke. Most of the time there's only Peggs around. And Garretty only comes in when he wants to bollock somebody.'

I hear myself speaking and I know, standing there alone on the MD's territory, how weak my arguments sound. I try to remember the pointed criticism Kath and the others made and I wish they were here now to help me out.

'Some days you can't find anybody anywhere when you want some help. All you get is, "Read your text books. Look at your computer." That's not right. I've not paid all this money for that.'

The front cover of my portfolio is sticky with sweat and my knuckles are white.

'I want some money knocking off.'

The MD rocks his chair back and forth. The mechanism still squeaks like a mouse every time he moves.

'Anything else?'

'It says on your website half past eight till five. We don't start till nine – half past ten on Mondays, and we finish at four every day. And on Fridays you send us home at two. It's ridiculous for the amount of money we've paid.'

I check the green carpet tiles again. They've not been glued down properly and as a result they're starting to curl up at the edges.

'It's nothing like what it says in your brochure or on your website.'

'Look. I know you've struggled to pay the final instalment. Is that what all this is about? You can't afford the final five hundred pounds and now you're trying to get the cost reduced?'

'Is it hell. I've got the money on me now.'

I flash the notes at the MD to prove I'm not lying. I can feel my face burning.

'It's a rip off. I could take you to Trading Standards for this.'

The MD pushes himself up off his chair, opens a gap in the blinds and surveys the near-empty car park.

'Let me tell you something.'

I'm wondering if he's going to talk to the window the whole time but after a few seconds he turns round.

'With every business I've set up, and I've done everything from IT to selling cars, I've taken risks and borrowed thousands of pounds.'

I can't prevent a little sneer developing on my face. Peggs told me that all the money to open the training centre came from the MD's mother. She's loaded, Peggs said.

'When I opened this training centre and the Health and Safety people came around and threatened to close me down unless I did XYZ, I didn't complain. I made the changes. When the price of copper almost doubled overnight, I didn't complain. I factored it in. When the government changed the rules on training grants, I didn't complain. I worked around it. I made things happen.'

Now I'm wondering if the MD is wearing a Superman vest under his sweaty blue shirt.

'I'm not on about running a business.'

'Let me finish. We offer far better value for money than any of the colleges in this area and better value than any of our local competitors in the private sector. Everything is accredited and monitored. Hundreds of students have successfully attended this training centre and every single one of them has left with a recognized qualification, a comprehensive set of reference manuals and a fully equipped tool kit, including overalls. Everything they could ever want to set up a successful plumbing business. We've received dozens and dozens of complimentary letters and emails.

'Here. This is just a selection,' the MD says and he brings out a file of correspondence from his drawer and fans out the letters like a magician with a set of cards. I try to read the upside-down writing but the MD closes the fan and files the lot away again. 'No one else has ever complained.'

I'm being made to look a fool by a fancy dribble of words. If this was a football match, I'd hit the MD hard with a tackle – man and ball.

'That's not what I've heard,' I say. 'I've heard you've had complaints on other courses about the same things that I'm on about.'

'Look. Take me to Trading Standards. Produce your evidence, and I'll tell them my side of the story. I know who they'll believe.'

'Don't worry, I'm going to. I'll tell them everything. It's daylight robbery.'

'I can't help you any further.'

The MD offers up the palms of his hands as if to show me he's on my side.

'Look. You're almost there. You've completed your training, you've passed all your assessments, and your portfolio is ready to be signed off. I don't want to have to make a report to the examining body but if you don't pay your final instalment today then you leave me with no other option.'

The MD sits down and taps his thighs as though I'm a pet dog and he wants me to jump up onto his lap.

'Come on, Phil. Make the payment and let's get your portfolio signed off. Then you'll be qualified and you can go out there and grab your share of the market. There's good money to be had.'

'How am I going to make a living after this? I can't even solder or bend pipe. None of us can.'

The money in my pocket presses against my leg. I stare out of the window to give myself time to think. If I pay up now, manage to get a few good plumbing jobs, then with any luck I'll be able to pay Gav back in a couple of months.

On the other hand, if I walk away and give up on my qualification until I can afford it, then I'll be able to give Gav his money back this afternoon. But how is walking away without a qualification going to help Gav find a job? It'd be the end of Steele and Son Plumbing before it had even got off the ground.

The MD starts tidying his desk as though he's preparing to leave the office. My neck is now as hot as my cheeks. The more I think, the more agitated I get. What if Gav really has got himself into some kind of trouble – big trouble? Bloody hell, Gav.

I wedge the portfolio under my arm and hold it as tight as I can against my sore ribs as though it's the most precious thing I own.

'I'm not paying up.'

The MD sighs and shrugs.

'It's your choice.'

2

Outside the reception office I'm still shaking and just about to go upstairs to the classroom to say goodbye to Kath and whoever's still hanging around when I remember to ring Deb.

'It's me, Deb. What's up?'

'Thank God you've answered. Those two blokes have come back to see our Gavin. They're with him now outside the garage.'

'Which two blokes?'

'Them that came to the house looking for him on Monday. I told you about them.'

'What are they doing?'

'I don't know. He rang me at the café and he sounded worried so I came straight home. I've been out to see if he's all right. He said he was but he was shaking and I've never seen him look so pale. I asked them what they were up to but they just ignored me.'

'Are they still there?'

'Yes. One of them's been driving our Gavin's car up and down the track.'

'Keep out of their way. I'm setting off from the training centre now. I'll be half an hour.'

I climb as fast as I can up the stairs to the classroom and find the last few remaining students clustered around a desk, chatting quietly about the prospect of finding work. I have to blink twice when I see Robert sitting next to Kath.

'I didn't think we'd see you in here this morning,' I say. 'You were in a right tacking last night.'

The blood must not be flowing to Robert's pale face because for once he doesn't blush.

'So I gather. Kath tells me I owe you a new pair of shoes.'

'Yes, you bugger. I nearly got thrown off the bus last night because of you. I smelt like a dog.'

Robert shuts his eyes and rests his head in his hands.

'Would you mind taking Kath to the train station?' he says. 'I think I'm going to be sick.'

Kath's tea cup is full and steaming. I could do without any delays.

'No, of course not. But we need to get off, Kath. I've got something of a mini crisis on back home.'

'No problem. I'm ready to go.'

'Have you got everything?'

'Aye.'

Kath lifts her rucksack onto her lap and pats the sides.

'Portfolio, hoover, ironing board, stilettos.'

I shake Robert's cold, damp hand and tell him if he ever intends to drown his sorrows again to make sure he gets rid of his guns first. Kath elbows me in my sore ribs and tells me to behave.

The van's a tip. There are empty pizza boxes and screwed up sandwich bags on the passenger seat and I scoop them up and throw them in the back.

'You ought to have kept your overalls on,' I say. 'It's a bit grotty in here. I've not had the chance to clean it.'

As we leave the car park, Kath tells me in a calm, unhurried voice to hang on a second to let an approaching car come past. I ignore her and pull out, my tyres screeching and my tools sliding along the van floor and crashing into the back doors. The station is only a mile and a half away and if the lights are on my side, I can be there in ten minutes.

'Well,' I say, trying to sound as though I have all the time in the world. 'How did it go last night at that Clickers nightclub?'

'It was a belter, Philip. They played some fantastic dance music.'

'Did many of our lot get in?'

'Aye. You couldn't move for them by twelve o'clock.'

There's only one person I want to know about and I don't have to wait long to find out.

'Young Simon's a character,' Kath says.

My smile is so forced, my mouth hurts. 'What do you mean?'

'He's a persistent wee laddie. He kept going on and on, all night long about a log cabin his parents own near Ben Nevis. He says he might be coming up next month to spend a few days there and if he does, he'll give me a ring and show me the place.'

Ben bloody Nevis, I say to myself, trying hard not to let my thoughts shape my face. It'll be the only place in Scotland he's heard of. I caught him telling the same story to a woman from Wales in the Bull's Head last night, only then the cabin was near Snowdon.

I'm just about to tell Kath but there's no need.

'He's a romancer,' she says. 'It's probably the only place in Scotland he's heard of. But I like him. We had a really good night.'

'I'm glad,' I say, at the same time thinking Young Simon's only a year or two older than our Gav. Miles too young for you, Kath.

The car in front drops down to fifteen miles an hour as we approach the second set of lights, even though they're at green. The driver looks to be in his seventies and just my luck, he's wearing a flat cap.

'Come on, bloody hell. Keep going.'

I nearly run into the car as it slowly turns off and I lean forward to ease my tense neck and cool my damp back.

'Have you got much on when you get back up to Scotland?'

'I've enough work to tide me over. Quite a few of my relations have been saving up jobs for me, ready for when I finished my training course. My cousin has went and bought a full bathroom suite ready for me to install. I'm hoping it'll see me through the first few weeks. How about you?'

'Oh, I'll be okay, once I've saved up enough money to get my portfolio signed off. If our Gav doesn't want to join me, I can always team up with a mate of mine called Barry. He's a top plumber. He's pulled out with work and he said I could give him a hand on a permanent basis if I wanted.' I surprise myself at how easily I lie to Kath about Barry and the prospect of work. Maybe it's because in my dreams everything works out fine. Who knows? 'Or I might give Robert a ring and team up with him. We've talked about it.'

'You seem to get on well with Robert. He's a lovely man. Did you know each other before you came to Plumbdeep?'

'No. I don't think I've ever talked to a farmer in my life until I met Robert on the course. Miners and farmers don't normally mix. They supported us during the strike, spuds and veg and all that, but I can't ever remember seeing one in person, never mind talking to one. They all keep themselves to themselves. But I like Robert. We get on okay.'

At last, we get through the final set of traffic lights. The train station is straight ahead.

'Are you out tonight, then, Kath? On the town?'

'Aye. I'm meeting up with my friends later. We'll be off down the city for a few drinks to celebrate me getting my qualification. Are you doing anything special?'

'I'll be out on the town with the lads. Can't wait.'

Another little lie. I know I'll be polishing my bike, under the fluorescent light, on my own.

'Here we are then.'

The drop-off zone is empty and I leave the engine running. A taxi pulls up right behind and a man carrying a briefcase gets out.

'It's been great having the little chats, Kath. It's helped a lot with our Gav and all that.'

My throat tightens. I can't believe it. What the hell's wrong with me?

Kath gathers the straps on her rucksack.

'I've really enjoyed it, as well. And I'll never forget that ride out we did with Robert.'

'Yeah, it was a good laugh.'

The taxi behind has been ticking over since dropping its passenger off and through the rear-view mirror I see the driver lean forward, arms resting on the steering wheel, letting us know he's getting fed up of waiting.

'When I get up to Scotland on the Flash, I'll give you a call if you like. Have a ride round those hills up there. See if we can find some more woods to ride through.'

The taxi beeps. Kath opens her door.

'I'd love that.'

I lean over and we kiss and instead of feeling good, I feel sad. Kath picks up her rucksack and I watch her disappear into the station. I hold my hand up and thank the taxi driver for his patience. I'm in the wrong and I know it.

3

Vehicles aren't allowed to turn right coming out of the station but there are no cop cars around so I ignore the warning sign and cut in front of a van forcing it to veer and stop across my path. The driver blasts his horn and puts two fingers up. I'm flat out down the dual carriageway, undertaking a lorry before swooping back to the outside lane to race past a line of vehicles. One of the cars in the line indicates and begins to pull out but the driver swerves back when I accelerate into the tight space. At a set of traffic lights, amber turns to red. I dash through, straining my stiff neck to check left and right. Opposite a bus stop, a double-decker sets off towards me as I overtake an articulated lorry. The passengers stare as I pass within inches of the window and through my mirrors, I see them turn their heads and follow the van's progress. When I get to my junction, I brake hard and turn onto the shared track without indicating, the van shaking and bouncing before skidding to a halt a foot off the back garden fence.

The garage is locked. The padlock is in place. I put my ear to the door. No sound. Everything looks normal. Washing on the line. Banging from next door's shed. Then the kitchen door opens and Gav comes sauntering down the path, hands in pockets, looking around the garden as though he's wondering whether the grass could do with a cut.

'What's going on, Gav? Are you all right, lad?'

Gav doesn't look up.

'I'm fine, Dad.'

'Where's these two blokes that's been pestering you?'

'They've just gone. It's all sorted.'

Deb comes down the path, rubbing her hands down the front of her apron.

'Have you seen what they've done to him? Show him Gavin.'

Gav raises his head. There is a gash above his eye leaking a thin line of fresh blood and his cheekbone is blue and swollen. I lift his chin up.

'How's that happened?'

Gav pulls away when I try to touch his eyebrow.

'It's somebody I know. They were just messing about that's all. But it's done now. They said I owed them some money but I've sorted it.'

Deb tries to dab the blood with a tissue.

'I've told him it wants stitching but he'll not go to the hospital.'

'Get off it, Mam. It's right.'

'And show your dad your hands.'

'It's nowt.'

Gav slowly puts his hands out palms up. His wrists are swollen and red.

'What's happened here?' I say and I try to hold his hands but he pulls them away.

'They wanted five hundred quid off me because they said I'd fiddled them but I haven't. When I told them I didn't have any cash on me they grabbed hold of my wrists and tightened them up in that vice in the garage to see if I was lying.'

I gently rub Gav's wrists. There are red grazes and white imprints where the jaws of the vice have gripped the skin. Gav seems unperturbed. Deb is more decisive.

'If they show their faces round here again, I'll smack them round the head with the yard brush. The bloody animals.'

She forces Gav to take the box of tissues.

'I'm going back up to the café to do some last-minute cleaning up. I'll be back in an hour. Give me a ring if you need anything, Gavin.'

Believe me, Deb's not kidding about the yard brush and I pity the two blokes whoever they are. I open the van door and grab my portfolio from under the passenger seat as though I'm snatching it out of Gav's hands.

'You'll be getting yourself into big trouble one of these days, lad, if you don't watch it. How many more times do I have to tell you?'

'Dad. I've got something to tell you.'

'If it's not good news,' I say, slamming the van door shut,' I don't want to know.'

'You know that money I lent you?'

'No, remind me.'

I pull out the five hundred pounds from my pocket and force it into Gav's hand.

'Here. I told you you'd have it back today.'

Gav doesn't even look at the bundle and he tries to push it back into my hands.

'You can keep it,' he says. 'You don't owe me it any more.'

I unlock the garage door, only half listening. He still hasn't put the money in his pocket but I'm not taking it back off him. Decision made.

'Look,' I say. 'I'm seriously thinking about selling the Flash. I've got to get that qualification if we're ever going to have a chance of working together. I know you're not hundred percent behind Steele and Son Plumbing but what else is there?'

I'm hoping to get some reaction but Gav won't look at me. Something's not right. What was that he said a few minutes ago?

'What do you mean I don't owe you the five hundred quid any more?'

When I lift up the door the garage sounds hollow. I switch on the light and wait for it to click and bang but I can already see something's wrong. Deb's cardboard boxes have gone and the garage sides are on view for the first time in weeks. But something else isn't right. The light flickers on. My trail bike is leaning against the bench. No Golden Flash.

'What's going off here, Gav? Where's my Flash gone?'

The blanket is lying in a crumpled heap in the middle of the floor and I lift it up, desperate for any sign of the bike.

'What have you done with it? I hope you've not been tidying up with your mother? You'd better not have, Gav, I'm telling you. Where've you put it?'

I march outside and check down the sides and the back of the garage. Nothing. The sidecar is still there, under the old carpet but there's no Flash. Nothing.

'Where is it?'

I push Gav out of the way and go back into the garage. Gav follows me. He's so close he almost treads on my heels.

'Dad, when they couldn't get any money off me, they took my car and they said I could have it back when I'd paid them.'

'What are you on about? Never mind your car, where's my bike gone?'

'They said they were taking your bike as well because I'd caused them a load of grief. I told 'em it wasn't mine but they just laughed at me.'

I glare at Gav and my words come out slow and deliberate.

'What do you mean they've taken my bike?'

'They threatened to do me in. I had to let them take it just to buy a bit of time otherwise they'd have taken it out on me.'

Gav looks mentally wounded and I know he's not telling the full story.

'I thought you said they were just messing about? Is it those pillocks you've been hanging around with? That Jason and that Ben character?'

'No, is it hell. They're my mates.'

'What about those nutters you saw in the club on Sunday night. Them you were trying to avoid?'

'It's not them, neither. These two blokes give us a few jobs now an' then – me, Jason and Ben. They kept saying I'd fiddled them out of five hundred quid but Jason and Ben said they'd not been chased for any money, and we do the same jobs together an' get paid the same money, so I don't know why they only picked on me.'

'Where are they from these two blokes that pay you all this money?'

'They own that garage where I had my interview.'

I throw my portfolio at the shelves at the back of the garage and it smashes into a jar of black engine oil.

'And where is this bloody garage?'

'Dad, they'll kill me if you go after 'em. Let it go.'

'Let it chuffing go? They've attacked you and threatened to do you in. They've taken your car. They've nicked my bike. And you say let it go.'

I kick the side of the garage and flakes of rust fall in one brief shower.

'Is that why you went missing on Sunday night? Because they've been threatening you?'

Gav scuffs the floor and nods.

'Why the hell didn't you tell me it was this serious?'

'I did tell you. But you don't listen.'

The marks on Gav's wrists, the trail of fresh blood trickling into his eyebrow, and the swelling on his cheekbone, make me feel sick and I slump on the milkcrate.

'Bloody hell, Gav. My Golden Flash.'

'What about me? If I hadn't lent you the five hundred quid for your training, I wouldn't have all this blood all over my face an' I'd still have my car.'

I sit motionless, my head in my hands.

'I thought they were going to set that mad dog of theirs on me, next,' Gav says, rubbing his wrists.

Silence. I look up.

'A mad dog? It wasn't a grey mongrel, by any chance, was it?'

'Grey and faulty.'

'Were they in a white van?'

Gav nods. I get off the stool so fast I knock it over.

'Don't tell me. One of them's a big ugly thug and the other one's a little shorthouse.'

Gav looks wary but nods again. I push him to one side and pull open the van door.

'Stay here. I think I know where these two blokes might be.'

'Where?'

'In a big house clowning around with a bent developer.'

Gav stops dabbing his eyebrow and jogs round the van to the passenger door.

'Hang on. I'm coming with you.'

'No, you're not. You're going to the hospital to get that eye stitched up.'

'I'll have to come with you. There's loads of white vans with two blokes an' a dog in. What if it's not them?'

4

We drive past the locked gates on Jagger's drive, slow enough to get a good view, fast enough to go unnoticed.

'That's them two, Dad. And that's my car.'

I park out of the way down a side street. Gav opens the passenger door and starts to climb out but I pull him back by his jumper.

'Stay here and keep out of sight.'

For the first time my head is held high as I approach the entrance. No sneaking up now. Jagger and his two side-kicks are leaning against Gav's car close to the locked gates. I grab hold of the bars.

'Your two mates have been threatening my lad.'

Jagger takes a long, slow drink out of a can of beer.

'Who? These two?'

The innocent expression on the men's faces wouldn't look out of place on a church wall painting. All that's missing is a halo above their heads.

'Don't be giving me all that bollocks. Them two.'

I point at Wiry and Heavy, my arm as straight as a spear.

'They've been in my garage and laid into our Gav. And they've taken his car – that one you're leant on. And they've taken my bike.'

Jagger takes another drink and tosses the empty can into Gav's car through the driver's window.

'What? That little pizza delivery thing you came round here on last week when you were pestering me for your money?'

'No. Not that one. They know which one I'm on about.'

Wiry flicks his tongue in and out like a snake sampling the air.

'I haven't seen no bike,' he says. 'I wonder if it's in here.'

As Wiry opens the rear door of the white van, the grey mongrel in the front compartment charges from one seat to the other, trying to rip down the metal grille partitioning off the cab. The van is empty.

'No. I can't see no bike in here.' Wiry slams the door shut and his face changes. 'But I tell you what. That car's ours until we get our fucking five hundred quid back.'

The tongue flicks in and out again. I have a good view of him now. I can't work out how hard he is but I mark him down as sneaky, always on the lookout, the type that only strikes from the blind side.

Heavy decides to join in the fun.

'Hey, it wasn't that pile of scrap his lad said we could have, was it?'

This man is big through weight training. Every inch of his physique suggests years of development to intimidate by bulk.

'My lad never said you could have that bike. That bike's got nothing to do with whatever it is he's supposed to owe you.'

'It could have been a bike now I come to think about it,' Wiry says. 'I wondered why it caught fire so easy. The petrol tank must have been full.'

Heavy saunters down the drive and jabs his finger through the gates into my chest.

'You want to tell that fucking lad of yours he's a very lucky boy. Nobody tries to do us out of money.'

I don't move even though the jabbing feels like a cold chisel being hammered into my breast bone. First rule – never back off. He's big enough to wipe the floor with me but I wouldn't give in. I knock Heavy's hand away.

'Don't touch our Gav again. Hear me? I'm warning you. He's done nothing wrong. He's only a young lad. You're nothing but a set of bullies, the lot of you.'

'Bullies? Is that right? Open these fucking gates, Jack.'

Jagger presses the remote control on his key ring and the gates begin to open. The electric motor whirrs a slow, even note. Wiry must have sniffed a fight and I see him sneaking down the drive, trying to hide behind Heavy's big frame. Even with good ribs, I know two is one too many never mind three. Heavy tries to speed up the opening gates by pulling on the bars. I stand motionless, fists clenched. Cars are passing. Witnesses. Maybe land one on this big ape then run as fast as I can down the road in the opposite direction to Gav and my van.

The bodybuilder shoves his bulky leg through the gap ready to attack. Then the motor noise changes and the gates begin to close. Jagger is pointing the remote control at me.

'I think it's time you fucked off,' Jagger says, 'while you can still walk.'

Chest out, shoulders back, I stare at Heavy and answer Jagger.

'Tell your two chimps to back off, then.'

Heavy is faster than I thought and before I know it his big hands are clamped around my throat. I can't breathe and I tear at his fingers and dig my nails into his flesh but there's no weakness in his grip. I grab the bars and try to straighten and lock my arms but there's no leverage. As my arms weaken, I turn my head and Heavy pulls my face into the hard steel.

'Keep your fucking mouth zipped before I pull you through these gates like a piece of fucking mincemeat.'

I thrash around for Heavy's face but the man leans back and his grip tightens. Then there's a blur. Someone, something, is striking the big man's arm.

Heavy tries to fend off the attack but the weapon keeps striking down and he has to release his hold on me. I can breathe again and when I look round, Gav is at my side, arm raised, threatening further blows, his face white with fear. Wiry, wild as the grey mongrel, barks at Jagger to open the fucking gates.

'Like father like son,' Jagger says, pushing himself away from Gav's car. 'They think they're on a picket line. Trying to bring the country to its knees. It was the hardest day's work you miners ever did, trying to stop the rest of us from going to work to make money. And then you all crawled back to collect your fat redundancies and your big pit pensions. For doing what? Fuck all.' He blows the dust from Gav's car off his hands. 'Let them go. I don't want any blood on my drive. What will the neighbours think?'

I don't move. Jagger probably thinks I'm stunned into silence. Frozen. But if he was closer, he'd see my face muscles tighten and my eyes sharpen their focus, and see the resentment raging under the surface.

Heavy rubs his big arm and threatens to put me and Gav six foot under. He swaggers back up the drive, head rocking from side to side, back so broad his arms are bent like a gunslinger's.

My lips are throbbing and I run my tongue around my front teeth. No gaps.

'You think you're ten ton you lot,' I say, spitting blood on the pavement.

Wiry shouts, 'Fire, fire. Bike on fire. Dinga-linga-ling.'

The gang of three laugh at my expressionless face. Gav offers up the money.

'I don't know what I'm supposed to have done to fiddle you but here's the five hundred quid. Let me have my car back.'

Wiry taunts him.

'It's six hundred now.'

Jagger tosses Gav's car keys to Wiry.

'Take the money off him. Let him have his little car back.'

Wiry snatches the five hundred quid out of Gav's hand like a monkey stealing food off a tourist.

'I'll get Jason to bring it round for you sometime,' he says, counting the notes. 'When I'm good and ready.'

Jagger kicks the front tyre of Gav's car and the steering wheel shakes.

'It's been a good afternoon,' he says. 'Five hundred quid in cash plus a valuable piece of scrap. And it's not over yet.' Jagger's smug smile turns into a hard stare. 'If you ever sneak into my property again or do anything to upset my kids again, anything, I'll break your fucking legs in two.'

When we get back to the van, I rub my sore ribs and inspect Gav's bloodied eyebrow.

'It's nearly stopped bleeding but it definitely needs a stitch. Come on. Let's get you to the hospital.'

I know things could have turned a lot nastier and I feel bad for putting Gav in danger. I place my hand on his shoulder and I have to breathe in and swallow hard to hold myself together.

'I'm glad you're all right, lad.'

'I'm glad you're all right as well, Dad.'

We leave the scene and join the main road, checking the mirrors every few yards to make sure nobody is following us.

'You made that gorilla let go quick smart, Gav. What did you clout him with?'

'This.'

Gav picks up a length of mangled copper pipe from between his feet.

'Bloody hell, Gav. That was my template for my new mudguard.'

'It doesn't matter now. You'll not be needing it any more.'

On the way to the hospital, I look right and Gav looks left as we search every field entrance and patch of waste ground for any sign of a burnt-out motorbike among the fly tipping. Gav rubs the grime off the inside of the passenger window and begins to yawn.

'It could be anywhere, Dad. We've no chance of finding it.'

'They can't have gone that far off this road. It's the main route between our house and Jagger's.'

We carry on searching for another mile and my eyes begin to water with the strain.

'That garage of theirs you were on about. Is it anywhere round here?'

'You're not going to their garage, are you? What if they've decided to take me car there? I've had enough beatings for one day.'

'Am I hell. Not with you, anyway. I was just thinking though. If it's not that far away, I could have a poke around the place while you're at the hospital. They might have dumped my bike there.'

'It's just off the next roundabout. About three miles down the road. It's in front of their scrap yard. But don't blame me if they turn up.'

'They've got a scrap yard? Why didn't you tell me?'

I get Gav booked into the crowded A&E department, promising to be back in half an hour to sit with him, and return to the roundabout.

There's no sign of a white van or Gav's car at the salvage yard. I tell the man who comes out of the cabin that I'm looking for a new gearbox for my van. The man points to where they're stacked and tells me to give him a shout if I need any help.

The open space in the middle of the scrapyard is surrounded by high banks of scrap vehicles. I feel as though I'm entering an arena and I keep to the edge. In the centre of the clearing, the jaws of a crane bite into a little green saloon then drop it into the mouth of a giant crusher. As the powerful hydraulic rams begin to close, the car boot slowly opens as though the vehicle is saluting its final farewell. When the crane swings away, a man in oily overalls steps forward and begins to sweep away the fallen debris. I call over to him.

'That looks like a scary job, mate. Do you get danger money?'

'Danger money? Not a fucking chance. A dump like this?'

My heart is racing but I force myself to look casually across the yard.

'It's a big place you've got here. Do you get many motorbikes in?'

'Odd ones.'

'What do you do with them?'

The crane swings back round with another car in its jaws and the sweeper steps aside and rests on his brush.

'Burn everything off like everything else in here. Then drop them in the crusher. It's all scrap.'

The man nods towards a plume of black smoke rising behind a caravan green with algae in the corner of the yard.

'I'm burning a few over there. Mopeds mainly and a few knackered off-roaders. I've just dumped a big bugger on the pile. Looked all right to me. Old but in good nick.'

The crane swings clear again and the man lifts himself off his brush.

'I said to the bosses, I'll have that bastard but they told me to torch it.'

I amble towards the caravan, hands in pockets, checking over my shoulder to make sure the crane driver and sweeper are occupied. As soon as I'm out of their sight, I run over to the smoking mound of bikes.

The Golden Flash is on its side on top of the heap. I try to grab the saddle, my other hand shielding my face, but the melted plastic sticks to my skin. I kick the back wheel, the tyre already down to the metal beading, but the bike's handlebars become entangled in the wrecks underneath. My hand is throbbing and the smell of burning oil and rubber tightens my chest. A short scaffolding pole is propped against the caravan, one end scorched. A poker. I ram it into the burning mass and try to lever the bike free. The whole pile sinks, sending flames and sparks and more jets of black smoke into the air, the sudden eruption of heat forcing me to take a step back. I run round to the other side, my trainers skidding on the hot ash, and dig the scaffolding pole in again. This time the bike shifts. I ram the pole in deeper, working it backwards and forwards, levering the Golden Flash off the pile and out of the fire.

5

In the garage Gav helps me lift what is left of the Flash onto the two blocks of wood. The bike is cold now. The bubbling hot rubber stench has gone and there's a dead smell, the kind that fills the air the morning after Bonfire Night. I check the damage from every angle, tapping and rubbing the scorched remains. Gav takes the hand brush off its nail above the bench and sweeps the black debris into a little pile.

'Will you be able to rebuild it, Dad?'

'I don't know. It's well gone. Well gone.'

'I can give you a hand. Learn a bit about renovating old bikes. I could look on the internet for all the parts – it can't cost that much. An' I could help you do up that sidecar you've got round t'back of t'garage. It'd make a cool advertising board. I can see a bright sticker running all the way down the side with Steele and Son Golden Flush Plumbing in a jazzy font.'

The lad's trying his best to lift my mood. He's full of enthusiasm and ideas but I'm too upset to think beyond the next few days. What have I been playing at? Putting my son's safety in jeopardy all for a motorbike. Why couldn't I walk away from Jagger and forget what happened all those years ago? Why didn't I sell the Flash when I knew I was going to be short of cash to pay for my certificate? I know the Flash is more than just a bike to me. It's been a lifeline to the pit and it's kept me from sinking into my own mineshaft. But I never thought it would get to this. Never.

'That would be great, Gav.'

I sit on the milkcrate and tell Gav about Jagger owing me five hundred pounds for the pond I built and how I got my own back by ripping out the liner that I'd paid for out of my own money. Gav wants to know what that has to do with him and the two blokes and the job he's supposed to have fiddled.

'It's a bloody con, Gav. They're having you on. They work for Jagger. He's told them to go an' get five hundred quid off you so he can get his pond fixed an' keep his kids happy.'

I spit on the garage floor and rub it in with my foot to show what I think of Jagger's ruthlessness.

'He's put the frighteners up you just to get at me. You're my lad. What hurts you, hurts me.'

Gav touches the dressing covering his stitches and a blot of fresh blood appears.

'I wonder what Jagger meant when he said it's not over yet?'

'I don't know,' I say. 'But it must have been his two heavies who beat me up on Sunday because that's what they said when they were kicking the hell out of me on the deck. Maybe Jagger's after my van and my tools next. Taking everything I've got left. But I tell you what, if him and his two hit men come after my van, I'll get missen a gun and lie in wait in the back of the van, and when they break in, I'll splat their big ugly kites all over the back doors.'

I'm pleased with the aggressive image. Then I think about the last time I fired a gun. It was at the city fair, when I was about ten years old. It was a thin air gun chained to a stand and I won a goldfish.

'Anyway,' I say. 'What sort of little jobs have you been doing for these two clowns that pay you all this money?'

'We deliver cars for 'em, that's all. Sometimes to other garages. Sometimes to their mates.'

My eyebrows jump so high they nearly reach my hairline.

'Deliver cars for that lot? You must be out of your head, Gav. It'll not have been cars you were delivering. Jesus. They're crooks.'

'They've always been okay with us, up to now. They treated us like brothers. And they must have trusted us because they asked us to set up their computer. Even the odd time when we had a problem delivering a car or collecting a package for them, they never threatened us or owt. They just said if we did another little job for them, everything would be okay.'

I throw my hands in the air at Gav's naivety. It's a release valve. Not just for the anger I feel at my son's involvement but also at the stupidity at my own dealings with Jagger.

'Another little job? And then what? Another little job? And then another little job? They'd have you by the bollocks. It's a wonder you haven't been shot. I thought you'd more sense, Gav.'

A ball rolls up to the garage followed a few seconds later by the two young lads. I'm still shaking my head at Gav's gullibility and my own recklessness as I tell them what happened to the bike. They stare at the blackened frame as though they can't believe it's the Golden Flash and they take it in turns to tell me what they know.

'We saw somebody put it in their van.'

'It wa' a white van.'

'We thought you'd sold it to 'em.'

'I said they were nicking it, didn't I? They nearly knocked us over.'

'I told you we should have got their number plate.'

Their genuine, uncomplicated concern acts like a tranquilizer, loosening the knot in my stomach and the tension in my jaw.

'Don't worry about it, lads. You did the right thing keeping out of the way. Me and our Gav are the only ones round here who don't know how to stay out of trouble.'

Deb comes down the garden path with a pot of coffee and a can of coke balanced on a tray. She hands over the drinks and asks the boys if they want a glass of juice. They say no thanks and as they run off down the track to resume their game of kick-the-ball-as-hard-as-you-can-against-the-garage-doors, Colin, next door appears in the doorway of his shed.

'Has something gone off?'

Deb says, 'Somebody's taken Phil's big bike and set it on fire.'

Colin takes his wooden ruler out of the narrow pocket down the side of his overalls and points it at the two lads playing on the track.

'It'll be them two little buggers that's done it, you watch. It's always the ones that can't wait to tell you who's done it that's done it.'

I wipe the spilled oil off the cover of my portfolio and stand the folder next to my BSA manual on the shelf above the bench.

'I've just realized, Deb. I never thought to ask them about your cardboard boxes. They'll be in the back of somebody's car by now, ready to be flogged off in a dodgy pub somewhere. At least I won't have to put all them chandeliers and tranklements up now.'

This silver lining makes my coffee taste a little sweeter. Then there is a hiss as Gav opens his can of coke.

'That's what you think, Dad. They're all upstairs in my bedroom.'

I bang my cup down on the bench and lose half my coffee.

'Do you know, I could have put money on that. Never mind my Golden Flash. Save your mother's boxes. That's all that matters.' There's no malice in my voice and when Deb and Gav laugh at me, I try to look offended.

'It's not my fault they set fire to your bike,' Gav says. 'You ripped out the pond liner.'

My mind flicks through various counter-arguments against Gav's cutting insight but I can't develop any and they evaporate half-formed. Deb looks confused.

'Ripped out what pond liner?'

'It's a long story,' I say. 'That bloke who owes me that money – him I've been chasing for months. It's Jack Jagger. Remember him?'

Deb remembers him, all right. I can tell by the way the confused look on her face quickly drains away.

'He's that developer who got our house for next to nothing when the building society took it back off us,' I say. 'Remember him? He rented it out for a while then sold it and made a fortune. I built a pond for him, and I paid upfront for the liner, like a dope, so when he wouldn't pay up, I ripped the liner out and brought it home. I'm going to sell it on the internet. Get a bit of my money back.'

'On the internet?' Gav says. 'I'm impressed, Dad.'

'That's why I got beaten up on Sunday night, and that's why he sent his heavies round to nick my bike.'

I think I'm winning Deb's sympathies but I'm wrong.

'Is that why our Gavin's finished up with stitches in his eyebrow? All because somebody who took advantage of us during the strike wouldn't pay you for digging a stupid hole in the ground.'

I don't want to antagonize Deb so I point at Gav.

'And because he's been daft enough to work for Jagger and his two cronies doing God knows what.'

'You haven't, Gavin? What have you been up to? What are you doing mucking around with the likes of that lot for?'

Gav snaps at his mother.

'It's work, isn't it? Better than doing nothing.'

'You must be mad.'

Now that Gav is on the ropes, I feel brave enough to own up to Deb about the size of my debt.

'And it wasn't just a few bob Jagger owed me for that pond, neither. It was five hundred quid. I've finished up with no plumbing qualification because of that crook, as if he hasn't made enough money out of us.'

'Well, I hope you've both learned your lesson,' Deb says. 'And don't you even think about trying to get your own back on this Jagger character again just because he's set fire to your motorbike. He's dangerous. I don't want him and his gang coming anywhere near our Gavin again.'

Deb tries to caress the edges of the plaster on Gav's forehead but he pulls away. She glares at me.

'All this aggro just because of you and your stupid ego.'

I put my head down. Deb's stare is more frightening than Jagger, his two henchmen and their mad dog combined.

Deb takes a step back and looks round as though she's engaging an audience and I know a lecture is coming my way.

'You still think you're twenty-one, that's your trouble. Trying to be a cocky young miner again. Fighting anybody that gets in your way or looks like putting one over on you. Riding off on your motorbike with your mates just to show off.'

'I'm not trying to be a cocky young miner again. I never was a cocky young miner. I had dignity. That's different. And all I'm doing now is trying to get back what's mine. That liner belongs to me, and if I could have ripped up all the flagstones and all the time and effort I put into making that chuffing pond for him, I would have done. The bastard.'

I look at Deb for a sign of sympathy for my actions or even understanding but her face remains set.

Gav says, 'He seemed a bit upset about his kids for some reason.'

'They were using the pond as a paddling pool, that's why,' I say. 'Tough.'

Deb folds her arms again, softly this time, and she looks sad.

'That's not on, Phil. I don't care who he is or what he's done, you shouldn't be upsetting his little kids.'

'Don't feel sorry for his little kids, or for him, neither. He didn't feel sorry for the miners when we were on strike and our little kids were suffering. When we were scratching abart on that muckstack in the wind and rain for bits of coal to stop us from freezing to death. And he didn't feel sorry for you, me or our Gav when he got our house.'

'I know,' Deb says. 'I understand all that. But you're putting us at risk with your aggression. What about our welfare? You've got to draw a line under the past at some point.'

I have no answer. I'm beginning to feel like a fool. A guilty fool. Doubting the reasons for my revenge. Deb turns her back and stares out onto the track. There's only the sound of carefree hammering from Colin's shed. More shelves, no doubt.

When Deb's in this mood, I have to keep quiet and wait for her to speak first. After a few minutes she turns round and collects up the empty coffee cup and coke can. It's a good sign. The storm has passed.

'I could do with a lift up to the café,' she says. 'I've got some ornaments to take up and put out ready for the big day tomorrow. I was going to take my chandelier up, as well. I was hoping I could get it fitted before it got too dark, but I suppose you're both too busy to give me a hand.'

'I'd gladly take you up, Mam,' Gav says, pausing until I look up. 'If I had a car.'

My head starts to itch and I rub the top of my scalp with both hands.

'Have a look at my head, Gav,' I say. 'Have I got two big donkey's ears sprouting out?'

As I drive the three of us to the café, I'm ordered by Deb not to go down any potholes in case the jolting damages the ornaments and the chandelier. On our way into the car park, we pass the new sign above the big window. Deb has decided to call her business The

Chandelier Café and I have to say it looks well, especially in the afternoon sun. Gav, Jason and Ben used their computer magic to produce the artwork and Charlotte and Ella painted the lettering in gold.

Deb unlocks the café's back door and as she steps inside, I hear her scream. I drop the cardboard box, cushioning it with my foot, and rush into the café.

'What the hell's up with you, Deb?'

Deb has her hand over her mouth. The plastic chairs and tables have been thrown into a heap in the middle of the floor. Legs have been wrenched off and thrown on the pile as though someone was preparing a bonfire. The fluorescent ceiling light, ripped out of its fixing, hangs by its cable and turns slowly in the draught from the back door. Tomato sauce has been squirted onto the newly papered walls and over the laminate flooring. As we stand in silence trying to take it all in, a chair leg falls off the stack and clatters onto the floor. Deb starts crying. I put my arm around her shoulder and try to stay calm.

'You've been shafted, love.'

'Why would anybody do this to my café? Why? Why me?'

The tears are running down her cheeks and I pull her into my chest and stroke her back. She holds on to me and I look over her head at Gav and feel helpless. Deb's sobs gradually ease and she relaxes her hold on me.

'What have I done wrong to deserve this? I've not fallen out with anybody. I've paid all my bills on time.' Deb looks around the café again, this time with a colder eye. 'Look at the mess. I'll never get it cleaned up in time for tomorrow.'

Cups and saucers have been swept off the shelves and I step over the fragments and check the till. It's empty. I close my eyes for a second and breathe in slowly.

'Was there any money in here, Deb'

'No. Why would there be? I'm not open yet.'

Despite the vandalism, I feel some relief. Deb is organized and could well have left a float in the till ready for her big day tomorrow. I slide the till shut.

'I'll bet that's why they've trashed the place,' Gav says, trying all the handles on the windows. 'They couldn't find any money so they've gone beserk. Whoever's broken in hasn't got in through the windows. They're all sound. I'll check upstairs.'

'The front door's not been touched, neither,' I say. 'The bolts are still drawn across. Was the back door locked when you opened up, Deb? Did you have to use your key?'

Deb still has the key in her hand.

'Yes. It was definitely locked.'

Gav comes running down the stairs, shaking his head.

'They haven't got in through the upstairs windows.'

There's a chair on the pile with its legs still attached and I lift it off and sit down to think.

'This is weird,' I say. 'No damage to the windows. No locks broken.'

Gav says, 'They must have had a key.'

'There's only one key,' Deb says, 'and that's this. Nobody else has got a key.'

I think Gav might be on to something.

'Not Sheila?' I say.

'Nobody. And why would Sheila do all this even if she had a key. She's as keen as me to get this place up and running.'

I keep nibbling, like a cop. Deb is in a fragile state.

'What about those two lasses? Them who did the decorating for you? Your mates, Gav. Charlotte and what's-her-name? You didn't lend them a key, did you?'

Gav jumps in before Deb can respond.

'They wouldn't do anything like this. They're my mates. They're not vandals.'

Deb's face hardens and I regret my clumsy questioning and blunt tone.

'Are you thick or something, Phil? I've told you. There's only one key. This one.' Deb catches her breath and wipes away the last of her tears. 'Anyway, you'd better phone the police. They might be able to find some fingerprints.'

I get off the chair and feel my jeans to see if there's any tomato sauce on them.

'I wouldn't bother,' I say. 'The cops'll not be interested if there's been no break-in, no money's been taken and nobody's been injured.'

Deb takes her coat off and rolls up her sleeves. She's back to normal. Action mode.

'We might as well start cleaning up, then. I'll see if Sheila's got some spare cups and saucers. And my mother's got some plates that she's never used. I'm opening up tomorrow no matter what.'

Gav helps Deb scrub the walls and I sweep the broken crockery into a pile. I'm about to start reassembling the heap of furniture when I notice a business card propped up against the hot tap on the kitchen sink.

'Looks like somebody's left us a calling card. Guess who, Gav?'

Gav steps over the pile of debris and reads the name on the card.

'So that's what he meant when he said it's not over yet.'

'You've got it.'

Deb throws her wiping cloth into the bucket.

'I say. Am I here or what? What are you two talking about?'

'Jack Jagger's done this,' I say, passing the card to Deb. 'He must have had a spare key.'

'How can he have?'

'Who's your landlord?'

'I've no idea. I've only ever met the letting agent.'

'I think you might find it's Jagger.'

I try to explain to Deb what kind of a man Jagger is and why he's wrecked the contents of her café. Why he's not satisfied with setting his heavies on me and Gav. Not satisfied with destroying the Flash. Not satisfied with stealing Gav's car and pocketing five hundred quid cash.

'He's done me, he's done our Gav, and now he's done you. All because, for once, somebody – me – dared to get their own back on the crook.'

The street light outside the café's front window has been on an hour by the time we finish clearing up and refitting the legs the best we can to the tables and chairs. Gav is standing on a table, I'm standing on the one next to him, and Deb is shining a torch at the ceiling.

'Be careful, Gavin,' Deb says. 'Make sure you don't drop it.'

'What do you think I'm doing, Mam?' Gav says, trying to support the chandelier with both hands and keep his balance while I connect the wiring. 'It's this table. It's like being on a trampoline.'

'Shine the torch round here, Deb,' I say. 'I can't see a thing.'

In her haste to take the torch round to the other side, Deb bumps into Gav's table and it's only his skateboarding prowess that prevents him from falling off and pulling the chandelier and the wiring out of the ceiling rose.

'Mother. Watch it.'

'Sorry.'

'Have you two finished?' I say. 'It's like working with Laurel and Hardy.'

When we settle down and stop blaming each other, I tighten the final bracket and tentatively tug the flex.

'I think that's got it. Let go of it, Gav. Steady. It weighs a ton.'

The new light fitting holds fast and Gav jumps off the table, his knees absorbing the dismount like a gymnast while I have to use a chair and Deb's shoulder to climb down, all the time looking up at the chandelier in case the chain fastening it to the ceiling snaps.

'Turn it on, Deb. And cross your fingers.'

Deb stands on a chair and shines the torch at the fuse box above the back door.

'Are you sure?'

'Course I am. Go on, turn it on.'

She flicks the little black lever. There is a click and the chandelier begins to glow, orange at first, and then soft and mellow as it gradually warms up. I watch Deb's face light up in wonder as she stares at the crystal pendants and the sparkle and flash of the gold-effect candles.

'Wow,' she says. 'That's fantastic. Look at the light in here, now. It feels as cosy as a front room. Come on, Phil, you've got to admit it. That beautiful chandelier's transformed this place. Even the front window looks good in this light.'

My legs are aching and I sit down at one of the repaired tables and rub my knees. Deb has recovered so now I can pretend not to be too impressed.

'I suppose it looks a bit better than that forty-watt fluorescent strip did.'

'It looks great. It'll look even better when Charlotte and Ella finish decorating and I've got all my other lights fitted and all my paintings and ornaments put up.' Deb does a little jig. 'It's wonderful. Better than I dared dream. And the women especially will love it. Does anybody fancy a drink to celebrate? I've made a fruit cake.'

Deb serves the refreshments and we sit around a wobbly table on wonky plastic chairs, chink cups and make a toast to each other. The tea is grand and so is the slice of cake and I tell Deb it's one of the best she has ever baked. Gav pushes his cake into his mouth, takes a gulp of coke and says he agrees, totally. The café is out of intensive care. Deb is happy and so I'm happy. Then as my tea and cake sink gently into my stomach, the little matter of my qualification rises up in my mind. It's like having a weight scale inside my head. For the last few happy minutes, the scales were balanced and I'd started to believe I would survive, then as the thought of finding work surfaced again the scales slowly tipped.

'I'm going to need a hand to earn a wage one road or another now, Gav. Try and get a few light building jobs or something. Just until I've earned enough money to pay for my portfolio signing off. It's either that or we both start working for Jagger.'

Gav doesn't respond to my joke. He continues to stare at the table top, rubbing his finger backwards and forwards, joining up the wet rings made by his can of coke.

'You'll have to start working with your dad, somehow, Gavin. We need to help each other from now on.'

'I know we do. And I will. Just leave me alone for a minute, will you.'

Gav is hurting. I can tell. Maybe it's because from now on there will be no more brown envelopes stuffed with cash from Jagger and his band. No more easy money to buy all that glitzy stuff that youngsters love to collect. Back to the soul-destroying reality of endless job applications and endless rejection. Or, worse still, he's in even deeper trouble with those tossers than he's letting on.

'Hey, lad.'

Gav won't look up.

'What?'

'Look me and your mam in the eye and tell us you've not been involved in anything dodgy with that set of crooks?'

It's a dumb question, I know, but maybe I'll be able to see something of the truth in Gav's eyes.

Deb says, 'Come on, Gavin. Be honest with us. We'll help you all we can.'

Gav's eyes flash from me to Deb and back.

'Have I hell. Do you think I'm that stupid? It's work I want, and freedom to go out and enjoy myself, not jail.'

I hold out my hand and eventually Gav shakes it without looking up.

Deb strokes Gav's back.

'We know you're not that stupid, love.'

Deb can't stop looking at the sky-blue wallpaper on the ceiling and I follow her gaze round the room, admiring the light cast by the chandelier on the tables and chairs and the laminate wood flooring.

'You can always come and work for me in here,' Deb says, still glowing. 'Both of you. There'll be plenty to do once I get it established.'

'You what?' I say. 'I'm not wearing a bloody pinny for nobody.'

I try to visualise myself at work in the café serving tea in tiny cups with dainty slices of fancy cake on patterned plates, the place full of customers laughing at me. The former-miner all dressed up like a fairy on top of a Christmas tree. But Deb's words make me feel guilty again. She didn't try to put me down like I would have done to her. It was a grown-up reaction. Maybe the café would be full of customers laughing with me, not at me. Maybe that's how it would be. Maybe she's right.

Deb looks at my glum face.

'For God's sake, Phil. Cheer up.'

I can't. I don't want to. Not yet.

'I'm thinking about all the damage that bastard Jagger's done to us. To me, to our Gav, to you and your café.' I try to take another drink but my cup is empty. 'I just hope it's all over. I just hope he's not going to start messing about with the café. Putting your rent up or something. Making it hard for you.'

'He's got two choices,' Deb says. 'But you'll not beat the likes of him with brawn. It needs brains.'

'I know that. That's where I'm snookered. Maybe it's about time I started using the old grey matter for once.'

Images appear in my head – the knife cutting through the pond liner, my hand crushing Garrett's hand, Gav's frightened face at the locked gates, the Flash on fire, Deb's tears in the café.

Deb puts her hands on my shoulders and tries to get me to look at her.

'Come on, Phil. We can get over this. We can make a go of it if we stick together. We got over the miners' strike, didn't we?'

I can't believe what I'm hearing. I'm down but I'm not out and I wriggle out of her grip. I know my responses are losing their power but I'm not giving in yet.

'Well, I haven't got over the strike. And I haven't forgotten it, neither.'

'I'm not saying I've forgotten it,' Deb says. 'What I am saying is we got through it and we're stronger for it. Let's build on what we learned during that year. How the men stuck together on the picket line and how the women stuck together in the soup kitchen. Let's build on that and make things better for all of us for the future. Not keep looking back and wishing we were still there.'

I feel myself closing up, shielding myself. I understand what Deb is saying – it makes sense. But it hurts because I can't accept it. Still can't let go of the past. Don't want to let go of the past. The pit was a big part of my life and my family's life, and a big part of the lives of every miner and his family. It was about earning a good living, about pride, about sticking together above and below ground, and about hope for the future, and I'm trying hard to hold onto those good times. Otherwise, what? Accept that I've wasted all these years by thinking too much about the past. That all those bastards who shut down the pits and now can't wait to bury every last structure of our mining landscape have beaten me and are still holding me down. No. It's not over yet. It needs one last effort.

I stop staring at the floor and search around the café for something to illustrate to Deb, to Gav, and yes, to myself, why I feel like I do. It's a half-hearted search and I can't find anything but I don't give up.

'You know that big green thing you see every time you look out of our kitchen window? It's not Ben Nevis. It's a muckstack. Never mind that bit of grass they've put on it and them silver birches they've shoved in. Our families built that muckstack. It's our history. In France you're not allowed to touch their muckstacks. They're sacred over there. Monuments to mining.'

Deb leans over me. Her face has taken on a sharp focus.

'Phil. I don't care what they do in France. A hill's a hill. Move on. Same with your bike. It's a bit of steel, for God's sake. You've already wasted half your life messing about with it.'

That stings and her words won't leave my head. I want to say yes, it's a bit of steel all right – a bit of *Phil* Steele, connecting me, the young fit miner to me, the worn-out former-miner. But I don't say anything. I can't.

Deb empties the cubbyhole of spare rolls of wallpaper and old magazines and packs them into the cardboard box.

I get up slowly, and it's not just the physical aches and pains that are causing my laboured movement. I speak quietly and for once without bitterness.

'Do you want me to take them back home with me?'

'You can do. Save me struggling.'

'Anybody want a lift back?'

'Not for me,' Deb says. 'I've a bit more tidying up to do in here before I open up tomorrow. I've just phoned Sheila. She's going to come round in half an hour and give me a hand. She says she'll have to bring her grandkids with her – she's babysitting – but she says she wants to make sure Soup Kitchen Part Two, as she calls it, doesn't get cancelled.' Deb smiles to herself. 'She's a fighter, that woman.'

'Gav? Do you want a lift?'

'No. I'm all right. I'll stay here and give my mam and Sheila a hand.'

Deb smiles again at the golden flash of the chandelier.

'I can't wait to see it in the daylight when the sun's shining on it. Everybody will love it.'

The joyful look on Deb's face makes me swallow hard and the sight of the stitches above Gav's eye makes me feel sad. I pick up the heavy box and ignore the pain in my back and neck.

'I think I've been a bit selfish, haven't I?'

Deb and Gav's eyes widen. This is new. I answer my own question.

'I've not meant to be. But I've not been seeing straight lately. All that money for that training course. It was my last chance to get a decent job with a decent bit of money to keep us all going before I get too old and decrepit to even get out of the house. But I'm like a spider in a bath. Every time I get near the top I slide back down again.' The box is getting heavier and I hitch it up for a better grip. 'And there's you making a right go of your café. I know I should be happy for you – I am happy for you - but it just makes me feel like I'm an even bigger failure.' I want to put the box down but it makes a good shield. 'I'd be lost without you, Deb. You know that, don't you?'

'You've a funny way of showing it.'

'I know I have. But I mean it. And I'm sorry, Gav, for not listening to you when you needed me and for putting you through all this bother with Jagger. I've been blind. Trying to stay in work. Trying to get a qualification. Trying to get the Flash finished.'

'It's all right.'

'It'll not happen again. I promise you, lad. I've learned my lesson. I need to move on. You and your mam come first.'

When I get back home, I tear two blank sheets of paper out of my portfolio and lock myself in the garage. The skeleton of the Golden Flash propped up on its wooden blocks looks stark under the fluorescent light. I settle myself on the milk crate and begin to write a letter.

Dear Missis Council Leeder.

You don't need to know who I am but it has come to my attension that one of your staff and a surtain property developer Mr Jack Jagger have been up to no good...

Twelve months later

Thursday

Gav is cleaning and refilling the salt and pepper pots and wiping down the plastic menus, and I'm giving the tables and chairs a final once over and checking that nothing lines up or looks too formal. Deb insists on making the café look as informal and friendly as possible so that, in her words 'My customers will feel at home and at the same time feel as though they are on a special day out.'

The café is opening at nine o'clock sharp this morning and we're all a bit edgy, especially Deb. The successful women-only day is running its first skills session.

When I'm happy with the look of the tables and chairs, I wash my hands in the sink at the side of the oven where Deb is baking scones.

'Hey, Gav,' I say, trying to sound bubbly for Deb's sake. 'We'd better not be upsetting your mam. It's pay day tomorrow.'

Gav looks at his own reflection in the big window, turns his baseball cap the wrong way round, and tightens the straps of his apron to accentuate his slim hips and waist.

'I know,' he says. 'I'm hoping we're going to get a bonus for good behaviour.'

'We ought to be getting a bonus for versatility, never mind good behaviour. Half a week in a pinny, half a week in overalls.'

Deb smiles to herself as she takes the tray of scones out of the oven and turns them around, the smell of warm fruit and sweet dough rising up to the sky-blue ceiling.

'Every day's a bonus when you're working for me,' she says, and she slides the scones back into the oven.

There's an A4 poster pinned to the notice board on the back wall and I cock my head one way then the other, lining up the horizontal and vertical edges, closing one eye, stepping back, then moving in for a closer inspection like an art critic.

'Does somebody keep moving this poster? I put it straight yesterday.'

'Stop fussing, Phil. You're making me nervous. It's fine as it is.'

'It's straight, Dad.' Gav says. 'It's the wall that's leaning. We haven't got time to knock it down and rebuild it.'

I want to reposition the A4 sheet but I know it's just nerves so I leave it alone and fold my arms.

'You made a good job of this poster, Gav,' I say, and I read the words again to myself.

Hello Ladies
On Thursday, as well as the usual chat, coffee and cake, we are trying out something new. We will be running an informal session on a topic that many of you have asked us to cover.
Sheila has offered to show us how to make a healthy meal for four using simple, everyday ingredients.
The session will take place in the back room of the café, starting at 10am and will last for about an hour. Please let Sheila know if you would like to join her.

Other topics coming soon by popular demand include:
Decorating for Beginners by *Charlotte and Ella*
Basic Computer Skills by *Gavin Steele*
Tips on How to Insulate your Home by *Phil Steele*
Basic Car Maintenance by dynamic duo *Jason and Ben*
Running a Business by *Deb Steele*
Arts and Crafts by *Arthur the Painter*

Keep an eye on the notice board for further details

Let's help ourselves and learn how to make things better.

From Deb and the team at the Chandelier Café

I untie the knot in my apron and hold the straps out like little wings as though I'm about to glide away.

'Is that it then, Deb? Have you finished with us? Does the room meet with your approval for the start of this momentous day?'

Deb inspects the furniture, pushing a chair closer to a table, removing a menu then putting it back in its holder.

'It'll pass.'

'Good,' I say, and I hang up my apron alongside Gav's in the cubbyhole. 'Just time for a quick coffee, Gav before we shoot off?'

Deb looks left and right out of the big window and checks her watch.

'Sheila should be here any minute. I hope she's not had a lie in.'

'Sheila?' Gav says. 'She only has four hours' sleep a night. She's amazing.'

As I put the kettle on, the back door swings wide open, Sheila almost falls in, escapes through the trap door in the counter, opens the cubbyhole door, hangs up her coat, grabs her apron, and shuts the door again before anybody can say a word. Her hair is dyed red now, still spikey, and she's wearing the red jumper with the white horizontal stripes that once belonged to Deb.

'Right, Deb,' Sheila says, quickly and expertly tying her apron behind her back. 'I've stopped smokin' for the day an' I'm rarin' to go.'

'Do you want a drink before you start, Sheila?' I say, unscrewing the coffee jar lid. 'You look as though you could do with some caffeine to fire you up.'

'I've had three already this morning,' Sheila says, and she rubs her hands together. 'Right, Deb. Do you need me for owt? Otherwise, I'm off into t'back room to prepare for my training session.'

'No,' Deb says. 'We're all set up to go. Are you getting nervous? I am.'

'Nar. Excited? Yeah. Nervous? Not a chance. Soup Kitchen Part Three here we come.'

As Sheila goes into the back room, the Brodworth Chronicle shoots through the letter box and skids along the sparkling laminate floor before coming to a stop against a chair leg.

'That paper lad ought to join the navy,' I say. 'He'd do well in the torpedo division.'

I pick up the newspaper and read the headline on the front page. My eyes slowly widen and I have to sit down and read it again.

'Chuffing hell. Come and have a look at this, you two. Jagger's trial's finished and he's been fon guilty.'

Deb and Gav press against my back and read the headline.

THREE FOUND GUILTY OF CORRUPTION

Local Councillor, Peter Hutchinson, Estate Agent, Martin O'Keefe, and property developer, Jack Jagger, were yesterday found guilty of corruption in relation to land and property dealings running into tens of thousands of pounds. All three are awaiting sentencing. Jagger was charged separately with intimidation and neglect in relation to his extensive portfolio of rented accommodation.

'I thought he'd get off with it, the slimy bastard, but they've nailed him. They've finally nailed him. He'll not be bothering us any more. Have a look inside, Gav. See if it says how they got him.'

Gav races through the pages, leaving me blinking to keep up, and then he folds the paper back on itself.

'It says here, "Jagger was on the verge of bankruptcy and desperate to purchase Valley Farm, which was owned by the council, in order to stay in business. His aim was to seek planning permission to convert the outbuildings into luxury holiday apartments and then sell the site at a profit to pay off his increasing debts. Jagger bribed councillor Hutchinson in an attempt to influence the planning department to approve his outline plans. Jagger also bribed estate agent O'Keefe in an attempt to rig the planned auction of the farm to enable Jagger to buy the property at a heavily reduced price, which would have deprived the council of thousands of pounds. The police began their six-month investigation after the new council leader received a tip off via an anonymous letter. The council confirmed the farm is no longer up for sale.'

'Wonderful,' Deb says. 'That means Robert and his mum and dad can keep their home.' She unlocks the front door and turns the OPEN sign to face the street. 'I'm glad Jagger and his motley crew have got their comeuppance. I wonder who sent the anonymous letter to the council.'

'It could have been somebody Jagger crossed,' Gav says. 'It sounds like he's been at it for a while. I'm glad I'm out of his clutches.'

I slot the Chronicle into the newspaper rack at the side of the cubbyhole, making sure the headline is on full view.

'I know this much,' I say, trying not to smile. 'Whoever's shopped him deserves a medal.'

I open the front door and step onto the pavement to breathe in the cold air. The sun is up but weak, not high enough to shine above the bank and the bread shop across the road. An old man walking alone on the other side of the street gives me a sideways nod without smiling and a builder I know drives by and pips his horn.

The big window looks good lit up. All the customers say the café with its golden chandelier, its candles and T lights, its string lights spiraling around the floor lamps, and its light-themed drawings and ornaments brings a little sparkle to their day, brightening up the betting shop, the mobility shop and the new charity shop, even extending its glow to the padlocked steel shutters on the latest businesses to close down.

I come back inside, put my hands on my hips and look around the bright, warm café. At the quality of the decorating. At the cosy furniture. At the hand-picked accessories and paintings. And there on the back wall, my plumbing certificate and the photograph of our Gav and me sitting on the Golden Flash.

'You've done a grand job with this place, love,' I say. 'I'm proud of you. And I'm proud to work for you.'

'Me too,' Gav says, and he turns his cap the right way round and smiles at his mother.

'Thank you very much,' Deb says. 'And you two haven't done a bad job, either.'

I nod to Gav and he runs upstairs. When he comes back down, he's hiding something behind his back.

'We've got a gift for you,' I say.

Gav brings out a bunch of daffodils tied with a yellow ribbon.

'For you, love,' I say, kissing Deb on the cheek. 'From the two men in your life.'

'Good luck with your new venture today, Mam.'

Deb smiles and gently rearranges the flowers.

'Thank you. They're lovely.'

'Picked fresh for you this morning,' I say. 'Grown in the richest soil in the land.'

'I ought to have known,' Deb says.

'I hope it goes well, love. Come on, Gav. Time you and me were off. See if we can find some work today.'

Thanks

My thanks to all those good folk who gave me feedback and suggested amendments: Ken Child, Jeff Halden, John Metcalfe, Jim and Hazel Reckitt, John Roberts, my sisters Sandra and Anne, my brother Jonathan and of course my wife Diane, the biggest influence of all.